THE GOOD FIGHT

By Danielle Steel

The Good Fight • The Cast • Accidental Heroes • Fall From Grace
Past Perfect • Fairytale • The Right Time • The Duchess • Against All Odds
Dangerous Games • The Mistress • The Award • Rushing Waters • Magic
The Apartment • Property Of A Noblewoman • Blue • Precious Gifts
Undercover • Country • Prodigal Son • Pegasus • A Perfect Life
Power Play • Winners • First Sight • Until The End Of Time
The Sins Of The Mother • Friends Forever • Betrayal • Hotel Vendôme
Happy Birthday • 44 Charles Street • Legacy • Family Ties • Big Girl
Southern Lights • Matters Of The Heart • One Day At A Time
A Good Woman • Rogue • Honor Thyself • Amazing Grace • Bungalow 2
Sisters • H.R.H. • Coming Out • The House • Toxic Bachelors • Miracle
Impossible • Echoes • Second Chance • Ransom • Safe Harbour
Johnny Angel • Dating Game • Answered Prayers • Sunset In St. Tropez
The Cottage • The Kiss • Leap Of Faith • Lone Eagle • Journey
The House On Hope Street • The Wedding • Irresistible Forces • Granny Dan
Bittersweet • Mirror Image • The Klone And I • The Long Road Home
The Ghost • Special Delivery • The Ranch • Silent Honor • Malice
Five Days In Paris • Lightning • Wings • The Gift • Accident • Vanished
Mixed Blessings • Jewels • No Greater Love • Heartbeat • Message From Nam
Daddy • Star • Zoya • Kaleidoscope • Fine Things • Wanderlust • Secrets
Family Album • Full Circle • Changes • Thurston House • Crossings
Once In A Lifetime • A Perfect Stranger • Remembrance • Palomino
Love: *Poems* • The Ring • Loving • To Love Again • Summer's End
Season Of Passion • The Promise • Now And Forever
Passion's Promise • Going Home

Nonfiction
Pure Joy: *The Dogs We Love*
A Gift Of Hope: *Helping the Homeless*
His Bright Light: *The Story of Nick Traina*

For Children
Pretty Minnie In Paris
Pretty Minnie In Hollywood

Danielle Steel

THE GOOD FIGHT

MACMILLAN

First published 2018 by Delacorte Press,
an imprint of Random House,
a division of Penguin Random House LLC, New York.

First published in the UK 2018 by Macmillan
an imprint of Pan Macmillan
20 New Wharf Road, London N1 9RR
Associated companies throughout the world
www.panmacmillan.com

ISBN 978-1-5098-0060-5

1 3 5 7 9 8 6 4 2

A CIP catalogue record for this book is available from the British Library.

Printed and bound by CPI Group (UK) Ltd, Croydon, CR0 4YY

To my wonderful, loving, brave,
and so greatly loved children,

Beatrix, Trevor, Todd, Nick,
Sam, Victoria, Vanessa,
Maxx, and Zara,

Be true to yourself, fight for what
you believe in and believe to be right,
and know that I love you,
with every ounce of my being.

With all my love, forever.

Mom/d.s.

Sometimes history takes things into its own hands.

—THURGOOD MARSHALL, civil rights hero and
ninety-sixth justice of the Supreme Court of the United States

THE GOOD FIGHT

Chapter One

Meredith McKenzie could remember almost perfectly the day her father left for the war in February 1942. In her mind's eye, she could still see the buttons on his uniform and how tall he looked and could almost smell his shaving soap when she kissed his face. If she closed her eyes, he was standing before her. There were other parts of the day she recalled less vividly. But she had a perfect mental picture of her mother crying, and her father's parents watching him go. Her grandfather had said it was a proud moment. Her father had enlisted as an officer immediately after Pearl Harbor, and had been assigned to the legal corps in Washington, D.C. He was thirty-seven years old, and her mother, Janet, was thirty-three. Meredith was almost six. Her father had promised that they could come to Washington to visit him as soon as he got settled, and her mother had clung to him with tears streaming down her face. Her grandmother had faced it stoically. They had come to the apartment to say goodbye. Robert had said that it would be chaos at the train station, and it wasn't as though he was going overseas, like many of the men who would be there.

After he left with a last wave and a smile, carrying his duffel bag, with his officer's cap smartly on his head, in his heavy coat, Meredith's grandfather had taken her for a walk to get some air, so Janet and her mother-in-law could talk, and Janet could compose herself before Meredith and her grandfather got back. Janet's parents had died many years before, and she had no other family, only her in-laws.

"You know why your dad is going away, don't you?" he asked her, as they walked along the edge of Central Park. She thought about it for a moment and then shook her head. Two of her friends at school had said that their fathers were enlisting in the army. But they were being sent to New Jersey for training, and then taking a big ship to Europe. Her daddy would be stationed in Washington, to be a lawyer, just like he was in New York. Her grandfather was a lawyer too. Her mother didn't work, although she had volunteered for the Red Cross, and so had Meredith's grandma. They were going to do it together, and Meredith's mother had already shown her the uniform she was going to wear. It made her look like a nurse. She said she would be helping with something called a blood drive, to help soldiers who would get hurt.

"Your father will be defending our country, to keep us safe from anyone who wants to hurt us, and he'll keep us free from bad people," her grandfather explained to her. "That's a very important thing to do. Freedom is the most important thing we have. Do you know what that means, Meredith?" he asked her solemnly, as they stopped and sat down on a bench in the park. Merrie thought about it and shook her head again. Her grandfather talked to her about important things that she didn't always understand, but she liked it when he explained them to her, and treated her like she was grown up. "Freedom means that we can do what's right and make our own choices and decisions, and no one can stop us or make us do something wrong. Sometimes we have to fight for freedom, like your daddy. If we're not free, we become slaves. There are bad people in the world, like Mr. Hitler in Germany right now, who want us to become their slaves. And all the free people in the world are going to Europe to stop him. They'll come back heroes when the war is over, just like your dad."

"Is Daddy going to meet Mr. Hitler in Washington?" she asked with interest, and Bill McKenzie smiled.

"I hope not. He's in Germany. Your daddy is going to do legal work for his country, the army, and the president of the United States." Meredith knew that her father and grandfather were lawyers, but she was never sure what that was, or what it meant. "Your dad might go to fight Mr. Hitler one day, but not yet. He has work to do in Washington first."

"Will you meet Mr. Hitler one day, Grampa?" she asked with interest, and he shook his head. She wondered if her grandfather was going to fight him too. He sounded like a bad person to her.

"No, I won't. I was in a war a long time ago, and I went to France." He had been in the First World War once the United States got into it. And he'd been one of the lucky ones who came back. He'd been two years younger than Robert was now when he went. Meredith's grandfather, William McKenzie, had just turned sixty.

"Can girls be lawyers, Grampa?" she asked after she thought about it for a few minutes.

"Yes, they can," he said firmly, taking advantage of the fact that they were alone. He knew Robert hated it when he said things like that to Meredith, but there was no reason she couldn't be a lawyer and join the family firm, where he and Robert worked. It was a big decision for a woman, and a choice she'd have to make. But Bill knew the war was going to change a lot of things, just like the last one had. Women would be joining the workforce, taking jobs that men held in peacetime. And one day, fields that had only been open to men previously would be accessible to women too.

Robert wanted his daughter to follow in the footsteps of her mother and get married, have children, and stay at home. Bill loved the idea of his granddaughter accomplishing more than that, although her grandmother had never worked. Bill had married her when she was nineteen. She had Robert at twenty, and had been a wonderful wife. But this was a new world, and a new generation, and Bill's dream for his granddaughter was that she would be part of a bigger life. They were fighting for all kinds of freedoms, not just in Europe, but at home.

"Maybe I'll be a lawyer too," Meredith said pensively, "or a doctor, or a nurse."

"You can do whatever you want," he said, as they held hands, crossed Fifth Avenue, and headed home. He liked his private moments with her. She was a bright child, inquisitive about everything and full of questions and ideas of her own.

Her mother and grandmother had tea and sandwiches and cookies waiting for them when they got back. Meredith was hungry after their walk in the cold. She ate two of the delicately trimmed sandwiches, and a cookie and a glass of milk. She went upstairs to play with her dolls then, while the grown-ups stayed to talk about the war. Later, she couldn't remember what happened after that, but she could always hear her grandfather's words echoing in her ears, about freedom, and telling her that she could do anything she wanted when she grew up, even be a lawyer like him and her father. It sounded just right to her.

Her mother visited her father in Washington every week, but she didn't take Meredith with her. Meredith stayed with her grandparents when her mother was away, and she didn't see her father again for several months, until he came home on leave. He was thrilled to see her, and he spent a lot of time talking to his father, and he was startled to realize that Meredith knew a surprising amount about the war in Europe. Her grandfather had explained it to her, and she had a good understanding of it for a child her age. Robert scolded his father for discussing it with her.

"You shouldn't tell her about the war, Dad. She's only six, she doesn't need to know."

"I think she does. Don't underestimate her. She's a smart girl, and I just tell her what she can understand in broad strokes, not the details. So what do you hear about how the war is going in Europe?" Bill was hungry for information. Everyone was.

"The Germans are punishing the Allies severely. Hitler is trying to take over all of Europe. Our losses are heavy so far, but so are theirs."

"Any word about your going overseas?" his father asked with a look of concern, and Robert shook his head.

"Not for now anyway. They're keeping me pretty busy at my desk. They still need a few of us at home, and I'm no kid, Dad. It's the young ones, the boys, they're sending into combat." The war was being heavily fought from the air, and men were being parachuted into Germany, Italy, and France. As an officer, and at his age, Robert

Danielle Steel

wasn't likely to be one of them. There had been talk about sending him to England, with a legal corps on loan to the Royal Air Force. But he wasn't assigned to the unit when they went.

Robert wasn't shipped to Europe for another two years, and went as part of the D Day operations in 1944. They sent him over in March, and he was with the landing operation of American, Canadian, and British forces on the beaches of Normandy in June. One hundred and fifty-six thousand men were among the Allied forces on D Day, and Robert was one of them. He remained in France afterward, as they liberated the country village by village, and at the end of the year, and into early 1945, he joined one of the units that liberated the concentration camps in Germany, which affected him profoundly. He saw Auschwitz after the Russians had freed it. He had never seen anything as horrendous in his life. And he was part of the unit that had freed Dachau. The prisoners they found, starved and suffering, literally died in their arms. They called for all the medical assistance they could deploy there, but it was too late for most of them. Corpses lay in stacks and littered the ground. Robert and the other men couldn't hold back their tears as they tried to help them. It brought home as nothing else could have the horrors of the war, and the crimes against humanity Hitler and his men had committed in Germany and all across Europe.

Before Robert returned from Europe, after France was liberated and the Germans had surrendered, he signed up for the legal team that would be prosecuting war criminals in Germany. He explained it to both Janet and his parents when he was back in New York. It was something he felt he had to do, to right the wrongs he had seen. Janet was sympathetic, but his father was somewhat stunned. They missed him at the law firm and Bill McKenzie had just been ap-

8

pointed a federal judge, which meant that no family member would be running the law firm in Robert's absence. But they had a competent managing partner who had things under control.

"How long do you think you'll be gone?" his father asked him.

"I don't know," Robert said honestly. "A year or two." Or longer. He couldn't judge it, and he didn't receive confirmation of the assignment for another month after he got home. It would mean staying in the army for the duration of the trials, which he didn't mind. And when he talked to Janet about what he'd seen in Dachau, with tears streaming down his face, she understood what it meant to him and agreed with his decision.

He got his orders to report to Nuremberg, where the trials would open and be held. They already had a prison full of men to bring to trial, with survivors of their atrocities to testify against them. Their crimes were legion and inhuman, the number of people they had killed astounding. Robert was to be part of the International Military Tribunal established by the Americans, British, Russians, and French, who collaborated to set the ground rules of the trial. There were four Allied judges and four main prosecutors. Sir Geoffrey Lawrence was the president of the tribunal. There were numerous attorneys of all four nationalities, and many assistants. Prosecutors and judges were designated. The trials were to be held at the Palace of Justice in Nuremberg. And there was a prison capable of housing twelve hundred prisoners. The American legal team alone consisted of 640 lawyers, researchers, secretaries, and guards. It was assigned the task of proving the conspiracy charges brought against the defendants.

With considerable negotiation, Robert was granted permission to bring his family, and housing would be provided. A number of houses had been rented for the officers, and a few were bringing their wives and children with them, though most members of the tribunal were not. Meredith was shocked when her parents said they were moving to Germany for a year or two, or maybe longer, and she would be joining them. She was nine years old and liked her school and her friends. She attended Marymount, and her grandfather told her that moving would be a wonderful opportunity to learn German, which sounded terrible to her.

"But they're bad people, Grampa! That's who Daddy has been fighting," she reminded him, as though he had forgotten.

"They're not all bad, Merrie. And many of them suffered at the Nazis' hands. The men who committed the crimes have to be punished. That's a very important assignment for your dad. You should be proud of him."

But for the first time, the war was going to affect her directly, and she was afraid to go there. "Why can't I stay home with Adelaide?" she begged, about their familiar, comforting housekeeper, who also cooked for them and had worked for them since Meredith was born. She loved sitting in the kitchen with her, helping her shell peas or clean string beans. Adelaide walked her to school in the morning, and had children of her own. Her only son had been killed in the war, and she had two daughters. And Adelaide loved Merrie. It had been decided that she would continue to care for the apartment while they were away, and they assured Meredith that she would be waiting for them when they came home.

"What if I forget how to speak English? And how will I go to school there?" Meredith asked, panicking, and her parents and grandparents reminded her again and again that it was a wonderful opportunity to learn more about the world, and for her father to help people, and it was a very special job.

Robert left a month before they did, and was working hard on his German to become fluent before the trials. Meredith and her mother arrived to find a small, tidy house that was simple but immaculately clean. The widow who owned it lived in the basement in an apartment she had created for herself, and was happy to rent her home to Robert and his family. She spoke no English but made delicious cookies, and had recommended a young neighbor girl, Anna, to cook and clean for them and help take care of Meredith. Anna had lost three brothers and her father in the war, was supporting her infirm mother, and was grateful for the wages Robert offered her. And he wanted her to teach Merrie German. If they stayed long enough, he hoped Meredith would transition from the school provided for the children of U.S. Army personnel to a local school, but Meredith didn't like that idea at all.

She looked at Fraulein Anna with suspicion from the moment they arrived. The pretty young blond woman chatted easily with her in German, pointing to things and telling Meredith the correct word. She wore her hair in braids and was very thin after the rigors of the war, but she was willing and kind. Within six months of their arrival, Janet discovered that she was pregnant, and was relieved that Anna said she would help with the baby too.

Meredith wasn't happy about it when they told her she was going to have a sister or brother. She was almost ten by then, and she told her parents that if they had to have a baby, she wanted it to be a girl. Robert and Janet discussed the possibility of Janet's going home to have the baby. Germany was still disrupted and many doctors had been Jewish and had died in the camps. Janet didn't want to see a German doctor, but the military medical corps provided all the care they needed, and she insisted that she didn't want to be away from Robert, and Meredith was doing well in school and making friends. The war trials had proven to be so complicated, with so many criminals to prosecute, that she didn't think Robert would be able to leave anytime soon. So they decided to stay, and the baby would be born in Germany. By then, Meredith and Fraulein Anna were fast friends, and Meredith was fluent in German. She transferred to the local school, as her father had hoped she would.

Their life was simple and comfortable in Nuremberg. Janet was happy there too. And when the baby was born in March 1946, everything went smoothly. They named the baby Alexander, and Merrie forgave him his gender and announced that he was her baby too. She helped Anna take care of him whenever she wasn't in school, and carried him around everywhere, much to the chubby little boy's delight. He took his first steps for Merrie, and he chortled whenever he saw her walk into a room, and squealed with delight.

Robert's parents had come to visit and see the baby as soon as he was born, and were thrilled with their new grandson. Bill accompanied his son to the courtroom for most of the week, and was deeply moved by the trials and the translation of the testimony. The horrors the witnesses spoke of were beyond imagining, and Robert would have found it overwhelming at times if he didn't take great satisfaction in being part of the team bringing the Nazi monsters to justice, to punish them for their crimes. It was deeply rewarding, and his father could understand why he stayed there. He had been in Germany for over a year by then, and there was no way of estimating how long it would take. But Bill assured Robert that the managing partner was continuing to run the firm admirably, and the partnership was thriving.

Robert was shocked at one of his father's suggestions. "You should let Merrie go to court with you sometime. This is an important piece of history. It would be good for her to see it." Robert could tell that he meant it, but in his mind it was out of the question, given the testimony they were hearing, the atrocities being recounted, and the occasionally graphic film footage and photographs they were shown, which his father wasn't aware of.

"You can't be serious," he said, horrified. "Dad, she speaks German. She'll know what they're saying." Bill had used the tribunal's very efficient translation system to help him understand the witnesses and had had tears in his eyes several times.

"All the better," Bill said with a look of determination. "And of course I'm serious. The entire world should know what happened. We can't ever let them forget it."

"She's ten years old." A lot of the testimony had been medical, as the victims described the experiments that had been performed on them, and the ghoulish surgeries. They had tried twenty-three Nazi physicians.

"If we don't want this to happen again, we have to shout it from the rooftops." He was pleased to note that there were more than three hundred correspondents from twenty-three countries covering the war crimes trials, and more than four hundred visitors daily.

"I don't want my ten-year-old child to know what those monsters were capable of," Robert said quietly.

"Why not? If you want her to make a difference in the world one day, she has to know what she's changing it *from*."

"I wish you'd stop trying to use her for your crusades," Robert said, irritated, as he spoke with feeling to his father. The trials were important, but not suitable for a child, in his opinion.

"She'll have her own crusades one day, or at least I hope she will," her grandfather said firmly. "The world is changing, and by the time she's older, women should have a voice in those changes. Why not hers?"

"That's not what Janet and I want for her," Robert reminded him, looking worried. "We want to shield her from the cruelties of the world. She doesn't need to ride into battle. Women don't need the hard life you think is so worthwhile to make a contribution to the world. She should get married and have children, and run a nice home for her husband, the way her mother does for me." He didn't consider what he said demeaning. It sounded right to him.

"Meredith is capable of more than that," his father said stubbornly. "Janet is like your mother. They're natural-born homemakers, and all they want is to focus on their families, an occasional fashion show at the Junior League, and their bridge game. Is that really what you want for Meredith, Robert? She's too bright for that. But you can at least influence her now, and open her eyes to the many things she can do in the world when she gets older."

"That wouldn't be a happy life for her," Robert said sternly. "If you get her wound up about a legal career, or righting the injustices in the world, and turn her into Joan of Arc or some kind of freedom fighter, she'll never have a husband and kids. That's a choice some women make, but not the life her mother and I want for her. It would be a huge sacrifice for her to make, and I won't let that happen," he warned his father. "You're a man, you can do anything you want. She can't." It was an eternal disagreement between them, and he didn't want his father influencing his daughter and pushing her into decisions she would pay too high a price for in the end. His father thought it was worth it. Robert didn't.

"You're behind the times," Bill growled at him. "The world has already changed more than you think. Women have a strong voice now and getting stronger."

"Not as much as you think. When we go home, she'll go to college like her mother, and get married. Don't turn her into a freak."

"You have a child with a bright mind and an adventuresome spirit," Bill said. "Don't turn her into a housewife with an ironing board in one hand and a baby on her hip. The world needs brave women, not just brave men, Robert. Look what you're doing here, bringing war criminals to justice." He was proud of his son for being part of history, and he wanted his granddaughter to follow in her father's footsteps one day, despite his objections or fears for her.

"I don't have to give up my wife and children to do what I'm engaged in," Robert reminded him. "If you want a revolutionary in the family, wait a few years and focus on your grandson. Don't fill Merrie's head with your ideas."

But he already had. Meredith had told Anna several times that she wanted to be a lawyer one day and fight for people who had been mistreated, like the Jewish people in Germany. The young German housekeeper looked embarrassed when she said it, and told her that no one had known how terribly they were treated in the camps, but when Meredith told her father, he said they had known more than they admitted, when they saw women and children and entire families cast out of their homes and dragged away or loaded into cattle cars and shipped east to the camps. Robert said that no one wanted to take responsibility for the horrors the Allies had exposed to the world, which were heartbreaking. It was why he was in

Nuremberg. The atrocities couldn't be denied anymore, and the criminals had to be brought to justice, and were now.

They spent four years in Germany, and Meredith spoke German perfectly, and loved her school and her friends and her life there. She was devastated when the war trials finally concluded and her parents told her they were moving back to New York. She looked and sounded like a German child by then. She was thirteen years old, and Alex was three and bilingual too. And even Janet had learned to speak enough German to get by in the shops and talk to people she met. Robert spoke it creditably, after hearing four years of testimony. They had condemned many of the accused criminals to prison sentences, and the judges had imposed the death penalty on a considerable number of the defendants, and they had been executed. But Robert was aware that, whatever they did to the Nazis, it would never make up for the number of people they had maimed, killed, and destroyed, the families they had wiped out, and the lives they had ruined forever. There was no way to undo the evil they had committed, or bring back the millions they had killed in the death camps. Their crimes were too hideous to believe. And Meredith had grown up hearing about them and understanding more than she probably should for a young girl her age.

It was a sad day for her when they left Fraulein Anna. Meredith wanted her to come to New York with them, but Anna was engaged to a young German by then who had lost an arm in the war, and they were getting married in a few months. His parents owned a bakery, and when the McKenzies left, she was going to work with them. Germany was slowly rebuilding, although signs of the war had remained. The country was still suffering, but they were trying to recover as best they could. Bombed-out buildings had been cleared away, and the Americans were helping them to rebuild.

Their time in Germany had been more pleasant than they had expected. They had taken several short trips to Paris, vacationed in Italy, and been to London a number of times, where the British were rebuilding too. There was an aura of new life after the war, and Europe felt more like home to her than the States. Meredith did everything she could to convince her parents to stay. She didn't want to go back to her old all-girls school in New York, with the nuns. She wanted to live in Europe, but Robert had a law firm he wanted to return to and a life to go home to, and he and Janet agreed that they wanted their children to grow up as Americans in the States. And a great honor had just been bestowed on Robert's father. He had been appointed to the Supreme Court by President Truman and confirmed by the Senate. The whole family was thrilled. Bill had been appointed to replace a justice who had passed away a month before, after serving for nearly a decade. It was time for Robert to become active in the firm now, no matter how much Merrie had come to love living in Germany.

Anna accompanied them to the Tempelhof military airport in Berlin, and she and the children cried when they left each other. Meredith felt as though she was going to a foreign country, not her own. They had gone back to visit only once in the four years they had been away. Robert's parents had come to see them in Nuremberg every year. Her grandfather had promised Meredith in a letter that she could visit him at the Supreme Court and attend his swearing-in, which was going to be exciting for her.

As they left Germany, Robert felt a surge of pride for what he'd accomplished at the war crimes trials. It was what he was most proud of in his life so far, and he left the country feeling he had done something to try to help Germany recover from what they had suffered at the hands of Hitler's government. And he had been treated with gratitude and respect everywhere he went. Now he was going back to a much quieter life at the family law firm in New York, helping his clients to plan their estates and investments. But he was ready for peacetime and an ordinary existence with his wife and two children. He was looking forward to civilian life. His commission was due to end as soon as they got back to New York. The war was finally and truly over for him now, after seven years. Only Meredith was deeply distressed to be leaving, and hardly said a word on the flight home.

Adelaide was waiting for them at the apartment when they got there, faithful as ever. She had aged a little in the past four years, and was a little rounder, but she held her arms open wide to Merrie. And after feeling shy and hesitating for only a second, Merrie slipped into them as though she had never left.

"Come to Addie, baby," she cooed to her as she hugged her, and Meredith smiled, remembering all the warm hugs she'd had from her over the years. "And look who's all grown up." Meredith's body had started to change, and she'd grown taller. She'd had her dark hair cut in Germany in a stylish pageboy that made her look older. Her long legs made her seem like a young colt. "I missed you, baby," Adelaide said to Merrie and smiled warmly. She'd made sandwiches for them, after the long flight, and a plate of cookies. Alex gobbled them up and watched her with interest, and thanked her in German.

"English, Alex," his mother reminded him, and they all smiled.

He looked confused for a minute and then said "Thank you," and looked around for Anna, and started to cry for her when he didn't see her. He didn't know Adelaide as Merrie did, and had only seen her during his one visit to New York. Meredith put her little brother to bed that night and tucked him in. Her parents were talking quietly downstairs about all the things they had to do now to settle back into their New York life. Listening to them, Merrie was homesick for Germany. She missed speaking German and her friends of the past four years, their Park Avenue apartment and the city no longer felt like home to her. She was a stranger here now.

Her parents didn't see it, but Adelaide did, and so did Meredith's grandfather, when her grandparents came to visit the next day. She had a decidedly European style about her that made her seem more grown up and sophisticated, and she was a very pretty girl.

"Does it feel strange to be back?" her grandfather asked her directly. He hated pretense and fakery and always cut to the chase. He was observant and knew her well, although he hadn't seen a lot of her in recent years.

"Very," she responded honestly. "This doesn't feel like home anymore. I miss Germany." He nodded as though that seemed reasonable to him, while both her parents looked surprised.

"That makes sense. You're a citizen of the world now. You'll go back and visit. You could do a junior year abroad when you're in college." That seemed like a lifetime away to her. "But first, I want you to come to my swearing-in and visit me at the Supreme Court. It's an exciting place. We make some very important decisions," he told her and she nodded. "I'm very honored by the appointment."

"And we're so proud of you, Grampa," she said, smiling at him.

"And slightly ashamed," Robert teased his father. Robert was a staunch Republican, as was Janet, and his father was a Democrat. "You couldn't switch parties and wait to be appointed by a Republican president, Dad? What am I going to tell my friends?"

"That they're damn lucky to have me there, to keep people like you from dragging our country back into the Dark Ages. It's a new world out there, Bobby, we have to move ahead with the times. Right, Merrie?" He turned to his granddaughter and she smiled. "You know why I'm there, don't you?"

She looked puzzled for a moment. "To make decisions about how the laws should be applied?" she said hesitantly, and he nodded.

"Yes. But I'm there to fight the good fight. To defend the people who need it and protect people from being discriminated against, or being abused by bad laws. You always have to fight the good fight, Meredith. That's what you're going to do one day," he said, putting an arm around her, and she smiled up at him. He was still her hero, and even more so now. Her father looked slightly exasperated. His father was always trying to turn her into a freedom fighter, even while she was still a child.

"You never change, do you, Dad?" Robert said, and his father laughed.

"On the contrary. My new job is all about change. The country is leaping forward, Robert, on every front. And we have to grow with it. I predict that we're going to see more change in this country in the next twenty years than we've ever seen before. And I'm going to be part of it. It doesn't get more exciting than that."

At the same time, Robert was about to take a giant step backward into the safety and familiarity of his pre-war life, in his old job at the family law firm. And he was going to uphold all the same traditions, while his father changed the future of the country from his seat on the Supreme Court. Somehow, Robert had the feeling that their roles should have been reversed. His father should have been upholding tradition and honoring the past, while he explored the future with fresh eyes. But that wasn't who they were.

"That's what this country is all about," Bill reminded his family. "We have to fight the good fight, to help the underprivileged, protect the rights of those who can't, and champion the underdog." As he said it, he looked at his granddaughter, who was nodding as she listened to him, and he knew his words hadn't fallen on deaf ears. However much her parents wanted to hold her to tradition, Justice of the Supreme Court William McKenzie had a feeling that wasn't going to happen. Not with this child. There was a fire growing in her that one day nothing would stop. And he had every intention of fanning the flames.

Chapter Two

C oming back to New York was lonely for Meredith, and something of a shock. She had lost touch with her old school friends
after she left. Alex was too young to know the difference, and adjusted to Adelaide quickly. She lavished affection on him, and he
lapped it up. Janet had gone right back to her old life, with greater
ease because Meredith was older and she didn't need to spend as
much time with her, and she hung out in the kitchen with Addie
most of the time anyway. And Janet knew that Alex was in good
hands. So she was free to play golf and tennis, and bridge with her
friends two or three times a week. Although she'd been sad to leave
their cozy family life in Germany, where Robert came home for
lunch every day and so did the children, she was enjoying being
back in New York.

And Robert was content being the senior partner of the law firm.
At forty-four, he had a comfortable career and a life he loved. And it
didn't do him any harm to be the son of a Supreme Court justice. He

was proud of his father, even if Bill wasn't a Republican, predictably all his friends and partners teased him about it. He claimed that his father was the only Democrat he knew. His prestigious place at the Nuremberg war trials enhanced his career too. Robert was an extremely respected attorney, and his colleagues and clients were happy to see him back.

Shortly after their return from Germany, they all went to Washington to see Robert's father sworn in as a Supreme Court justice. They left New York on the train, and the entire event fascinated and thrilled Meredith, who was so proud of her grandfather. Her mother and grandmother had new dresses for the occasion, and wore beautiful hats, and Meredith had a new dress too. Her grandfather had explained to her all about the Supreme Court, and had shared some of the building's history with her, and given her a little book about it, which she had studied diligently. She informed her parents on the trip down from New York that the Supreme Court Building had taken three years to build, was completed in 1935, fourteen years before, and was designed by architects Cass Gilbert Sr., Cass Gilbert Jr., and John Rockart. But nothing she had read about it had prepared her for the beauty and grandeur of the impressive structure and surroundings the morning they arrived for her grandfather's swearing-in.

The exterior was made of Vermont marble, and the finest natural materials of the country had been used. There were four inner courtyards of crystalline flaked white Georgia marble, each with a central fountain, and the walls and floors of all the corridors and entrance halls were of creamy Alabama marble. The wood used in the offices throughout the building was American quartered white oak. Meredith remembered all the names of the different kinds of marble from the book she had read, but seeing them in front of her was a stunning experience.

The main entrance to the building faced the Capitol Building. The Supreme Court Building was designed to harmonize with the important monuments around it. There was a 252-foot-wide oval plaza at the front of the building, and flanking the shallow steps that led to it were a pair of marble candelabra with carved panels depicting Justice holding a sword and scales, and the three Fates weaving the thread of life. Fountains, flagpoles, and benches lined both sides of the plaza. Janet had to urge Meredith to keep up with them, as she stopped to stare at the majesty of it all. And on either side of the main steps there were seated marble figures, and Merrie informed her parents that the statues were by James Earle Fraser, and that the female figure on the left was the Contemplation of Justice, and the male figure on the right was the Guardian or Authority of Law.

The pediment at the main west entrance was supported by sixteen marble columns. On the architrave above was carved "Equal Justice Under Law." And capping the entrance was Robert Aitken's sculpture group representing Liberty Enthroned, guarded by Order and Authority.

Double rows of monolithic marble columns flanked both sides of the main corridor inside—the Great Hall—rising to a coffered ceiling. Busts of all former chief justices were set alternately in niches and on marble pedestals along the side walls.

"Will they put a statue of Grampa there one day?" she asked her father, staring at them.

"I'm sure they will," he said, smiling at her, touched by how avidly she had studied every detail about the art and architecture, and how reverent she was. She wanted to visit the old court chamber, the original one, in the Capitol too, but they didn't have time that day. Her grandfather promised to take her on her next visit.

At the east end of the Great Hall, the doors opened into the court chamber. It was a huge room eighty-two feet wide and ninety-one feet long, with a forty-four-foot ceiling that soared above them. Its twenty-four columns were Old Convent Quarry Siena marble, from Italy. The walls and friezes were of Spanish ivory vein marble, and the marble floor borders were from Africa and Italy.

Meredith and the entire family stopped and stared with awe at the raised bench, behind which the nine justices normally sat. The bench and all the furniture in the courtroom was a rich mahogany. And the attorneys who argued cases occupied tables in front of the bench. They would then address the bench from a lectern in the center, which Robert pointed out to them. And there was a bronze railing to divide the public section from that of the Supreme Court bar. Press would be seated on red benches on one side of the courtroom, and identical red benches on the opposite side were for guests of the justices, and black chairs in front of the benches were for officers of the court and important guests.

The main floor of the building was divided between the justices' chambers, conference rooms, and offices for law clerks and secretaries. The offices of the marshal and the solicitor general were on the main floor as well, along with a lawyers' lounge, and the justices' robing room.

Robert and his family stopped when they reached the justices' conference room, where his father would take the first oath that morning. The chief justice, Fred Vinson, was going to administer the constitutional oath, and family members could attend. Bill had asked his son to hold the Bible for him, which was a tradition, and several associate justices would be in attendance. Meredith stood riveted as she watched the proceedings, and was silent and solemn as they moved to the west conference room with the small gathering of Bill's family and friends, for the chief justice to administer the second oath, the judicial oath, which would conclude the official proceedings of the day. The formal investiture would happen several months later in the courtroom, at a special sitting of the court. After Chief Justice Vinson administered the second oath, Bill posed for photographs with his family and the other justices present.

Meredith thought that being there was the most exciting day of her life, and there was a luncheon afterward at the Mayflower Hotel for her grandparents' friends. Meredith watched the other guests with great interest, and the family went back to New York the next day on the train. She knew she would remember every detail of the day forever, and she hugged her grandfather extra tight before they left.

"I'm so proud of you, Grampa!" she whispered fiercely, with a look of immeasurable admiration, and he held her and smiled for a moment, with a knowing look.

"I'm going to be proud of you one day too, Merrie." As he said it, she knew she wanted to live up to his faith in her. She just didn't know how she would do it yet, but hoped that one day she would.

After the exciting days of her grandfather's swearing-in, her thoughts turned to going back to school in September, and she felt glum again. She wasn't looking forward to it. She was going into eighth grade at Marymount, where she'd gone to school before. It was the same all-girls school she'd attended from kindergarten until they left. She liked her coed school in Germany much better, and having friends who were boys as well as girls. Everything about being back in New York felt like a return to her early childhood, and she had started growing up in Germany, she was a teenager now, and wanted a change. She had five more years to attend at Marymount before she'd graduate from high school.

The final weeks of summer seemed interminable. They had rented a house on Martha's Vineyard for a week, as they always did, and another one on Cape Cod after their trip to Washington. It was fun playing on the beach with Alex, and she made friends with some girls her age staying in nearby houses, but it all seemed boring to her now. She'd had more fun in Italy and the south of France during her summers in Europe, but she didn't say that to her new friends.

In the fall, she started eighth grade at Marymount, and Alex started nursery school. There were different teachers, but the classrooms were familiar and looked just like the ones Merrie had attended in the lower grades before they moved. She missed speaking German more than ever. For lack of anything else to do, she applied herself to her schoolwork and got good grades, which pleased her parents. She made a few friends, and reconnected with some of her old ones, but her life experience was different now, and broader than the girls her age. She cared about social and political issues, which set her apart too. By the time she'd been back for a year and started high school, Germany seemed like it was a lifetime away. Her parents acted as though they had never left the States and thought that Meredith had adjusted well. They had no idea how lonely she was at times, and how out of step she felt with her classmates. Alex had forgotten all his German after a year. They'd received Anna's wedding pictures, and she wrote to tell them she was expecting a baby, and sounded delighted about it.

Meredith visited her grandparents in Washington several times, and her grandfather had her come to his chambers at the Supreme Court, which fascinated her. She wrote a paper about it for school, and told her classmates she wanted to be a lawyer one day, like her father and grandfather. They laughed at her when she said it. They all wanted to get married and have babies. Only about half of them wanted to go to college, and only because their parents said they should. The other parents didn't care. They thought girls didn't have to go to college, as long as they got engaged within a year or two of high school graduation. The goal for their daughters was marriage, not an education. Meredith couldn't imagine anything dumber than not going to college and just getting married and having kids. She wanted to do a lot more with her life than that. She stopped talking about law school, because her classmates all thought she was weird when she said it. And her parents didn't like the idea either. Her grandfather was the only one who thought it was the right path for her.

She signed up for some volunteer work at school, but the only thing her parents would let her do was tutor younger students, which she didn't love. She had hoped to do something more interesting like serve meals at a soup kitchen, but they thought she might catch an illness from the people there. None of the options seemed meaningful to her, and high school felt like a desert she had to crawl through in order to get to college, but her parents had strong opinions about that too. They wanted her to go to an all-female college, either Vassar or Wellesley. Her mother had gone to Vassar, so they put a lot of pressure on her to choose that. It was an excellent school for women, and she couldn't think of where else to go. She would have liked to try for Radcliffe, the sister school to Harvard, but her father told her that her mother would be really upset if she didn't follow tradition. To make them happy, she applied to Vassar and got in, so her fate was sealed. She was going to Vassar in the fall, just as her mother had done. It felt like a cookie cutter life to her, following in her mother's footsteps. She was determined to be her own person, but didn't know how to break out of the mold. Her parents had such rigid ideas about what was expected of her, and she didn't want to disappoint them. But she didn't want to be her mother either. She dreamed of getting more out of life than a husband and children, and playing bridge.

She was fiercely excited two weeks before her high school graduation when the Supreme Court ruled for integration of white and colored children in schools, in the *Brown v. Board of Education* case, striking down the earlier *Plessy v. Ferguson* decision, which was in favor of segregation. It was a landmark ruling and Meredith called to congratulate her grandfather.

"It was the only proper thing we could do," he said reasonably, and Meredith told him how proud she was of him. The case had been presented to the Supreme Court three years in a row, and chief counsel for the NAACP Thurgood Marshall had argued eloquently in front of the Supreme Court. Chief Justice Earl Warren delivered the court's final opinion. Meredith had even caught a glimpse of her grandfather on the news on television that night. She was bursting with pride that he had been part of it.

He and her grandmother attended her high school graduation, and afterward they took her to Europe for a month as their gift to her. She had a fantastic time with them. She wanted to go back to Germany to see her friends, but it wasn't on the itinerary, and her grandparents told her maybe another time. She would have liked to see Anna, their old nanny, who had two children by then, and they looked sweet in the pictures she sent. They were both girls and were towheaded blondes just like her.

In Paris, she stayed at the Ritz with her grandparents and went to museums every day. Her grandfather took her shopping and bought her a beret. They went to Notre Dame and Sacré-Coeur, and had lunch in bistros and cafés. She loved being with them, and from there they went to London and visited the Tower of London, Westminster Abbey, and the Tate Gallery, and they took her to several plays and a production of the Royal Ballet. After that they traveled to Rome and Florence, to visit churches and art, and the monuments of Rome. They ended the trip in Venice, where they rode in gondolas and wandered the streets for hours. It was the best present of her life, and she loved being with them. She felt like a world traveler again, and was starting to get excited about college. Even if Vassar hadn't been her ideal choice, it was still her first step in adulthood. The school claimed that it encouraged independent thinking and hard work, which made it slightly more appealing to Merrie. Her brother, Alex, was eight by then and sad that she was leaving, but she promised to come home often to see him, and said he could visit her at college.

The summer flew by once she got home from Europe. Adelaide helped her pack her trunk. And she got a polite letter from the girl who was going to be her roommate, who was from North Carolina. Her mother and grandmother had gone to Vassar too. She'd sent a photograph, and she was very pretty, with long blond hair.

Meredith had everything ready for her departure, and it all went smoothly until the night before she left, when her mother mentioned that she'd have to come home for several rehearsals for the debutante ball where she was being presented right before Christmas. And she said they'd have to shop for a dress. Meredith looked across the table at her in horror and shook her head.

"I'm not doing that." She had told them that before, but her parents were sure she'd come around. Meredith thought it was a ridiculous, archaic, snobbish tradition, and said she wasn't going to be paraded around in a white dress, with a bunch of giggling girls looking for husbands. It always happened during the Christmas holidays of a girl's freshman year of college, or the Christmas after their high school graduation if they hadn't gone to college. Normally, the girls were eighteen, which was customarily the right age to "come out." Meredith had been telling her parents for years that she would never do it. And now her mother acted like she'd never said it before.

"Don't be silly, Merrie," her mother said, looking nervous. "All the girls love it, you'll have a wonderful time. You'll have to come down from school one weekend so we can look for a dress."

"I'm *not* doing it," Meredith said again. "It's stupid, and a throwback to another century. The purpose of it originally was to marry girls off. I'm not looking for a husband." She glared at both of her parents. "It's a travesty, with more important things happening in the world. The segregation of white and Negro children in school was ruled illegal by the Supreme Court, and you expect me to look like an idiot as a debutante." She had discussed the case in depth with her grandfather for months, and the impact it would have on schools in the South.

"Your mother did it, and she looked beautiful," Robert said nostalgically, ignoring her comments about the landmark decision. The two issues were not related as far as he was concerned, although he knew Meredith was far more interested in politics and civil rights than picking dresses, which she considered irrelevant.

"Did you go with her?" Meredith looked surprised, distracted for a moment, and her mother smiled.

"Your father was escorting another girl. He was incredibly handsome in white tie and tails. We met that night. It was magical. A friend's brother was my escort. Who do you think you'd want to take?" Janet acted as though Merrie had made no objection to it.

"I said I'm not going." She was sullen to the point of rude, as she glared at them.

"Your mother came out at the same ball," her father reminded her gently, and her mother looked hurt.

"It's a lovely Cinderella night," her mother added.

"The purpose of which is to find a husband," Meredith said stubbornly. "I'm going to law school. I'm not getting married."

"Of course not. But that's no reason for you not to come out."

"I'm not coming out," she said again, and her brother watched her, puzzled.

"What are you coming out of?"

"Nothing," Meredith said, left the table, and stormed up to her room. They couldn't force her. She wouldn't let them. She didn't see them again until morning, when she came down for breakfast before they left for Poughkeepsie. Both of her parents were taking her, and Alex too. He wanted to see where she was going to school, and her mother said she was planning to walk the campus for old times' sake, and see what had changed, after they settled her in. The subject of the debutante ball did not come up again. There was plenty of time to discuss it, Janet had said to Robert. They thought she was nervous about school, and didn't realize how serious she was about not making her debut.

Her father went to get the car from the garage he used a few blocks away. He had rented a station wagon the day before, and the doorman helped him slide the trunk into the back, and put both her smaller valises on top of it, along with a bedspread, a small colorful rug, and two spare pillows. Her bedding was in the trunk, and some posters she wanted to put on the wall. The brochure and advance material had suggested that the rooms were small and not to overdo the decorating. She would have a small closet, a chest of drawers, a desk, and a chair, and she had brought a portable typewriter with her that her grandmother had given her. Her father had reminded her to bring her tennis racket. And she was going to buy a bicycle in town to get around the campus.

She had selected all her classes, and was taking all the required subjects to get them out of the way, and a German literature class that interested her as her only elective. She had kissed Adelaide goodbye the night before, since she wasn't working that day because they were leaving, and had given her the day off. Meredith felt sad as she left the apartment. She knew her life would never be quite the same again. Her carefree childhood days were over.

It took them two and a half hours to get there, and the countryside in the Hudson Valley was pretty. She had visited the school the year before when she decided to apply, and she had agreed that it was a lovely campus.

West Point, the military academy, was the nearest boys' school, and Yale was unofficially their "brother" college. Vassar was the second of the Seven Sisters colleges. They had mixers on campus regularly so the girls could meet male students from other schools. There were no sorority houses at Vassar, nor eating clubs or societies, unlike some other colleges. They believed in equality and treating everyone fairly so no one would feel excluded. Meredith's only real objection to it was that it was an elitist all-female school, but it was her mother's alma mater, and she didn't have the heart to let her down.

She was lost in her own thoughts as they reached the campus. She was wishing she was back in Germany. She would have preferred to go to college there, but her parents wouldn't agree to it. They didn't want her so far away at her age, and wanted her to have an American college experience, particularly at an outstanding school with such strong traditions. She was still hoping to return to Germany for junior year.

The Main Building came into sight, which was prominent on the brochure with its Second Empire–style palatial structure. The residence halls were built around the quad. She had been assigned a room in Lathrop House. There was a long line of cars driving onto the property, and Alex looked around as though they were landing on the moon.

"It's all girls here, huh?" he commented. The only men in evidence were the arriving students' fathers and brothers and a few male workers handing out name tags and dorm assignments. At first glance, Meredith felt suddenly overwhelmed and wished she'd gone to another school, where there were male students, and everyone didn't look so fancy. She saw girls in skirts and sweater sets, with saddle shoes, getting out of cars. Their hair was perfectly done, and she noticed that a few of them wore a string of pearls with their sweaters. Meredith was wearing a Black Watch kilt, navy sweater, and flat shoes, and wished she didn't have to get out of the car. She wanted to go home. Her mother had worn a new pink suit, and her father and brother had worn suits and ties to help her move in, as did all the other male relatives assisting the arriving freshman girls.

Robert got Alex to help him pull the trunk and suitcases out, while Janet and Meredith went to get her room assignment. The smiling young man she got her dorm keys from told her where the building was and how to get there. And then the four of them set out to find her dorm, with Alex and Robert carrying the trunk.

As soon as they reached Lathrop House, Janet pointed to her own freshman hall across from it, as Robert and Alex headed into the building and struggled up the stairs. Her room was on the second floor, so they didn't have far to go, and as they walked into the room, they saw that half of it was decorated in pink, and there was a teddy bear sitting on a pink bedspread on the bed. The other half of the room was bare, waiting for Meredith to unpack her things, and she was suddenly nervous about the girl she'd be rooming with. What if they hated each other?

Janet got out the keys to the trunk when Alex and their father set it down, while Merrie sat down on the bed and looked carefully around the room. Beyond the window, she could see the campus, it looked venerable and distinguished with handsome old trees. She could hear women's voices everywhere, in the halls, in the other rooms, on the stairs, and outside as they stood beneath Merrie's windows, and suddenly everything she'd brought with her seemed wrong. All the decorative items she'd packed were bright red. Her bedspread, some throw pillows, and even her typewriter all clashed with the powder pink of her roommate's childlike treasures. Meredith's choices were bolder, just like her points of view.

Meredith unpacked photographs of her family first, all in red frames, including a photograph of her grandfather in his robes when he'd been sworn into the Supreme Court, and several of her parents and Alex, and one of Anna and her two little girls in Germany. The photograph was a way of bringing a piece of her German life here.

She and her mother hung her clothes in the small closet, while Robert put a small record player under the desk with her Frank Sinatra records. They put the red rug down, spread the bedspread on the bed with the pillows, and put the posters over her bed with tape. One was a photograph of a German castle, and the other was a movie poster of Audrey Hepburn in *Sabrina,* which she had seen that summer and loved. Her roommate had posters of Frank Sinatra, Doris Day, and Judy Garland over her bed, so they had all the current movie and singing stars covered.

Within an hour, the room was set up, Meredith was unpacked, and there had been no sign of her roommate yet. They were about to leave the room when she came sailing in, breathless from running up the stairs, and smiled at Merrie. She was a pretty blonde with a long pageboy, and was much better looking than her pictures, with a startlingly good figure for a young girl, and a heavy southern accent when she greeted everyone.

"Hi, I'm Betty. I'm sorry I wasn't here to welcome you. We went to the cafeteria to get some lunch," she explained. "My parents just left." She clapped her hands excitedly when she saw the record player. "I didn't think I'd have room for one." She smiled at Alex, who was fascinated by her. She was wearing a tight pink sweater and a slim gray skirt, with the saddle shoes that all the girls seemed to be wearing, except Merrie.

"We were just going to take a walk," Meredith explained shyly, somewhat bowled over by her effusive roommate. "My mother wants to take a look, for old times' sake."

"So did mine. She met my dad while she was going here. She dropped out after freshman year and they got married. And then I came along." She beamed at them, as Meredith tried not to stare at her voluptuous chest. She looked like a movie star. None of the girls at Marymount had looked like that. The nuns forced them to be much more restrained. "See you when you get back," she said, as they gathered up their things to leave. "Maybe we can listen to some of your music then," she said, as she took a pack of cigarettes out of her purse and a pink ashtray out of a drawer and set it down on her desk. "I hope you don't mind if I smoke." She looked very sophisticated as she lit up.

"No, it's fine," Meredith said, somewhat stunned by her. She had a lot of personality, and seemed warm and friendly and very southern and was anything but shy. "See you in a while."

Meredith followed her family down the stairs, glancing at the other girls moving in or going back down the stairs in pairs with their new roommates. She couldn't imagine being close to someone like Betty. She was very different from the girls Meredith knew at school, and seemed a lot older and more glamorous. She had noticed that Betty was wearing makeup, and all Meredith had brought was a single pink lipstick, which was the only one she owned. Betty looked like the kind of girl that boys would be crazy over, and Meredith suspected she'd be engaged by Christmas, or the end of freshman year, like her mother. Meredith never knew what to say to girls like her. She had nothing in common with them and felt awkward when she compared herself to them. For a minute, she wished she had gone shopping with her mother, as Janet had suggested. She'd bought a few new sweaters, but mostly brought comfortable old clothes.

They walked around the campus until her mother had seen everything she wanted to, and then they hugged Meredith. She waved as they drove away, and she wandered back to her dorm, feeling lost and lonely, wondering what she was doing there. She felt like the ugly duckling in the midst of a flock of glamour girls. She noticed a thin, pale girl with her blond hair in a long braid sitting by herself on a bench as Meredith went back to Lathrop House. Their eyes met for a moment, and the girl smiled, and Meredith wondered if she felt as out of place as she did. She was wearing a simple pleated skirt, a dark sweater, and loafers with navy knee socks. She looked like the girls Meredith had known in Germany, more serious and subdued than the students here, and she seemed more European.

When Meredith went back to her room, she found Betty and three other girls listening to her Frank Sinatra records. The album covers were on the bed, along with a Nat King Cole record she really liked, and Buddy Holly.

"Is this okay with you?" Betty asked over her shoulder, Meredith said it was, and sat down on her bed to listen too. The girls left a little while later, and didn't ask Meredith to join them. They seemed to already have plans, and one of them said to Betty that there was a mixer planned that weekend with the freshman boys from West Point. They all squealed with excitement at the news, and Meredith felt like an outcast before she even started.

She skipped dinner that night and stayed in her room, and it was right before curfew when Betty came back. She disappeared to the bathroom with her bathrobe and makeup case, and came back with her hair in pin curls. Meredith went to get ready for bed then, and when she returned Betty was reading a movie magazine with Grace Kelly on the cover. She'd been in two movies that year, *The Country Girl,* and *Rear Window* with Jimmy Stewart. Meredith had seen *Rear Window* with a friend from school, and had loved it. Betty showed her photographs in the magazine of Grace Kelly on the Riviera with Cary Grant, filming a new movie that summer, and gave it to Meredith to read when she was finished. The two girls didn't seem to have much in common, but Meredith tried not to be daunted by her. Betty was wearing a frilly nightgown, and lit another cigarette as she lay on the bed. Meredith was wearing a faded flannel nightgown she'd had since Germany and still liked, even though the cuffs were frayed and it was a little small.

"Smoke?" Betty offered her the pack of Lucky Strikes, and took out her pink lighter, and Meredith shook her head. She had never tried and was afraid it might make her sick if she did. Betty looked like one of the popular girls in a movie, and Meredith didn't know what to say to her. She was so beautiful and had all the accessories and mannerisms of someone girls would follow and men would fall in love with. Meredith had never aspired to be one of those girls. She'd had friends who were boys in Germany, but she'd never had a boyfriend or a date, and going to an all-girls school, didn't have any opportunity to meet any. She'd never been boy crazy, and studied most of the time, to maintain her good grades. "My mama said she had a lot of fun when she was here," Betty said as she put out her cigarette, and it was easy to believe, if she looked anything like her daughter.

They lay silently awake in the dark for a long time, without saying anything, as Meredith wondered if they'd become friends or be like ships that would pass in the night, each of them observing the other like a rare specimen they had never seen before, and they'd be sharing the room for the rest of the year. Meredith had her own natural beauty, but she was totally unaware of it, unlike Betty's looks, which were carefully studied to make her appear sexy and appealing. Meredith felt like an alien from another planet next to her. What boy would want to meet a girl like her, when they could have Betty, ripe for the plucking? But Meredith didn't really care. She hadn't come here to meet boys, but to learn, get her degree, and go on to law school after she got her bachelor's degree. She wondered if she'd make any friends at all, or if she'd be an awkward outsider forever, wherever she went. And as she puzzled over it, she drifted off to sleep.

Chapter Three

Meredith wore her dark hair in a long, sleek ponytail down her back, with a kilt and a black twin set her mother had packed for her, knee socks, and loafers as she hurried off to class the next day.

Betty was wearing a soft pink cashmere sweater, a circle skirt in the same shade of pink, and her saddle shoes with short white socks. Her hair hung in waves and soft curls to her shoulders after the pin curls of the night before. And she'd worn just a touch of pale pink lipstick. There was no dress code, so they could wear whatever they wanted. *Vogue* had recently praised the fashion sense of the typical Vassar girl, so the students on campus had set a high standard to live up to, which Merrie was determined to ignore.

Betty met up with two other girls in the hall, and they went to orientation together. Meredith walked down the stairs alone and consulted a map of the campus to figure out where she was going. She saw the girl with the long braid walking ahead of her, heading for orientation too. They sat in the same row in the auditorium, but didn't speak to each other, and listened to all the speeches and introductions, and then left the hall with all the other freshman students. Meredith could see Betty on the other side of the building, and her group of followers had grown. There were six or eight of them walking together to their English class. Meredith had to consult the map again that she'd brought with her. The building she was going to was farther away, for her German literature class, and she was surprised to see the girl with the braid walk in ahead of her. This time they smiled at each other when they sat down in class.

The room was small. There were ten students, and the young woman who taught it had a noticeable German accent, and kept everyone's interest for the ninety minutes she spent with them. She said they were going to be reading the classics and greats of German literature: Franz Kafka, Rainer Maria Rilke, Hermann Hesse, Thomas Mann, Günter Grass, Hoffmann, Freytag, and Irmgard Keun. Meredith was sorry they couldn't read them in German, and she was considering buying some of them in the original, but was afraid her German was too rusty now to do so and get the full meaning, although she was still fluent enough to hold a conversation with ease. And she wrote to Anna in German.

She was excited about the serious nature of the course, and she liked the professor, who was a woman in her late thirties and made her description of each book they would be reading sound fascinating. Meredith was disappointed when the professor said the time was up and dismissed the class, and Meredith stopped and thanked the professor in German. The teacher looked at her in surprise and smiled, and they chatted for a few minutes, as the young woman with the braid walked slowly by. She looked as though she would have liked to join them, but didn't dare.

She was standing outside when Meredith came out, and looked at her with her shy smile.

"Are your parents German?" she asked her in German, and Meredith smiled back as she shook her head. She loved being able to speak the language again, which reminded her of the happiest days of her life so far. She had felt so comfortable and at ease in Germany, more so than in the States since she'd been back.

"No. We lived there for four years. In Nuremberg. Are your parents German?" She continued speaking German to her, which seemed comfortable for both of them. The young woman seemed to hesitate before answering the question.

"No," she said firmly, "they're American. But I was born there. In Berlin. Your German is very good," she complimented her.

"I don't get a chance to speak it anymore. I was fluent when I got back five years ago. I loved living there."

The girl with the braid nodded, and then spoke in barely more than a whisper. "I used to love it too. I came here nine years ago." She had obviously come at the end of the war, or just before, Meredith calculated easily.

"Where are you going next?" Meredith asked her.

"Math class," she said with a sigh.

"I have English. I think they're in the same direction. My name is Meredith McKenzie," she volunteered then, and the other girl stuck out a polite hand to shake hers, which was something one rarely saw between women in the States but was common in Europe, where everyone either shook hands or kissed.

"Claudia Steinberg. How do you do?" It seemed like providence that they had met, in their first class, and could speak German to each other. "My parents don't really like me speaking German," she said wistfully. "They want me to be American now that I'm here, but I miss speaking my own language."

"I miss speaking your language too," Meredith said, and they both laughed. "Did you and your family come over after the war?"

Claudia shook her head in answer. "No. I came," she said clearly, offered no further explanation, and Meredith sensed that she didn't want to share more. They chatted about the school and the dorms on their way to class. She was in the same house as Meredith, on the floor above.

"Do you like your roommate?" Merrie asked, and Claudia shrugged.

"She's not very friendly so far. We haven't really talked. My parents were here yesterday to bring me. And she was busy too."

"Mine looks like a movie star," Meredith said, smiling. "She seems okay. She wears makeup and smokes and reads movie magazines. I think she came here to meet boys."

"She won't meet any here," Claudia said, laughing, referring to the all-girls school.

"She wants to go to the mixers. Her mother got engaged while she was here, and I think she has the same thing in mind."

"I didn't really want to come to a women's school, but my mother went to school here, so they insisted," Claudia said cautiously.

"So did mine. I'd rather be in a school with men too, not for romance, but it's just more interesting to have a male point of view in class. And I like having men friends. I'm tired of being with women all the time. I went to an all-girls high school in New York. I had much more fun in school in Germany."

44

Claudia didn't respond to that, and by then, they had reached the math building and she had to go.

"Do you want to have lunch?" she asked Merrie before she left, Meredith nodded, looking pleased. She liked Claudia, and they had more in common than she did with Betty the blond bombshell.

"I'd like that." They made a date at the dining hall at noon, and then both of them hurried off to their classes.

Meredith found her English class far less interesting than her German literature class, and the professor very dry. Her mind was wandering for the second half of the class, and she almost fell asleep. She left quickly when it was over and hurried to the dining facility, where Claudia was already waiting for her.

"The professor let us go early," she explained. They went to choose their meal then. The food looked adequate and wholesome, and they came back to the table after they'd both signed for their lunch with their campus account.

Claudia asked Meredith about life in Germany right after the war. Meredith told her she hadn't been there since 1949 when they'd left, but she had loved living there.

"They did a lot of reconstruction while we were in Nuremberg. The city was very badly hit and almost destroyed by the Allied bombing raids, but the rebuilding went pretty quickly. The Germans are hard workers."

"Some of them," Claudia said cynically. "Did your father do business there?" She was intrigued by Meredith and how well she spoke German, as though she had always lived in Germany or been born there.

"No, he was in the army. He's a lawyer. He was on the legal commission of the Nuremberg war crimes trials. It kept him there for four years."

"They did a good thing bringing the Nazi criminals to trial," Claudia said with feeling.

"I thought so too," Meredith agreed. "I was very proud of him, and he loved it. He didn't talk about it much at home. And my brother was very young. He's only eight now. He was born in Germany. But he's forgotten all his German. Do you still have relatives there?" Meredith asked her conversationally. Claudia looked at her with eyes that told a thousand stories, and then finally she spoke in her soft voice.

"I was liberated from Auschwitz at the end of the war," she said quietly. "My whole family died at the camp. Two sisters, a brother, and my parents. I don't know how but I was the only one who survived. Perhaps because I was old enough to be strong, and not so young they sent me to the gas chamber. I was ten when the camp was liberated. I was placed with an organization that was sending Jewish orphans to America and finding families to adopt them. At first we were all so sick, they couldn't send us to America for a while. I was adopted when I was better by a wonderful family in New York. My new mother gets upset when she thinks I'm too attached to my German roots. She wants me to forget all about them, but I can't. It would be a dishonor to my family not to remember what happened to them."

Meredith couldn't help wondering how she had survived it, and was silent for a long moment, in awe of this girl.

"My father was among the American soldiers who liberated Dachau," Meredith told her. "He said it was the most horrifying thing he'd ever seen."

"It was," Claudia confirmed. "But now it feels like it happened to someone else. I've been here for nine years. That's a very long time. I'm nineteen, how old are you?"

Meredith was stunned into silence for a moment by what Claudia had told her, and then said she was eighteen. Claudia lifted up the sleeve of her sweater then, as they talked, and showed Meredith the number tattooed on the inside of her forearm. Merrie stared at it in respectful silence. Claudia said she had been out with her nanny when the whole family had been picked up. Neighbors had hidden her for nearly a year, but they had been afraid they would be discovered and had moved her to a different location, where she was found anyway and sent to the same camp as her parents. Her mother and two younger sisters and grandparents had been dead by then, gassed almost immediately after they arrived. Her older brother and father had been forced to do hard labor, and both had died of typhus shortly before the camp was liberated. She had lost them all and had no other family. Eventually, after the war, she had been sent to America, to be adopted by the Steinbergs. They had two daughters who were close to her age, slightly younger. Claudia said they had been nothing but kind to her, but she could never forget her own family and how they had died. She thought about them every day.

"I feel guilty in places like this," she admitted to Meredith. "Everyone is so comfortable and so spoiled, and they don't know how lucky they are. I want to write a book about the war, but not until I'm older. I want to be a journalist after I graduate. I will write the truth about what it was like one day." Meredith nodded, bowled over by her. Claudia was so real and so honest, yet still so gentle and had suffered so much. But she didn't seem angry or bitter, or even shattered by it. She was a testimony to the strength of the human spirit, and Meredith sensed something very powerful within her to have survived it. After what she'd been through, nothing could hurt her or stop her or destroy her. It was an inspiration to listen to her, and painful to imagine what had happened to her. And now this slight, quiet girl was here, a survivor of one of the worst camps. It made everything else seem insignificant, and a girl like Betty and her pin curls and movie magazines ridiculous, and yet Claudia had gone on to lead a normal life.

"I don't usually tell people," Claudia said, looking faintly embarrassed. "My American parents don't like me to. But I can't be silent about it. People need to remember what the Nazis did to the Jews, little children and old people and women. They took everything from them, their jobs, their homes, their families, their lives. That should never be forgotten."

"No, it shouldn't," Meredith agreed with her solemnly.

"One day, I will put it all in a book," Claudia repeated, looking thoughtful, and Meredith nodded. It sounded important to her too.

"My grandfather always says you have to fight the good fight, for justice for everyone, especially people who can't defend themselves. He says we have to make a difference in the world. I want to do that one day, but I'm never sure how. He's a justice of the Supreme Court, so he can make a difference by interpreting the law and making important decisions, but so far, I don't see what I can do to change anything."

Meredith was still waiting for some kind of sign from the universe to show her what to do. She hadn't found her own path or any of the answers yet. The only thing she did know was that the life her parents wanted for her, to get married and have children as her end goal, just wasn't enough. She wanted to accomplish more than that, and

Claudia did too. Meredith was glad that they had found each other, and on the first day. Now she had a friend at school. "I want to go to law school after we graduate," she said. "I want to defend people who are disadvantaged in some way, and have no one to protect them."

That sounded like a good idea to Claudia too. "I want to tell the truth with my words," she said as they left the cafeteria.

"I have to go to the library to get some books for my English class. Do you want to come?" Meredith invited her. Neither of them had class that afternoon.

"Sure," Claudia agreed, and they fell into step beside each other. They found the library, and Meredith got the books she needed, and they both checked out the first book they'd been assigned for their German class. And then they walked back to Lathrop House together. Claudia stopped at Meredith's room and looked around, but Betty was out, so Meredith couldn't introduce them. A few minutes later, Claudia went back to her own room upstairs. They agreed to meet at the dining hall for dinner that night. For the first time in years, Meredith felt as though she had made a friend. She hadn't felt a bond with anyone she went to school with since she'd left Germany, and had felt like an outsider all through high school. And now, on her first day at Vassar, she had met this extraordinary girl who was a survivor and wanted to make a difference in the world too. It seemed like the hand of destiny that they had met.

They talked about their families in New York that night at dinner, and their parents' expectations of them. Claudia said that the Steinbergs were very important at their temple, Temple Emanu-El on Fifth Avenue. They wanted her to marry someone important in the Jewish community, preferably a doctor, a lawyer, or a banker, and they had warned her not to go out with any Christian boys while she was at Vassar, which seemed silly to her. She didn't want to get married, and she was there to go to school. And they had warned her to stay away from Bohemians, presumably from other schools. They thought them unsavory and unwashed. She thought her parents' outlook was limited and a little ridiculous, but she knew they meant well and wanted the best for her.

"My parents don't want me to go to law school," Meredith sympathized. "They think it will stop me from getting married, that I can't do both, have a husband and family and be a lawyer. They think it's a choice. My grandfather thinks law school is a great idea, but my parents don't. They want me to play bridge every day like my mother," she said in exasperation, and Claudia laughed.

"Mine plays bridge all the time too. And she shops a lot. My sisters do too. They think I'm weird because I'd rather read a book, or write one eventually. I tried to write poetry, but I'm not good at it. I went to a poetry reading in Greenwich Village, and my parents had a fit. And my father thinks jazz musicians are all on drugs. They don't like black people either. I think that's why they want me here, because even if most of the girls are Christian, there's no one for me to date."

Meredith smiled at that. "Not according to Betty and her pals. They're all expecting to meet the man of their dreams at the mixers with the boys from nearby schools, and maybe they will. But there's a lot I want to do before I think about getting married." And then she remembered the debutante ball where they wanted her presented at Christmas, and she told Claudia about it, who listened with interest.

"It might be fun," she admitted. "You could wear a beautiful dress. It sounds very fairy princess." Her eyes looked dreamy as she imagined it, from Meredith's description.

"That's not what I want to be when I grow up. And they all do it to find a husband. That's the whole point of events like that. I'm surprised your parents don't want you to come out too."

Claudia looked startled as she said it. "They don't allow Jews to be debutantes," she said with certainty. "No matter how much money their parents have. My mother told me that, otherwise I'm sure they'd make me do it too." But Claudia sounded as though she wouldn't mind. The big white dress was the lure, almost like a wedding. And she liked to dance.

"Is that true?" Meredith was shocked. It had never occurred to her. "Jews can't be debutantes?" She knew black girls couldn't be presented. But Jews?

Claudia nodded.

"That's disgusting. Why not?"

"It's just the way it is. It's always been that way, I think. They can't join certain clubs, or buy apartments in some buildings. My parents wanted to buy an apartment on Fifth Avenue, and they were turned down. They bought one on West End Avenue instead, and we have a very nice place. My father was so angry about it, he bought the whole building. Negroes and show business people can't buy in fancy buildings either. Harry Belafonte owns the building next to ours."

"That's like Germany during the Nazis," Meredith said with a look of outrage, and Claudia shook her head seriously.

"No, it's not. It's a lot different not being able to join a Gentile club, or buy an apartment, than not being able to practice law or medicine, or having your home taken away from you and looted by the SS, and losing everything you own, and being herded into a cattle car to be killed in a death camp. We have our own clubs and buildings. Maybe it doesn't matter. But no one is killing Jews here,

51

or dragging them through the streets." She said it sadly, remembering the terrors of her childhood and the family she had lost.

"It's still discrimination, and it's very wrong. If I can come out, and I don't even want to, why can't you?"

"I just can't. It's not a matter of life and death." Claudia knew the difference, and it didn't bother her not being a debutante. She had never expected to be.

"But it could be one day. Maybe that's how it starts. Why should Jews be treated differently?"

"They have been throughout history. That's what the state of Israel is all about, a safe haven for Jews." It had been established six years before and recognized by President Truman, who was a hero in the Jewish community. "My parents give a lot of money to Israel," Claudia commented, and it made Meredith wonder where her parents stood on the issue. They never talked about it, so she didn't know. "My father says it's very important to support Israel, and they need our help. They went there last year. I wanted to go, but they wouldn't take me. I was in school, and they didn't want me to miss any of senior year."

Meredith was fascinated by what she was saying and the questions it aroused. Claudia had a much broader view of the world, on certain subjects anyway. Meredith felt as though she had led a very sheltered life, and in many ways she had. Her parents were ultra traditional in their lifestyle and ideas, although she assumed they were sympathetic to Jewish people, given how hard her father had worked at the Nuremberg trials, and having seen concentration camps firsthand. How could he not be sympathetic after that? Obviously, he was.

While Meredith and Claudia discussed more serious issues, the rest of the girls only seemed interested in the upcoming mixer that weekend and the boys they were going to meet. Betty and the clique she had formed as soon as she arrived spent days choosing what they would wear, borrowing clothes from each other and talking about their hair. Betty had found a new way to pin curl hers, and had discovered some curlers at the local drugstore that would give her more waves. The dresses they had picked out were sexy and showed off their figures, and Betty had the perfect high-heeled shoes for her outfit and a short swing coat the same peacock blue color as her silk dress. They were in a frenzy of excitement over the boys they were about to meet from West Point.

Meredith watched the comings and goings from her room with a combination of dismay and amusement. She was sure she hadn't brought the right thing to wear, and didn't even own it, and she didn't want to go anyway. She said as much to Claudia. Claudia's roommate was out a lot of the time, and to get away from "Betty's girls," Meredith preferred to go upstairs to visit Claudia instead of wading through the crowd of giggling girls in her own room. They used her record player all the time and she didn't care.

Claudia stunned her the night before the event. They'd been at school for a week by then, and Meredith liked most of her classes, but Claudia was the only girl she wanted to hang out with, and Claudia felt the same about her. She was concerned that the other girls wouldn't want to be friends with her because she was Jewish and most of them were Christian, which Meredith told her was paranoia but secretly wondered if it was true. She'd overheard one or two nasty comments about the Jew on the third floor, and was afraid it was Claudia, but she didn't tell her, and didn't want to hurt her feelings.

"I think we should go," Claudia said, as she lay on her bed, and Meredith sprawled in the room's only chair, with her long legs stretched out ahead of her.

"Go where?" Meredith looked distracted. She was thinking about a paper she had to write for their German class and wasn't sure exactly how to approach it, and she wanted to impress the teacher.

"To the mixer," Claudia said in a soft voice.

"Are you crazy? Why? I'm not looking for a husband, and neither are you."

"No, but it might be nice to meet some boys. There are a lot of girls here."

"That's for sure," Meredith commented and rolled her eyes. And most of them were like Betty, boy crazy, and more worried about their hair than their grades. Vassar was a serious school that offered a great education, but the freshman girls were notoriously more excited about the coed social events than their studies. Supposedly, they eventually settled down, especially once they were engaged. "Why would we go to the mixer?" Meredith looked baffled. She didn't want to meet a bunch of snobby boys or would-be soldiers at West Point. If she met a boy, she wanted it to be someone interesting, intellectual, smart, and different. And Betty and their crowd had made it seem like a circus. Nothing about it appealed to her.

"I think we should. We might make some new friends, boys for a change," Claudia said. Meredith thought about it for a minute and wasn't convinced.

"You really want to go?"

Claudia nodded. "It'll be fun to get dressed up. My mom made me pack a couple of nice dresses for social events."

"My mom did too. I didn't want to, and she insisted." They exchanged a smile. Their mothers sounded similar, no matter their religion, it didn't seem to make much difference in their concerns for their daughters. They both thought their mothers worried too much.

They debated for a while, and Claudia finally overcame Meredith's objections. The following evening, they were dressed and ready to get on the bus to go to West Point. Claudia and Meredith sat at the rear. Claudia had worn a navy silk dress that showed off her slim figure, with a white silk coat over it, and she was wearing a small hat and gloves and high heels. Her dress had long sleeves. Her mother had taken her shopping at Bergdorf Goodman for her school wardrobe. She had her long braid wound into a small bun at the nape of her neck. She looked very pretty. Meredith had worn one of three black dresses she'd brought, and her heels weren't as high so she didn't look too tall. She was also wearing a short fur jacket that had been her mother's and made her look very grown up. Betty and her crowd had gone all out, and looked perfect with dresses in jewel colors, or white or black, high heels, dressy coats, evening hats and gloves and small evening bags. And their hair looked glamorous in a variety of styles it had taken them hours to achieve.

The cadets at West Point were about to receive the best that Vassar had to offer with three busloads of very attractive young women who had made every effort to impress them. The boys in dress uniform were waiting for them in long formal lines when they arrived, as the girls stared at them in delight and whispered to one another. The chaperones were right behind them, to keep an eye on them all night and see that everyone behaved like the ladies and gentlemen they were supposed to be, and looked like in their dress uniforms and pretty dresses, whether borrowed or owned by the girls wearing them.

"I feel stupid," Meredith whispered to Claudia, as they got off the bus after the hour's drive from Vassar. But she had to admit, the cadets looked very handsome, and were offering the girls an arm to escort them inside to the ballroom, where refreshments had been set out. The West Point band was going to play dance music for them until midnight. The uniformed West Point chaperones greeted the women from Vassar with amusement, knowing that their charges would keep them busy all night. And whether in uniform or not, they were a bunch of eighteen-year-olds out to have fun and get away with whatever they could.

"They look nice," Claudia said, glad they had come. It felt good to get dressed up, and she told Meredith she looked very pretty in the black dress. Several of the young men had already noticed them, as they all chatted for a while and helped themselves to fruit punch.

"They're all going to grow up to be killers one day, in some war or other," Meredith said cynically, and Claudia scolded her.

"Well, they're not killers yet. Be nice, Merrie." They exchanged a smile, as a particularly good-looking young cadet with blond hair and blue eyes approached them and introduced himself. His name was Seth Ballard, and he seemed riveted by Claudia, who blushed when she introduced herself, and Meredith smiled. The freshman boys had arrived at West Point as recently as the girls had arrived at Vassar, and they talked about their schools back home. Seth was from Virginia, and had just the faintest trace of a southern accent. His father was a retired colonel, and his grandfather a general, and his family had a horse farm in Virginia. He was third-generation West Point.

"We're second-generation Vassar," Claudia said, referring to herself and Meredith.

"How do you like it?" he asked them politely, and they said they did, and their classes were interesting so far. He left for a few minutes to find a friend to bring over to introduce to Meredith, and as soon as he left, Claudia asked Meredith quietly in German what she thought of him.

"He seems pleasant, and he's handsome. But he doesn't look Jewish." Meredith grinned at her, and liked the fact that they could speak a language no one else understood, so they could say whatever they wanted.

"You sound like my mother. Who cares? I think he's really cute," Claudia responded.

"If you get engaged freshman year, I won't be your friend anymore," Meredith warned her with a smile.

"Don't be stupid!" Claudia said, as Seth came back to them with a tall redheaded boy with freckles whose name was Christian. He was from Boston, and said he was second-generation West Point. He was very polite, and both boys asked them to dance when the music started up, and monopolized them for most of the evening. Magic didn't happen between Christian and Meredith, but she had a good time with him. He was intelligent, and the oldest of six children. When the evening ended he said he hoped to see her again. She doubted they would, except at another mixer. Seth walked Claudia all the way to the bus and looked totally besotted with her, as he stood and waved while she disappeared with the chaperones and other girls.

"You were a big hit!" Meredith said in German as they took their seat in the back of the bus again.

"He's so polite. I really like him," Claudia said, looking starry-eyed. "He said he'd come to visit me at school sometime."

"Your mother will kill you. He must be Episcopalian for sure."

"Oh, shut up." Claudia grinned mischievously. "He just wants to visit, not propose."

"Give him another week," Meredith teased, and they chatted happily all the way back to school. Meredith admitted that it had been fun, and Christian had been interesting to talk to. He told her all about their classes and training at West Point, which sounded incredibly rigorous to her. It made Vassar seem like summer camp for girls.

The two girls left each other outside Meredith's room, and Claudia went upstairs to hers. Betty came in a few minutes later, and looked victorious. Three boys had asked to visit her, and during a break, she had chatted with one of the boys in the band. He was a senior, and wanted to see her again too. The evening had been a smash hit for her, and there was another mixer planned in a month or so with Yale. She planned to have a boyfriend by Christmas, she told Meredith, and a fiancé by June. She was on a mission, and so were her friends. They'd had a good time. The West Point cadets had been very hospitable to the Vassar girls. Meredith had enjoyed the evening too.

The following weekend, Meredith's parents came to visit her for Parents' Weekend, and she introduced them to Claudia. Meredith told them afterward that Claudia was German but didn't mention her war experiences, or that she'd been adopted by Americans. The subject seemed too serious to just mention casually.

Her family walked around the campus together, and she told them about her classes. They took her to dinner that night, and the next day they left, satisfied that she was adjusting and making friends. She promised to come home for a weekend soon. Her mother wanted to take her shopping for her coming-out dress, and Meredith didn't argue about it with her. It would be nice to go home for a weekend and see Alex too.

When she got to New York three weeks later, he was ecstatic to see her. She'd asked Claudia if she was going home for the weekend, but Seth Ballard, the West Point cadet, was coming to visit her on Saturday, and she didn't want to miss it. She was excited to see him, and he'd called her several times on the phone in their residence hall since the mixer. He obviously had a crush on her, and he was taking her to dinner on Saturday night. Claudia had gotten permission for it. They had a two-hour pass for dinner in town and had to be back by eight o'clock. The rules were very strict, and any infraction would result in not getting a pass the next time she asked.

Robert and Janet were happy to see Merrie too, and the subject of her debut didn't come up until dessert on Friday night. Alex had already left the table by then, and Janet listed all the stores they were going to visit the next day to find the dress. Meredith looked at her seriously and took a breath.

"I told you, Mom, I'm not going to make my debut. I don't want to, and I don't believe in it. I won't do it."

"What do you mean you 'don't believe in it'? What's that supposed to mean?" Her mother looked confused.

"They don't let Jews come out at the cotillion, do they?"

Her parents both looked shocked, as though she had slapped them.

"What does that have to do with anything? We're not Jewish," her mother said tartly.

"No, but it excludes Jews. And Negroes, I assume. It's a discriminatory event, and I don't want to be part of it."

Her father looked furious as she said it. "Did your grandfather tell you that?" he asked pointedly.

"No. We didn't talk about it. I just know from girls I've met at school that Jews are excluded. I don't think that's right. And the whole premise is wrong. I'm not looking for a husband, and I don't want to be part of some kind of cattle call to show me off like a cow at auction."

"Oh, for God's sake," Robert said, annoyed by the whole conversation and her stubbornness. "You wear a white dress, you look beautiful. You make your bow. And you've been officially presented to society. What's wrong with that? And what difference does it make if there are Jewish girls in it or not? We're not prejudiced. Why are you making such a fuss about this, Merrie? And no one is auctioning you off. It's a party, that's all."

"The purpose of which, historically, is to find a husband. I don't want one. At least not yet. And not for a long time. I have better things to do with my life first, like law school."

"Making your debut and going to law school are not incompatible concepts or mutually exclusive," he pointed out.

"A debut is superfluous. And no, you're not prejudiced, Dad. You spent four years prosecuting war criminals for crimes against the Jews. So why would you endorse a party that excludes them?"

"I'm sure there are Jews there, for Heaven's sake."

"But not the debutantes. Doesn't that seem wrong to you?" She was putting him on the spot, and her mother hadn't said a word. She had no idea what to say or how to respond, and left it to Robert to deal with her. She hated arguing with Meredith.

"Yes, if you put it that way, it does seem wrong. But there are clubs that don't accept Jews either. It's always been that way," her father explained calmly.

"That doesn't make it right. And buildings where they can't buy apartments. What about this one? Can Jews buy apartments in our building?" She wasn't letting up, much to her parents' dismay. She was asking pertinent questions.

"I have no idea," he said, looking uncomfortable. In fact he did know, and they couldn't buy in the building, but that had no bearing on whether Meredith made her debut or not. It was important to Janet, and to both of them, that she do it. It was a tradition they followed and believed in. And he didn't want to lose that argument over whether or not Jews could buy apartments in their building.

"You seem to have gotten very political since you went away to school, Meredith. Who've you been talking to?"

"Claudia, my best friend at school, is Jewish. She's German. Her whole family died in Auschwitz, and she survived. She was adopted by an American family after the war. You met her when you visited me."

He was silent for a moment, faced with the memories Meredith had revived, and visions he would never forget. "That's a terrible thing, Merrie. I can't disagree with that. But coming out is an old tradition. And the cotillion is a very old club, of old New York families. One day, there probably will be Jewish debutantes presented. But that hasn't happened yet, and this is important to us. I'd like you to put your political principles aside on this and do it, to make your mother happy. It's not a lot to ask."

He tried to reason with her and remain gentle about it, and his wife looked at him gratefully. She had no idea what she'd say to her friends if her daughter didn't come out. There was no possible excuse. They would be a laughingstock, or a pariah, if people knew the truth, that Merrie had refused.

"It *is* a lot to ask. You're asking me to forget my principles for a night, for a party. That's not right."

"I'm asking you to do it for your parents, for us. Even your very liberal Democratic grandfather would like to be there and see you come out. He's still part of the Establishment too. And he goes to the cotillion every year. He'll be disappointed not to see you there, and so will we."

Meredith was quiet for a long moment and looked at her mother, with tears in her eyes. Meredith could see it really was important to her, and with a heavy heart, feeling as though she had betrayed everything she believed in, Meredith stood up and stared at them both.

"All right. I'll do it this time. But don't ever ask me again to violate what I believe in. I'm doing it for you, but I won't do it again. I have to stand for what I believe in. I won't sacrifice my integrity even for you." It was a major declaration at eighteen. Her father nodded agreement, and she left the table without saying another word. A moment later, they heard her door close firmly, as Robert let out a sigh and glanced at his wife.

"This is all my father's fault, and the liberal ideas he gives her about fighting for causes. She's too young and impressionable for that. He's going to turn her into a revolutionary if he's not careful, and he'd probably be pleased."

"Thank you" was all Janet could muster, deeply grateful that they weren't going to be publicly humiliated by Meredith refusing to come out. And she cleared the table, thinking about the dress they would buy the next day.

Chapter Four

On Saturday morning, Meredith and her mother took a taxi to Bergdorf Goodman and went to the bridal department, where the debutante dresses were sold. Janet was planning to make a day of it, and visit all the department stores with bridal departments before picking the dress they liked best. It felt like a dress rehearsal for a wedding to Meredith.

She chose the second dress they showed her at Bergdorf's. It was simple and understated, not too low cut, as was proper, with a big bell skirt and a small waist. It was white taffeta with little cap sleeves, and it looked beautiful on her. Janet would have preferred something a little more elaborate with beading or lace or embroidery, or a sash at the waist, but the one Meredith had picked was striking in its simplicity, and with her dark hair swept up she looked like Snow White in it. She was going to be a beautiful debutante whether she approved of the event or not. Not all the girls who came out were beautiful. Many were heavy, had bad skin, or were unattractive, but it was their night too and it had a Cinderella quality to it for all the girls.

They went to the shoe department next and chose high-heeled white satin shoes, and long white kid gloves in the glove department. Her outfit was complete by one o'clock. She didn't even need the dress fitted. It was perfect and looked like it had been made for her. Even the length was right when they went back and tried the shoes with it. Janet was enormously relieved, and they went across the street to the Plaza for lunch afterward in the Palm Court, and by three o'clock they were home. Her mother had rattled on all through lunch about the dress and the event, and spoke of little else.

Janet had reminisced about her own experiences at Vassar too, and Meredith told her about the mixer she'd gone to at West Point. In answer to her mother's questions about whether she'd met any cadets she liked particularly, she said she hadn't. Janet admitted to having a beau there for a few months early in her freshman year. She had been swayed more by the uniform than the man. And then she had met Robert. Her grandparents had given a ball for her, and she had come out at the cotillion too, for good measure. Robert and his best friend had been escorts at the cotillion, and she said it had been love at first sight. They had gotten engaged six months later, and married three years after, when she graduated from Vassar. Robert had just finished law school then and joined his father's law firm. Meredith was born three years later.

Like most women of her generation, Janet's course had been set early on, and never wavered. And she was still happy with Robert more than twenty years later. She had never questioned her path or her decisions. She had done what was expected of her all her life and had no regrets, and neither did Robert. She was forty-five years old, but she appeared older, as did Robert at forty-nine. She had a matronly style that suited her, and a conservative attitude. She never challenged her beliefs, or his, and even going to Germany with him for four years had seemed like the right thing for a good wife to do, and she had enjoyed it. Robert made all her decisions, which was comfortable for her, and what she expected, and so did he. She never challenged his wisdom or authority over her.

Meredith loved her parents, but she couldn't imagine choosing a man at eighteen and living a life based on what her parents expected of her, without questioning all of it or making decisions of her own. Her grandfather was the only renegade among them, and was frequently criticized for it and thought to be eccentric, although his own wife followed him without question too. His willingness to confront everything and swim against the currents had taken him to great places, and had served him and the country well. He was the model Meredith would have preferred to follow, but women didn't do that or have the opportunities men did, unless they were willing to become total outcasts, which Meredith didn't aspire to either.

She wanted to be her own person, respect her own values, fight her own battles, and make her own decisions, and she didn't see why that was so difficult for women and considered unacceptable. Why weren't they allowed to have their own ideas too? Why did everything have to be decided by their husbands? Whenever something came up in her parents' lives, her father made the decision, and Janet always seemed grateful that he did. She never wanted to take matters in her own hands or do something different. All she wanted was to be protected, to bend to him, and be the passenger not the driver.

Meredith couldn't imagine living that way, or following any man blindly. She wondered if she would ever meet one who would accept her independence and free thinking. She could only respect a man willing to fight for what he believed in, and who wanted her to do the same without trying to control or quash her. She wanted to be a person willing to fight the good fight, as her grandfather said, and even die for her beliefs. It didn't seem compatible with marriage, and certainly not one like her parents'. But she wasn't interested in looking for a man anytime soon. Her freedom of choice to follow her own path was far more important to her than marriage.

On Sunday morning, her father played golf early, as he always did. Alex had spent the night at a friend's and wasn't home yet. And her mother was playing tennis at the club with a friend and said she'd be home by noon. They were all going to have lunch together, and then Meredith would take the train back to Poughkeepsie. She had nothing to do that morning, and was having breakfast in the kitchen. Adelaide had made her irresistible pancakes, and she asked Merrie if she ever went to church. The family went from time to time, but her father liked to play golf on Sundays. Meredith hadn't gone to church yet at Vassar. As always, even about church, her mother did whatever her father wished. He was never a tyrant, he was simply used to being in charge of all their plans.

"Do you, Addie?" Meredith asked with interest, as she finished the pancakes. It was still early, and she was going to read the Sunday paper before everyone got home.

"I love going to my church, when I'm off on Sundays," which wasn't a regular occurrence. Adelaide beamed as she said it. "I go to a church up in Harlem with a gospel choir. It's like listening to an-gels singing," she said with a rapturous expression, and Meredith smiled.

"I'd really like to go with you sometime. I love gospel music."

"I'll take you anytime you want, when I'm off," she offered gener-ously, and Meredith looked at her watch as she said it. It was only nine-thirty, and the others weren't due home till at least noon or even one o'clock. Her father was only playing nine holes of golf that day so he could have lunch with her, although he usually played eighteen.

"Do you want to go now? What time does it start?"

"Ten-thirty. I'm not dressed for it," but she had a coat to put over her uniform, and because it was Sunday, she'd worn a hat.

"You look fine," Meredith assured her.

"You don't think your mama and papa would mind?"

"Why would they?" Meredith couldn't imagine it. It was church, after all. What did it matter where and with whom? She went to put on a dress and coat, and a small hat. She grabbed her bag and gloves and put on heels. Adelaide was excited at what they were about to share. So was Meredith. It was an adventure, and much more inter-esting than going to the family's usual church.

They took the subway uptown to Harlem and walked to the Abys-sinian Baptist Church just off 138th Street. It was the first black Baptist church in New York State. When they got there, Meredith saw families and swarms of people entering the church and greet-ing each other. Adelaide met several people she knew and intro-duced Meredith. She realized immediately that she was the only white person in the church, but she had expected that to be the case and wasn't surprised or bothered by it. She felt comfortable with

Adelaide, and everyone was friendly to her, although a few seemed curious.

They slid into a pew toward the middle of the church. The sermon was energetic, and the congregation was enthusiastic and responsive, and Meredith loved it. There was an atmosphere of joy and life in the church that she'd never experienced or seen before. Halfway through the service the music started, and the rafters shook with the beautiful voices. It was the most moving thing Meredith had ever heard. There was a soprano soloist who ripped your soul out, and a baritone who had a voice worthy of the Metropolitan Opera. The choir was amazing. Meredith didn't want to leave the church and wished it would go on forever, and Adelaide was thrilled by how much she loved it. An hour later, they were back on the sidewalk, and Meredith felt as though she'd been to Heaven and just flown back. She knew it was a moment she would remember for the rest of her life and thanked Adelaide profusely.

"I can honestly say that's the most beautiful thing I've ever heard," she said, deeply moved by it, and hugged Addie, who looked proud and pleased to have shared it with her. Adelaide said goodbye to the friends she'd seen there, and they took the subway back downtown, with Meredith still floating from the music.

They walked into the apartment five minutes before noon. Her mother came back ten minutes later, and Alex was dropped off by his friend's parents. Her father arrived at twelve-thirty, pleased with his golf scores. They sat down to a lunch of Addie's cold chicken and a variety of salads shortly after one. Everyone had had a good morning and was in a happy mood, especially Meredith, after church.

"What did you do this morning, Merrie?" her mother asked, handing her the bowl of potato salad, and Meredith helped herself.

"I went to church with Addie," she said, looking blissful at the memory of the exquisite music. And everyone she'd met there had been welcoming and kind. No one had reacted badly to the fact that she was the only white woman there. On the contrary, they seemed happy to see her, had been universally friendly, and thanked her for coming afterward.

"That was nice of you, dear," her mother said blandly. "I didn't know she went to church." Her mother had never asked. She planned meals with Addie and gave her instructions. She never asked about her personal life, or habits.

"We went to her church, the Abyssinian Baptist Church in Harlem," Meredith said as though it were a common occurrence, but as soon as she said it, both her parents stopped eating and stared at her.

"You did *what*?" her father asked, as though she had just told them she had walked down Park Avenue naked.

"I went to church with Addie," she repeated. "They have an incredible gospel choir."

"Were you the only white woman there?" Robert asked, and Meredith nodded. Adelaide was in the kitchen and couldn't hear them.

"Yes, I was," Meredith said, as she took a mouthful of potato salad. "People couldn't have been nicer."

"Are you insane?" her father whispered to her, and her mother glanced at her in horror. "You could have been killed. You can't just wander into a colored church. That's not safe."

"It was perfectly safe. And the music was gorgeous," Meredith said, digging her heels in and shocked by their reaction. "Nobody was the least bit menacing. There was nothing scary or dangerous about it. It was beautiful, that's all it was. And a lot more moving than our church."

There was silence at the table after that, and no one said a word for the rest of lunch. When they got up from the table, her father motioned her into his study, where he faced her with a combination of fury and terror.

"Meredith, I forbid you to ever do anything like that again. I'm sure Adelaide meant well, but she put your life in danger taking you there. Do *not ever* go to Harlem again."

Meredith was so stunned by what he said that she didn't know how to answer him.

"I don't want her to get in trouble," Meredith said, worried about Addie. She didn't want her father to fire her, or even scold her. Meredith had wanted to go with her and had suggested it herself.

"She won't, but you will if you ever do anything like it again."

"I don't understand. Because it was Harlem? Because they're Negroes? Is that what this is about? I always thought that you were so liberal. Maybe not as much as Grampa, but that we were normal people. Now you want me to come out at an event that excludes Jews, and you forbid me to go to a colored church in Harlem, which was as safe as our own church down here, maybe more so. The people were nicer. Who are we, Dad? Are we prejudiced? Do we hate Jews and Negroes? I don't understand," and she truly didn't. There were tears in her eyes.

"You need to stay with your own kind, Meredith. You don't belong in Harlem."

"They are 'our own kind,' they're humans. Your heart bled for the people you liberated from Dachau. But now you don't want to go to parties with them? Or have me go to church in Harlem? I didn't go to some kind of drug den, I went to church, Dad. No one is going to kill me there."

"Don't be so sure," he said, frowning sternly. "I want you to promise me you won't go back."

"I promise," she said, because it was easier than fighting with him, and she wasn't going to join Addie's church, but she had loved going with her. And she was sad that her parents couldn't understand that.

She went to her room and packed her bag, and left an hour later to catch her train. She gave Alex a big hug, kissed Addie, and said goodbye to her parents, but there was a tangible distance between them now. They had become strangers, and they seemed to share none of the same beliefs. It was the first time she had seen it so clearly. A door had slammed shut between them.

She thought about how different she was from her parents all the way back to Vassar on the train, and she couldn't get it out of her mind. When Claudia stuck her head through the door to her room, she saw that Meredith looked serious and upset.

"How did it go? Who won about the dress?" she asked her.

"I picked one with my mom at Bergdorf's. I said I'd do it. It means so much to her, I gave in. I took the second one they showed me. The first one had ruffles on it, which I just couldn't do. I don't care. But they're not the people I thought they were," she said sadly, as Claudia came in and sat down, worried about her. She told her then about going to Harlem with Addie, and her father having a fit about it.

"My parents don't like colored people either, except in the kitchen.

It's their generation," Claudia said, more willing to accept their limitations than Merrie was. "They think they're dangerous."

"So I'm only supposed to talk to white Christians for the rest of my life? And you can only date Jews? Why are they all so prejudiced?" It seemed so limited to her, and so wrong.

"They grew up that way. It seems normal to them, even if it shocks us." She smiled at Meredith. "You're not wrong about how you feel. They just don't see it that way. And I know you want to fight the good fight, but maybe not quite so hard. Maybe you need to fight a little more gently for what you believe in."

It wasn't bad advice, but Meredith didn't want to hear it. "I hate the hypocrisy, the pretense of how open-minded and liberal they pretend to be when they really aren't. How was your date with Seth, by the way?"

Claudia's face lit up when she was asked. "Seth is wonderful. He's the sweetest man I've ever met." Meredith smiled at the look in her eyes. "He said he'd take me to dinner again sometime soon. We had a really fun time."

"Did you tell him he'll have to convert to Judaism?" Meredith teased, and Claudia laughed.

"Not yet. I thought I'd save that for the second date."

She told Meredith all about it then, while they had dinner in the dining hall. But Meredith was shaken by her weekend with her parents. She was discovering things about them that she never knew. Their prejudices were so ingrained in them, they didn't even see them, and Meredith couldn't tolerate their belief system. Standing up for her beliefs had become all-important to her. More than ever.

Her father had a similar reaction after she left, and was upset too. He could tell that Meredith was changing and slipping away from them. "My father has ruined her," Robert said to Janet after dinner that night, after Alex had gone to his room. "She wants to break down all the barriers and change the old rules. But they're there for a reason, to keep us all in our place and where we belong, and others on the other side of those barriers. If she spends her life as a revolutionary, she's going to be a very unhappy woman. It's fine for my father to think that way, but not a woman, and certainly not a girl her age."

Janet nodded and didn't say anything, as she thought about it. But she knew he was right. He always was. "She'll outgrow it," she reassured him. "She's doing her debut. Sooner or later, she'll meet a man who'll calm her down, and she'll settle into the life she was born to." Janet didn't look worried about it, as she tried to soothe him.

"I'm not so sure," Robert said, still shaken by the idea that she'd gone up to Harlem and been the only white woman in a black church. He'd never been to Harlem in his life. "She's way too brave and open-minded for her own good. She could get hurt that way. She doesn't realize the risks she's taking."

"Maybe she does," her mother said thoughtfully. "The world needs more people like her, but I still don't want her to be the one blazing trails. Let others do it. And she'll settle down once she meets a man. A good man will tame her. She'll get busy with a husband and kids, and she won't have time for these battles."

Robert looked at his wife strangely. As far as he was concerned, the world as he knew it did not need to change, nor rabble-rousers to upset the balance. The old ways worked best. And Meredith was just going to have to learn to accept that. Hopefully soon.

Chapter Five

Two weeks after Meredith's weekend in New York, there was another mixer, with Yale this time, which was two hours away, but very appealing. Claudia and Meredith decided to go, since the one at West Point had actually been fun. Claudia had had dinner with Seth again. They were getting to know each other, and it was rapidly turning from friendship to romance, faster than Claudia had expected and Meredith thought wise. He knew about her history by then, and how she had come to the States. She had shown him her tattoo, and he had cried. And he was planning to take German next semester. Claudia's parents knew nothing about him, and Meredith was worried about her. There was no point getting serious with him. The relationship couldn't go anywhere. Her parents would never allow it. Claudia knew it too, but couldn't seem to stop the tide, and didn't want to.

"Does he know your parents won't let you go out with Christians?"

Claudia nodded, trying not to think about it. "I told him. I think he believes we can figure it out later. But they'll never agree. I don't think they'd even accept a convert, or maybe they would. I don't know. We shouldn't need a marriage license and parental consent to have dinner," she said, frustrated about it, but she was falling in love with him, and he was head over heels for her. "His parents won't like it either," she told Meredith. "They're staunch Episcopalians, and he says his family is somewhat prejudiced. But they're intelligent people, and Seth thinks he can reason with them once they know me. I'm not so sure." She had dealt with anti-Semitism all her life in its most extreme forms.

"Are you planning to meet his parents?" Meredith looked stunned. They'd only had two dates, and been to the mixer together.

"Not now. And not for a long time. Maybe in a year, if we're still dating. But we talk about it. My parents don't want me to get married now anyway. They want me to get an education." She and Meredith had that in common. Most of the girls they went to school with were more interested in finding a husband than learning anything and getting a degree. Betty, Meredith's roommate, was making a full-time job of it, which was just as well since her grades were mediocre and Meredith didn't think she'd make it to sophomore year. If she found a husband, it wouldn't matter. That was the only diploma she wanted, a marriage license.

Claudia and Meredith went to the Yale mixer together. Claudia had a date with Seth the next day and was more excited about that, and Meredith didn't think the men looked too enticing as they stood around the punch bowl and chatted. Claudia and Merrie were talking about the book they were reading for their German lit class when a good-looking blond boy came over and interrupted the conversation. He acted as though he knew them, but he didn't. He looked like an overgrown kid, and acted like one.

"So, should we put gin in the punch bowl?" he whispered. "I dare you." He looked and sounded so ridiculous that both girls laughed.

"I don't know about you," Claudia said to him, "but I promised my parents I'd graduate from Vassar. I don't think getting kicked out first semester of freshman year would thrill them."

"Me too," Meredith said regretfully.

"We could go outside and drink it. I hid a bottle in the bushes." Claudia rolled her eyes, and Meredith laughed at him. He was wearing a suit and tie, but he looked faintly rumpled and as though he had dressed in a hurry. "Clearly, you have no desire to get drunk with me. What should we do instead? I'm Ted Jones, by the way. My entire family has gone to school here, the men anyway. Four hundred generations of them. There's some building here named after me. Or, actually, I think I was named after the building. No imagination in my family. Very boring people, all of them." Meredith had come to realize that her parents were too. The only interesting member of her family was her grandfather. "What are you beautiful girls doing at Vassar?" he asked them. "Trying to find a husband or get an education?"

"Education," they said in unison, and he looked disappointed.

"That's terrible news. You must both be smart. Smart women never like me, they see right through me." He was totally absurd and frivolous, but fun to talk to. "I've been trying for years to become the black sheep of my family. But I haven't succeeded yet. It's still a work in progress. I haven't done anything bad enough. I'm trying to, though. I almost got arrested last year, but the policeman knew my father and felt sorry for me. Where are you both from, by the way?"

"New York," Claudia spoke for both of them.

"Perfect. I'm from Connecticut. We can meet in New York for dinner over the holidays. Girls from New England are too uptight, California girls make me nervous, and southern girls terrify me, so that leaves both of you. Regionally, you qualify. We're a perfect match. Now you just have to figure out which one of you wants me."

"I think I almost have a boyfriend," Claudia said, laughing.

"Almost is not enough," he told her and turned to look at Meredith, who was eyeing him with a mixture of amusement and disapproval. He was unabashedly silly, but something about him touched her. There was an appealing innocence to him. "That leaves you. What are you doing for the rest of your life?" he asked Merrie.

"Avoiding men like you, I hope." She laughed at him.

"Very sensible of you. But . . . don't be too hasty. I'm very personable and easy to get along with. I was captain of the swim team in high school, and I'm planning to play basketball here if I make the team. I'm not demanding. I have a decent allowance that can take you to dinner, and my parents gave me a very nice car for my eighteenth birthday. It's at home in Greenwich, along with my dog Butch, a black Lab. I would make an excellent boyfriend. And I'm good with parents. They usually like me, even if their daughters don't."

"The offer is almost irresistible," Meredith said. "But I don't want one. How are you as a friend?"

"Almost perfect. I give great advice and listen for hours to your love troubles without falling asleep. I can change a tire for you, and lie to the chaperones for you if you disappear into the bushes with some other guy. I'm virtually flawless as a friend. And for a small additional fee, I lie to parents too, to cover for you if you go to a sleazy motel with some guy for the weekend."

"You're hired," Meredith said to him. "I'd much rather have a friend than a boyfriend. How are you at math? We're both having trouble with our math classes."

He looked chagrined for a moment. "Unfortunately, I flunked math two years in a row in high school, and only got in here by the skin of my teeth. If it weren't for my family applying pressure on the school and making a large donation, I wouldn't have made it. I plan to coast for four years on that gift. Sorry, ladies, no math."

"That's a serious black mark against you. We'll consider your application and get back to you," Meredith said blithely, laughing at him.

"Damn, I thought I almost had it nailed."

"You did. But that math component counts for half the grade."

"Shit." He said it with feeling, and all three of them laughed, as a young man a head shorter than Merrie came over and asked her to dance. Ted could see immediately that she didn't want to, and he stepped in before she could even answer. "I'm sorry," he said to him. "We just got engaged half an hour ago. Betrothed to each other at birth, you know how that goes. We're getting married over Christmas. Our parents are thrilled." Ted stood beaming at him, and Merrie's would-be suitor looked slightly confused, apologized to Ted, and moved on.

"That was actually very good," Meredith complimented him. "You did that really well."

"I told you, I'm flawless as a friend. So do I get the job?"

"Yeah, I think maybe you do. You make a good bodyguard too. You should come over and visit us sometime at school. I have a sexy roommate you might like. She's looking for a husband. Tall blonde, great figure." As she said it, she noticed Betty in the crowd around the punch bowl and pointed her out to Ted. He looked hesitant.

"I don't know. She looks like she means business. My mother warned me about girls like that. She looks like she wants a ring and the whole shebang."

"Definitely," Meredith confirmed.

"I don't think I'm ready for the big time yet."

"Neither are we." Meredith smiled at him. He asked her to dance after a few minutes, and he was a terrific dancer. They came back breathless half an hour later and had had a good time. By then, Meredith had told him she wanted to go to law school, and he said his father wanted him to go into banking.

"I want to do something more fun. Like professional roller-skating. Or parachute jumping. Maybe surfing in Hawaii. Banking is so boring. My father is a banker and he never has any fun. What does your father do?"

"He's a tax attorney and estate lawyer," Meredith answered.

"Mine's an investment banker," Claudia added.

"It's all so boring," Ted commented. "I want to do something I enjoy when I grow up. If I grow up. I haven't made up my mind yet about that. At least I don't have to think about it for the next three and a half years. I'm here to have a good time." He was honest about it. Meredith was more interested in getting good grades, and Claudia was too. The idea of going wild for four years hadn't occurred to either of them.

He danced with Meredith again before the evening ended, and

walked them both to the bus. His tie was askew by then, and he'd taken his jacket off. He was hot from dancing, and he promised to visit them at Vassar soon. They waved to him from the bus, and Claudia looked at her and raised an eyebrow.

"He's pretty cute, and very entertaining. You're really not interested?"

"No. How could you ever take him seriously? But he would be great to have as a friend."

Claudia nodded in agreement. Seth was much more grown up than Ted, and serious when he needed to be. Ted was the class clown, but they liked him.

"What about him as your escort to the debutante ball?" Claudia suggested, and Meredith laughed.

"My parents would kill me, and they've already set up one of their friends' sons as an escort. I've known him forever, and he's fatally dull, but he's very proper, and he goes to MIT. He wants to be a physicist. I'm not sure Ted would behave at a debutante ball, although he'd be a lot more fun." It was going to be a very formal event, with the women in ball gowns and men in white tie and tails.

Both girls went home for Thanksgiving, and Claudia invited Meredith over to meet her parents and sisters. They were extremely polite to her and very pleasant, but in their own way, they were as serious and conservative as Meredith's parents. But it was nice seeing Claudia at home. They sat in her room and talked for a long time. She said she was in love with Seth Ballard, although they'd only been dating for two months and hadn't seen a lot of each other. But he called her every day at school. She had no idea what she was going to say to her parents. Nothing for the moment. And he wasn't telling his either. Which seemed like a recipe for heartbreak to

Merrie, with disapproving, prejudiced parents on both sides. It sounded too Romeo and Juliet to her.

The time between Thanksgiving and the deb ball over Christmas break went too quickly for Meredith. Her parents had invited a dozen friends to sit at their table. Meredith went to the rehearsal with her date, Josiah Appleton, on her first day back from school, and he was as dreary as she remembered. The night of the ball, she looked beautiful, and curtsied impeccably to the four hundred guests in the ballroom at the Waldorf Astoria, where the cotillion was held. She came gracefully down the stairs, holding her small bouquet of white roses after she made her bow. And she spent the rest of the evening talking to her parents' friends, meeting up with girls she hadn't seen since high school, and drinking champagne.

Josiah got blind drunk with his friends and had to be sent home, and she didn't care. She went home with her parents at two in the morning, having fulfilled their dream of seeing her as a debutante, which meant absolutely nothing to her.

Her grandparents had been there, and her grandfather had danced with her and told her he was proud of her.

"Why, Grampa? This whole thing is so meaningless and stupid."

"We all need a little tradition in our lives to anchor us. And you made your parents very happy. Some battles just aren't worth fighting. You have to know how to pick them. Don't wear yourself out on the small stuff, Merrie. Save yourself for the big stuff."

She was still waiting for the right fight to come along, but it hadn't yet. She could see what was wrong with the world but not how to right it. She hoped to have figured it out by the time she finished law school, but for now her life was still a blur without form.

She called Claudia the next day and told her all about the party, and Josiah getting drunk and having to go home. But on the whole it had gone smoothly, and wasn't such a big deal or so terrible after all. She hadn't loved it, but she'd survived it.

The girls agreed to go shopping in a few days, after the holiday. And Seth had called Claudia several times at home.

Meredith was surprised when Ted called her. He had come in from Greenwich for the day, and offered to take her to lunch. She met him at the Carlyle Hotel, and they had an elegant meal in the hotel dining room. Afterward he walked her home. She liked seeing him away from school. It solidified their friendship, and he made her laugh more than ever. He admitted that he'd had a girlfriend at home, a girl he'd dated all through high school. Their parents were best friends and she wanted to get married, but he didn't. She had decided not to go to college, and he wasn't ready to make a commitment. He wanted to be free to enjoy college life, date other girls, and meet new people. He said he knew that if he married her, he'd be stuck in Greenwich forever and become a carbon copy of his parents, which was the last thing he wanted. He wanted a more exciting future. Meredith said she didn't want to become her parents either. She was hoping that law school would make her entirely different from the women she knew. She didn't realize it, but she already was.

He kissed her on the cheek and told her he'd see her back in school in January. After she left him, she found a plastic frog he'd slipped into her pocket, and she burst out laughing.

The rest of their freshman year flew by. Meredith and Claudia signed up for all the same classes for second semester, and spoke German whenever they were together. Ted came to visit them from time to time. He was dating as many girls as he could, and Claudia's relationship with Seth was getting more and more serious. He had told her he wanted to marry her one day, although neither of them had figured out how to make that happen. But they had three more years to solve the problem of how to convince their parents. Claudia admitted to Meredith that it was getting harder and harder not to go to bed with him. Meredith advised her strongly against it. If she got pregnant, it would ruin everything, and their parents would go crazy. And she'd have to drop out of college, or risk her life getting a dangerous illegal abortion. Having sex with Seth just wasn't worth it. Claudia agreed, but it was getting increasingly tempting.

At the end of the school year, Meredith and Claudia left together to go back to New York. Meredith was going to Nantucket and Martha's Vineyard as she did every summer. And the Steinbergs were going to their house on Long Island. Seth would be in Virginia, so they couldn't see each other, which Claudia said would be agonizing.

She and Seth devised a plan to meet in New York for a day, but it fell through at the last minute, when the Steinbergs went to Long Island earlier than planned. Claudia told Meredith it would be a long, sad summer without him.

Before they left for Martha's Vineyard, Meredith went to visit her grandparents in Washington for a few days, and her grandfather invited her to visit his chambers at the Supreme Court. She'd been there before, but it always thrilled her, and excited her about the power of the law again.

Her grandfather explained to her in broad terms the different cases they were working on, and introduced Merrie to three of the justices. It made Meredith prouder than ever to be his granddaughter.

She went back to New York on the train that night, and a few days later, she and Alex and her mother left for the Vineyard. Claudia had invited Meredith to spend a few days with them in August, and she was looking forward to it. The Steinbergs were nice people, had gotten used to her, and always welcomed her warmly. One of Claudia's sisters was leaving for college in the fall, to go to Wellesley, and her youngest sister was in high school. The Steinbergs never treated Claudia differently or as though she was adopted. She had become their beloved oldest daughter, and acted accordingly. She felt guilty not telling them about Seth but knew that she couldn't. Her being in love with a Gentile would have broken their hearts, and she couldn't do that to them. At least not yet.

Meredith met a boy she liked in Martha's Vineyard that summer. He was a junior at Harvard, visiting friends of theirs. They went out a few times, and kissed on the beach in the moonlight, but it was more fun than serious, and he promised to invite her to Cambridge for a football game that winter. It was the perfect summer romance, and nothing meaningful happened. They were just two young people having a moment together, without deeper implications, although her brother teased her about it. He was nine years old, and disgusted when he caught them kissing.

She had a letter from Betty when she got back to New York after Labor Day, saying that she had gotten engaged over the summer and wasn't coming back to Vassar. She was getting married in December and needed time to plan the wedding. Her mission had been accomplished. She was marrying a banker from Savannah, she said in her letter. He was twenty-five years old and worked at his father's bank. She would be nineteen when they married, and she was excited about moving to Savannah. She wished Meredith luck and said it had been nice rooming with her. Meredith called Claudia as soon as she read the letter and told her to write to the housing office immediately to ask to move into Merrie's room, and she would do the same.

"She's an idiot to drop out of college and get married at nineteen," Claudia commented. "And she can't even be pregnant, if the wedding isn't for another four months." A lot of girls had to get married.

"That's all she's ever wanted," Meredith told her.

"How stupid. And now what? She has babies and plays bridge for the rest of her life?" Claudia said in disgust.

"That's what most women we know do," Meredith reminded her. And their mothers were no different. It was exactly the life that neither she nor Claudia wanted, and why they were in college, not to find a husband and join the ranks of bored housewives.

When they went back to school they were thrilled to see each other and to share a room. Ted came to visit them that weekend and said he'd had an uneventful summer working for his father in Greenwich. And Seth took Claudia to dinner. They had missed each other unbearably all summer. He had called her whenever he knew her parents weren't around. They came back late for curfew the night they had dinner, and Claudia got a warning slip when they let her in. She promised never to do it again, and said they'd had a flat tire on the way back from dinner, which was the excuse everyone used. Meredith guessed that they'd lost track of time in the back of Seth's car, and hoped it hadn't gone too far, but Claudia promised they'd been good. And she looked flushed and happy to have seen him. The summer had seemed endless to both of them.

Meredith and Claudia took all the same classes again, and went to fewer mixers sophomore year. They already knew a lot of people in neighboring schools, and Claudia saw Seth every chance she could. And Meredith had dinner with Ted whenever he didn't have a date. He told her about all his romances, which never seemed to last more than a week or two. As he admitted himself, he had great opening charm but no staying power. And as soon as the girls he dated talked about looking for a serious relationship, he ran for the hills, or back to Meredith for a friendly dinner.

"I don't know why you don't want me," he complained occasionally. "We get along perfectly, and we have a good time together."

"That's the whole point. It works perfectly as a friendship. Why screw it up with sex and romance?" she said sensibly. Besides, she knew him well enough now to realize that he was flaky and unreliable and didn't know what he wanted to do with his life after he graduated. The last thing she wanted was a confused man on her hands. She was still trying to figure out her own life.

He had just come to see her after the Thanksgiving weekend, and she and Claudia were in the visiting room, when a news report on television mesmerized her, and everyone in the room stopped talking. A forty-two-year-old colored woman named Rosa Parks had refused to give up her seat to a white passenger when ordered to do so by the bus driver, and had been arrested in Montgomery, Alabama. Buses were segregated, whites at the front of the bus and colored persons in the rear, and once the white section was full, Negro passengers were expected to give up their seats to them. The woman had refused and been arrested and removed by police. Public outcry from the Negro community had been instant. A boycott had been declared against the Montgomery bus system, and it was disclosed that the woman was a member of the NAACP, dedicated to equality between the races. The protest was being organized by a young Baptist minister named Martin Luther King Jr. Something told Meredith that the story was going to be a very big deal. She and Claudia watched the newscast and were still talking about it when they went back to their room. The news report said that Rosa Parks was not the first Negro woman to refuse to give up her seat and be arrested, but it was the most powerful and public response of its kind, with the boycott of the bus system, which would cripple the city.

"It's time that they do something about segregation in the South," Merrie said to Claudia, who nodded in agreement. Only a month before, the Supreme Court had ruled that segregation of public recreational facilities was unconstitutional. "My grandfather and I have talked about it. He said it's going to happen, but when it does, it will be a bloody battle, and neither side is going to give in easily. Do you realize that minister organizing the bus protest is only six years older than you are?" Claudia was twenty. And Martin Luther King Jr. was only twenty-six years old. "Rosa Parks must be a brave woman." She was set to stand trial four days later.

Meredith thought about it all night, and went into the sitting room to watch the television there several times in the course of the next few days. The bus boycott in Montgomery had taken hold. Seventy-five percent of the people who rode buses in Montgomery were said to be colored, and without their business, the bus companies would be hurting soon.

Four days later, on December 5, Rosa Parks was fined fourteen dollars and convicted of breaking the laws applicable to colored passengers on public buses. The boycott continued, and Rosa Parks became a household name as people all over the country talked about her, the bus boycott in Montgomery, and the young minister who quietly but with determination continued to organize the protest of the laws that applied to colored people on buses, in Montgomery and throughout the South. Meredith couldn't wait to discuss it with her grandfather when she went home for Christmas, and they spent most of Christmas dinner talking about it until her father complained that they'd heard enough about it and it wasn't suitable dinner conversation, particularly on Christmas. It was the only topic that interested Merrie.

"What do you think is going to happen, Grampa?" Meredith asked him after dinner. "Do you think they'll change the laws now?"

"Not yet, Merrie. It's going to take time and probably a lot of bloodshed before it's over. And it will land in our laps at the Supreme Court again eventually," which Meredith found even more interesting. She had heard the young minister speak on TV, and found him compelling and inspiring. She wished she could be in Montgomery so she could see what was happening. The bus boycott had garnered more publicity than any other act of protest so far. The eyes and ears of the country were riveted to it.

And in the end, her grandfather's prediction was right. A bus segregation case was brought before the Supreme Court in November 1956, a year later, and they ruled that segregation laws on public buses were unconstitutional, upholding an earlier decision by a Montgomery district court that had been appealed. It was a landmark decision that began to unravel segregation laws throughout the South. The boycott lasted for 381 days, and successfully challenged the existing segregation laws. Rosa Parks became a national hero for her courage, and was held up as a role model in the black community.

Meredith followed every detail of the case for the entire year, and Claudia wrote several articles for the Vassar newspaper. Meredith talked about it again at length with her grandfather during Thanksgiving dinner, a year after Parks's protest, after their landmark decision in the Supreme Court. It was a highly volatile issue. Northerners thought the Supreme Court ruling desegregating public transportation was the right one, while southerners thought it an outrage. It was Meredith and Claudia's junior year at Vassar by then, and they were still roommates.

Nothing major had changed in Claudia and Meredith's lives. Meredith had met a boy at one of the interschool social events and dated him for a few months, but it fizzled out during the bus boycott, since he was from Mississippi and told Meredith he didn't like her politics. She didn't like his either and didn't miss him after he stopped calling her. Claudia was still deeply involved with Seth. Meredith knew they were meeting in motels on weekends and pretending to be married, and Meredith was praying, as Claudia was, that she didn't get pregnant. They had vowed to confront their parents and marry after graduation, which was still a year and a half away. They longed to be out in the open with their relationship, and to be married, but felt it wisest to wait until after graduation.

And Ted's friendship with Meredith had deepened. He was as confused as ever about his future. All he knew for sure was that he didn't want to work in his father's bank, or marry his high school sweetheart, but he still spent time with her whenever he was in Greenwich because it was easy, and he worked at his father's bank in the summer. He felt like he had no other options, and he didn't have the imagination to find them. The path of least resistance always seemed to be the one he chose.

Meredith spent July and August on Martha's Vineyard with Alex and her parents, and Claudia was on Long Island with her family, separated from Seth for yet another summer. They went back to Vassar in the fall of their senior year, and within days of their return to school, the nation was once again mesmerized by news reports that shocked everyone. Nine students in Little Rock, Arkansas, had presented themselves for admission to all-white Central High School, and had been refused entry. The governor, Orval Faubus, had called out the National Guard to stop them, in the presence of an angry mob of white onlookers, determined to stop the colored students from entering the school. Nineteen days later, black lawyer Thurgood Marshall got an injunction to remove the National Guard, and the Little Rock police escorted the nine teenagers into the school. And at the urging of Martin Luther King Jr., President Eisenhower ordered the Little Rock schools desegregated and provided protection for the nine students for the remainder of the school year.

It was another major leap forward for desegregation, which once again made Meredith wish that she could be there. She said as much to Claudia as they watched the news on TV, and Claudia told Meredith she was crazy. It wasn't her fight, and there was a good chance that someone was going to get killed in Little Rock with tension sky-high between whites and Negroes. It was a dynamite keg waiting to explode.

"It's *everyone's* fight," Meredith corrected her. "You can't just watch this on TV, or write about it later, like some historical event you're not part of. You have to stand up and fight for what you believe in," she said heatedly, and as she watched the nine students walk into Central High School, with tears pouring down her face,

90

she knew that one day she would be there for fights like this. The universe was finally beckoning to her. She had waited her whole life to be part of something that was important and made a difference. It was time now for her to stand up and take her place.

Meredith got into heated discussions with other students about the cruelty, immorality, and illegality of segregation. And when she got home for Christmas, she was outspoken about the vital importance of change now, arguing that it could no longer be postponed or delayed. She thought it barbaric to keep people in segregated conditions, with public bathrooms, buildings, medical facilities, schools, and different forms of transportation. She felt it was the last vestige of slavery in this country, and that it was time to stop it. And again and again, she found herself watching and reading Martin Luther King Jr.'s speeches and being deeply moved by him. He was an extraordinary orator, and everything he said made sense to her. She also became an avid fan of the American Civil Liberties Union, and she sent them several contributions, sacrificing her pocket money and allowance to do it. Claudia commented that if people in Europe had spoken up for the Jews as ardently, Hitler wouldn't have been able to exterminate six million of them.

It was during spring break from Vassar, two months before graduation, that Meredith went to the office of the ACLU and applied for a job. She said she was willing to do anything they needed her to do, from pouring coffee to protesting. She warned them that she was planning to go to law school in a year, but after graduation, she wanted to work for them until then. She filled out an application, and they promised they would get in touch with her.

She took the train back to Vassar and told Claudia what she'd done. Claudia wasn't surprised. She still had to find a job herself for after graduation, but her parents wanted her to take the summer off and think about it in the fall. They were encouraging her to do charity work instead of looking for employment, but she wanted a job, preferably with a newspaper or freelance, and to write a book about her war experiences one day. She told Meredith she'd die of boredom if she wasn't working, and that playing bridge and being on charity boards with wealthy women wasn't what she wanted to do with her life. She was worried that Meredith's work for the ACLU could be dangerous, but Meredith didn't mind. She insisted that there was a risk in anything worth doing, and she was willing to take it on. She hadn't told her parents about her plans, she wanted to wait and see if she got the job before tackling that.

But Claudia couldn't make firm plans yet anyway. Seth was going to tell his parents about them as soon as they both graduated in June. He had decided he didn't want a life in the military, which would be a blow to them too. He had an eight-year military obligation to fulfill after West Point, five years in the army and three in the reserves. It was possible to get out of it, though costly and his parents would view it as a disgrace. As a result, Claudia didn't know if she'd be going home with him to Virginia now, staying with him in New York, or living on an army base, if his parents refused to pay to release him from his commitment. She couldn't look for a job until she knew. The only thing they were sure of was that they were getting married. But their parents' reaction was uncertain, and so was where they would be living once they were married. They wanted to get married as soon as possible. She was sure her parents would be reasonable once they saw how much they loved each other. Seth's family was harder to predict.

Two weeks later, Meredith got the call that she'd gotten the job at the ACLU. She told Claudia immediately. Her plans were taking shape, and she was going to tell her grandfather at graduation. She knew he'd be proud of her.

On graduation day, both girls were nervous. They were leaving the safe comforts of Vassar, which was like emerging from the womb. Meredith was planning to inform her family about her job, and she knew her parents would be concerned. And Claudia was waiting to hear from Seth after he told his parents. He was going home to Virginia with them straight after his own graduation, and intended to tell them about Claudia when they got there. The graduation ceremony at West Point was an elaborate and lengthy affair, and she knew he wouldn't have time to call her before they flew back to Virginia that night. The shock for them would be that he wanted to marry a girl they'd never met, of the Jewish faith, and abandon the military career he'd prepared for for four years, which was an important tradition for them.

But he was sure he could convince them of what an extraordinary woman she was. He was going to share with them everything she'd been through during the war. She deserved a happy life now, and he was going to give it to her. And if obliged to, he would fulfill his military commitment, but after that he wanted a civilian life with her. He still had to find a career path, but with her plans to work for a newspaper, Claudia would be busy. And in a few years, he wanted them to move to Virginia and start having babies, if they waited that long. They were both twenty-three years old, old enough to know what they wanted, and they had been together for the entire four years they'd been in college, and had never wavered once in their devotion to each other. They knew it would be a strong argument to both sets of parents, and the fact that they loved each other. Neither

Seth nor Claudia doubted that their families would come around, although they knew it wouldn't be easy at first. Seth said his parents were reasonable people and would love her when they met her.

Meredith and Claudia hugged after the graduation ceremony, and they had tears in their eyes. They had grown up together over the past four years, and hated leaving each other now, to live with their respective families in New York.

"Did you tell them yet?" Claudia whispered to her, meaning the job at the ACLU.

Meredith shook her head. "Tonight at dinner. Have you heard anything from Seth?"

"He's not going to sit down with them about it until tonight, when they get back to Virginia. I don't think I'll hear from him until tomorrow."

Both women joined their families then. Everyone went out to lunch with their parents, and afterward picked up their things and headed home.

The McKenzies got back to their apartment at six o'clock, and they had reservations at 21 at eight. It was Robert and his father's favorite restaurant, and one of the most popular posh dinner venues in New York, with delicious American food and terrific steaks. Meredith couldn't believe she'd graduated, and now she could go out and live her life and do everything she'd dreamed of. She'd been waiting for this for years. She finally felt all grown up.

The Steinbergs were eating at home that night, and had planned a dinner for Claudia the next day. Her parents had told her over and over again how proud they were of her. She went to her room and lay down before dinner, thinking about Seth and what he was saying to his parents in Virginia. She was sending him thoughts of love and strength. Once they knew their children were getting married, both sets of parents would have to meet. She could hardly wait to introduce Seth to her parents, once they got over the fact that he wasn't Jewish. They had gotten used to Meredith in the past four years and were very fond of her. Claudia knew they'd adjust to Seth too. The whole world didn't have to be Jewish, even if all their friends were.

The McKenzies walked past the statues of jockeys that lined the entrance of 21. The dinner for Meredith was in an elegant wood-paneled private room. The whole family was present, including her grandparents, and a few of her parents' close friends. It was a festive occasion with flowers on the table, great wines, and a delicious dinner. There was a cake for Merrie at the end of it, in the shape of a mortarboard with her name on it, and "Congratulations" written across it in gold icing, which the pastry chef had made especially for her. Her father took photographs of her with it.

They drank champagne with the cake when it was served, and after all the plates had been set down, Meredith tapped her glass with her knife to get everyone's attention.

"I have an announcement," she said, almost glowing with pleasure. Everyone wanted to hear what it was. Her parents knew it wasn't an engagement since she didn't have a boyfriend, much to her mother's disappointment. In four years of college, she hadn't met a boy she cared about deeply. Her mind was always on other things, either causes, or her studies, or her friends. Her dedication to her studies had paid off, since she'd graduated cum laude, which was not easy to achieve, particularly at a school like Vassar.

"I wanted to let you all know that I'm not going to be one of those deadbeat graduates lounging around the living room and watching TV. I have a job, and I start next Monday." A ripple of pleasure and admiration ran through the assembled company, waiting to hear the rest of her news. "I'm going to be working for the ACLU until I go to law school, I hope in a year."

She was beaming as she said it, but there was not a sound in the room. Her mother looked like she was about to cry, and her father's face had gone pale. Their friends didn't know how to react and took their cues from Meredith's parents, who were visibly distraught at the announcement. Only her grandfather was smiling and raised his glass to her.

"Well done, Merrie. Good luck to you. We're very proud of you. You go get 'em!" She smiled back at him, but the look on her parents' faces chilled the mood immediately. They said absolutely nothing. Her father signaled for the check and paid it, and a few minutes later everyone stood up to leave. She saw him say something angrily to her grandfather, and by then Janet was crying, and Meredith's grandmother was trying to comfort her. The two women were very close, and very similar in character. Both were quiet and passive and supportive of their men. Bill's mother had always been like a mother to Janet too, since she had lost her own.

"How could you?" her father said to Meredith after the guests were gone, as Alex watched them intently. He was twelve years old, and he wasn't entirely sure what the ACLU was, except that he thought they organized protests of black people in the South who were fighting segregation, but he couldn't understand why his sister would work for them, since she wasn't black and lived in New York.

"What are you doing working for an organization like that?" her father asked, as her mother sobbed audibly. "What are you going to do, plan protests and marches and get arrested?" He knew they defended civil liberties, but they were most active about desegregation these days.

"I'll do whatever they assign me to do," Meredith said quietly. "I'll be working in the New York office, unless they need me to help elsewhere. There's plenty to do here, on a variety of issues. Daddy, times are changing, they have to. Segregation is an ugly part of our history. We all have to work against it now."

"Let the government and the southern black ministers do that. Can't you get a decent job doing something else?" he said angrily. "Look at what you've done to your mother." He pointed to his wife, who looked like she was melting.

"It's the job I wanted. And the work I want to do, fighting injustice and discrimination. It's important work. I want to be part of the changes in this country. That's where the future is, for all of us."

"Not to me. Tell that to your grandfather. You're not some black woman sitting on a bus, Meredith. You come from a good home."

"That's the whole point, Dad. People like us have to take a stand too. It's not just someone else's problem. The laws in this country have to change, and it's people like us who can change them. And Grampa," she said proudly. Her grandfather was watching the exchange between father and daughter and said nothing.

"*You* don't need to be part of it. Besides, it's dangerous."

"So is crossing Park Avenue," and then she started to get angry too. "You used to be courageous, Dad. What happened to you? You fought for all those people who survived the camps, to get them justice. Do you not want desegregation? Would you rather keep things the way they are?" She'd never even thought of that before. Maybe he was a racist.

"Maybe I would. Maybe it's simpler not to turn everything upside down all the time. It's been working like this for a long time."

"Working for who? Not for colored people. Can you even imagine what it must be like to live with segregation? To be discriminated against for your whole life? I can't. I've never lived it. But I sure want to help them change it. I believe in what I'm doing, and I'm sorry if you don't."

"No, I don't. You're a rabble-rouser, Meredith, and you're naïve. You don't understand the risks you're taking. You want to make a career out of making trouble. That isn't what your mother and I want for you."

She thought about it for a minute and nodded. "I know you don't, Dad," she said sympathetically. "You're right. I do want to make trouble for all the people who are persecuting others, and keeping them down, underpaying them, and treating them like they're less than human. That can't seem right to you. It has to stop, Dad. Someone has to stand up to them. And not just colored ministers. Everyone. It's time to fight the good fight, and that's what I'm going to do. I'm sorry you and Mom don't like it, but that's who I am. And it's who you used to be too. Who do you think I learned it from? Not just from Grampa. You fought for the victims and underdog too. And now it's my turn. I'm sorry if you don't like who I turned out to be. Thank you for dinner," she said and turned and left the restaurant.

She walked all the way home from 21 back to their apartment, and it took her almost an hour. It was a cool June evening, and she thought about what she had said to her father. She believed every word of it.

When she got home, her parents' bedroom door was closed, and neither of them came out to see her. They were heartsick over her decision to work for the ACLU, but that was what she was going to do. There was no turning back now. It was time to fight for those who needed it, just as her grandfather had encouraged her to. She had waited four years for this, and now she had graduated and was on her way. And like it or not, by word and example, this was who they had taught her to be. It was a bitter pill for her parents to accept her as she really was. They still thought they could change her and make her follow their path and not her own. But it was too late for that now.

Chapter Six

Claudia was up at six-thirty in the morning, waiting to hear from Seth. She was sure he was still sleeping. She stayed near the phone all morning, and was tempted to call him. She had his number at the farm, but she didn't want to interrupt him if he was still discussing things with his parents. By eleven, she was literally shaking, and had snapped at both her sisters when they asked why she was sitting by the phone. At noon he called her, and she was relieved to hear his voice.

"I was so worried about you," she said the minute she heard him, and pulled the phone from the hall table into her room. It had a long cord so her sisters could use it too. Her parents had their own line for their private use. "How did it go?" she asked, as soon as she got the phone into her room, so her sisters couldn't listen in. "Were they very upset?"

"They were pretty shocked," he admitted, sounding beaten down. "You know how southern families are, they think people have to marry someone just like them. I guess it never occurred to them that I could fall in love with a woman of another religion, or from a different background than theirs. And Jewish is pretty out there for them. Even fancy southerners can act like rednecks at times."

"So what did they say in the end?" She couldn't stand the suspense, and he sounded exhausted. It had been a rough night, much rougher than he wanted to tell her.

"Claudia, I don't know how to say this to you, and I didn't want to tell you on the phone. My mother cried all night. We had to call the doctor. She's not as young as yours." He was the youngest of four sons. "My father has a heart condition, and she thinks it will kill him if we get married. They called in two of my brothers and we nearly came to blows. I love you, with every ounce of my being, but this will destroy my family." He was crying by then. "They're just not going to let this happen. My brothers said they would kill me first, and my parents said they'd never see me again. I can't do this to them, or to you, to bring you into a family that would hate you and never accept you. I never realized they would feel this strongly about it, or I wouldn't have let it go on for four years," he said miserably, sobbing between sentences, and so was Claudia by then. They were going to get married. That's what he had said. How could he turn around like this and let them bully him out of it?

"Just because I'm Jewish?" Her voice was a croak when she asked him.

"Jewish, German, the Jewish family who adopted you, the concentration camp. All of it. It's all foreign to them. They don't understand who you are."

"Will they meet me?"

"Never. They're southerners, and military. And my mother said she would die if our children were Jewish." And Claudia's family would die if they weren't. She and Seth had agreed to it two years before, in the isolation of their relationship, without their families involved. "And they aren't crazy about my not wanting a career in the military," but that was the least of their problems. "Claudia, I love you, but I can't do this to them."

To them? What about to her? She felt dizzy and sick as she listened to him. "What are you telling me? That it's over? Just like that? You tell them we're getting married, they go crazy because I'm Jewish, so you dump me over the phone?" She wanted to fight, but she couldn't. They had him in their grip and had convinced him in a single night.

"I didn't have the strength to come to New York today. We fought about it all night." But he didn't have the guts to fight back, or to stand by her and what they felt for each other. He had given in. They had won. "It's over," he confirmed. "We just have to learn to live without each other. There's no other choice." He seemed entirely willing to accept it, although he was crying as he said it.

"We could stand up for what we want, and what we believe, and our love," Claudia said, sounding desperate.

"I just can't do that to them," he repeated.

"But you can do it to me?" she said, feeling sick.

"I can't help it. We're young, we'll get over it. They won't. And I owe them a lot: my life, my education. I can't just walk out on them if they won't agree to our being together."

"So now you marry some southern Christian girl because they tell you to? What happens to me?" She was sobbing uncontrollably. She had never thought he could do this to her. And what if she'd gotten pregnant in the past two years? Would he have dumped her then too? Apparently, he would. She realized now how lucky she had been that she hadn't. She would have been faced with an abortion or a baby born out of wedlock, because she was a Jew. Overnight he had turned into a stranger. She wasn't good enough for him.

"I love you. You're the only girl I want to marry, but I can't. I can't do this to my parents," he said again.

"So what happens now?"

"We go on with our lives, without each other." He made it clear, and had stopped crying.

"Will I ever speak to you again?" she asked in a whisper that nearly broke his heart more than it already was.

"I don't think we should," he said sadly. "It'll only make it harder. The only thing left to say now is goodbye." She sat crying into the phone, and then pulled it away from her ear as though there were a dagger in it, and, staring at the phone as she did it, she silently hung up. He had said all she could stand to hear. She waited a few minutes to see if he'd call her back, but he didn't. She dialed Meredith immediately. Fortunately, she was home and answered the phone. Everyone was out, and she was still recovering from the explosion at 21 the night before.

"Are you busy?" Claudia was frantic, and Meredith frowned when she heard her.

"No. Why? What's wrong?" She'd never heard Claudia like that before. She almost didn't recognize her.

"Can I see you?"

"Sure. Do you want to come here?"

"No, meet me in the park."

"Did you hear from Seth?" Meredith had a bad feeling, listening to her. Claudia sounded as though her whole world had collapsed, or as if she was running from something, running for her life.

"I'll tell you when I see you." They agreed to a meeting place, and fifteen minutes later Meredith was there. They came from opposite sides of the park to the boat pond in the middle. Claudia arrived two minutes later, at a dead run, and almost knocked Meredith down when she flew into her arms, sobbing.

"Oh my God, what happened?" Meredith was horrified at the condition she was in. They sat down on a bench together, and Claudia poured out the whole story. Four years of a serious relationship, plans of marriage, and it was over in a single night with his parents. "All because you're Jewish? That's ridiculous." But apparently it wasn't ridiculous to them, or to him, since he had agreed to give her up, and then called to say goodbye.

"I hung up," she sobbed in Merrie's arms. "I didn't know what else to do. There was nothing left to say."

"I would have hung up on him too, after I told him to screw himself." She was furious on her friend's behalf and wanted to shake him. Claudia looked absolutely destroyed. She hadn't expected this to happen. He hadn't warned her that he might give in to them. And there was nothing she could do now, except what he had told her: they had to forget each other and move on, because he didn't have the guts to stand up to his parents and marry her.

They sat in the park for two hours, with Meredith's arms around her while Claudia cried. And then, slowly, Meredith walked her home. Her parents' party for her was that night, and Claudia had no idea how she would get through it. Meredith left her outside her building, and Claudia stumbled in looking like someone had died.

Her mother heard her come in, and came to find her in her room. She was sitting on a chair, staring into space, with a ravaged expression. Her mother hadn't seen her look like that since she'd arrived from Germany when she was ten. And she'd had nightmares for two years.

"Where were you? We've been looking for you for an hour. I wanted to show you how pretty the flowers look for tonight."

Claudia nodded, fighting back tears again. She didn't want her mother to see them. "I was with Meredith. We went for a walk in the park."

"Is something wrong?" her mother asked pointedly. She could see that there was, and also that Claudia didn't want to tell her. Claudia didn't think she ever would. They would never know about Seth. There was no point upsetting them now, telling them she'd been in love with a Christian and hidden it from them for four years.

"No, I'm fine," Claudia said, steeling herself to go to see the flowers. She had no idea how she would face the party that night. She didn't want to see anyone. And she kept telling herself that if she could survive losing her whole family, she could survive losing Seth, but she was devastated.

She told her mother the flowers were beautiful and went back to her room as quickly as she could. Meredith called to check on her, as she sat crying in her room again. It was the worst day of her life since coming to America. Meredith felt desperately sorry for her. But there was nothing she could do to help her. Seth was gone, and Claudia was going to have to live with it, along with all the other losses in her life.

*   *   *

Claudia was quiet and ghostly pale at the party that night, and her mother checked to see if she had a fever. She looked sick. She didn't eat any of the food on the buffet. And more than once her mother thought she looked like she was going to faint. Somehow she got through the evening, and thanked her parents for the beautiful party. Everyone congratulated her, and she didn't care. She just wanted to go back to her room, curl up in a ball, and die.

She called Meredith after everybody left, and they talked for a while.

"So what do I do now?" she said miserably. She wasn't going to be getting married. All her plans for the future had evaporated that morning, talking to Seth.

"Get a job, maybe," Meredith suggested cautiously. "You wanted to work for a newspaper." Claudia nodded, thinking about it. They were going to Long Island for the summer, and she had wanted to start looking for a job in the fall, if she and Seth had stayed in New York.

"I'll think about it," she said to Meredith. After they hung up, she stood in the bathroom and stared at herself in the mirror. She looked like someone had died. She lay in bed afterward and thought about Seth, realizing that she would never see him again or hear his voice. She used to feel that way about her parents. Now she felt that way about him. She wanted to hate him, but she didn't yet. She still loved him. She closed her eyes and tried not to think. She thought of her parents, who had died so long ago. And her sisters and brother. She could barely remember them. And then she thought of Seth, and told herself that he was dead now too. It was the only thing that she could do. She had to forget the past four years and everything they had meant to her. And whether she wanted to or not, whatever happened, she had to go on living. However much she had loved him, she couldn't let him destroy her. He wasn't worth it. No one was. She felt dead inside when she went to bed, and sobbed herself to sleep.

When Claudia woke up the next morning, it felt like an elephant was sitting on her chest. The terrible weight of grief and loss, and knowing something awful had happened, hit her from the moment she opened her eyes.

She forced herself to get out of bed, put on her bathrobe, and go to the kitchen. She still looked deathly pale as she picked up the newspaper and made herself a cup of coffee. She sat staring at the newspaper without reading the words. She had no idea what to do now. She had left her summer open so she and Seth could make plans. Her family was going to be on Long Island, and she wanted to be with them. It would give her time to figure out what to do next without him.

She called Meredith, who was staying in New York for the summer and starting her job in a few days. But Claudia didn't want to be in town with nothing to do. She wondered what Seth was going to do now, and imagined he would stay on the farm with his parents. He had two months off after graduation before he had to report to begin a Basic Officer Leader Course. He had told her he didn't want to stay in the army as a career, but he had given in to them on that too. She had never expected him to surrender so easily and abandon her so completely. He wasn't the man she'd thought. At twenty-three, he didn't have the guts to fight his family when they opposed his plans to marry the woman he said he loved. Or did he really love her? Now she would never know.

"What do you want to do now?" Meredith asked her when they spoke.

"Get a job, I guess." She'd been planning to do some freelance writing, but she didn't have the energy to do it now. She needed time to catch her breath. "I think I'll go to Long Island, and send out some applications and get serious about it in September." She had the luxury of time. They both did, since their families didn't want them to work, and would have been happier if they didn't and concentrated on finding husbands instead of jobs. "Will you come out for a weekend?" Claudia asked, sounding lonely and lost. She felt totally broken by what Seth had done.

"Of course. Take care of yourself now," Meredith urged her. She'd had a terrible shock, after everything else she had suffered in her early life. She didn't deserve this, Merrie thought. No one did. To be betrayed and abandoned by the man you loved, when you thought you were getting married. Maybe it would be a blessing in the end. She hoped so for her.

Claudia hung around the apartment for the rest of the day, and decided to send out her applications and CV sooner rather than later. She sent letters to the employment offices of all the major newspapers, and included half a dozen articles she'd written for the college paper. Other than that, she had a bachelor's degree from Vassar and included on her CV that she spoke fluent German, which would be useless to them anyway. She hoped they'd at least be impressed by the college she had graduated from, and would like the articles she'd written.

Three days later, after having lunch with Meredith, she left for

Long Island with her parents and sisters. Her father commuted in the summer, and took the month of August off. She begged Meredith to come for the weekend as soon as she could. She said her family would be happy to see her, and Meredith was her only close friend, and the only one she could talk to about Seth. She and Meredith had talked about getting an apartment together once they both had jobs, but neither of them could afford it for the moment, and they knew that their parents wouldn't approve. Nice girls lived at home until they were married. But it was something to think about for later on, now that Claudia wouldn't be getting married.

As they drove to Long Island, with the station wagon full of their belongings and the housekeeper driving behind them in another car with more, Claudia stared out the window, thinking about her life. A week before, she thought that all her dreams had come true and she had a happy life with Seth ahead of her. And now it was all smashed to pieces, in rubble at her feet. She knew that one day there would be another man, but she couldn't imagine it and didn't want to. A lone tear slid down her cheek, for all the people she had loved and lost.

In Seth's case, it felt like a tragedy, but she knew it wasn't. She had lost far more important people in Germany. This was just a broken heart, even if it felt like the end of the world.

Chapter Seven

Once Alex and her parents left for Martha's Vineyard, and Claudia was on Long Island, Meredith was lonely in New York. Her job at the ACLU was not as exciting as she had hoped. They used her for a spare pair of hands in the office. She did a monumental amount of filing, cleaning up, serving coffee to all the people who worked there, buying pastries, and keeping the coffee machine clean. Sometimes they sent her out to get them lunch. She was basically an errand girl, but she assumed that one of these days they'd let her do something more interesting. If not, it was going to be a long, tedious year. They were not only wasting her time but her brain. But she didn't have the skills yet to work on the legal team, or the experience to be a secretary. It made her hungrier than ever to go to law school so she could do something meaningful and use her mind.

For lack of anything better to do, she called Ted in Connecticut and asked him if he was coming into the city and wanted to have lunch. He sounded thrilled to hear from her, and said he had some errands to do for his father later that week, and could even have dinner with her. They made a dinner date for Thursday at P.J. Clarke's.

It cheered her up immediately, as soon as he walked through the door. She'd been standing at the bar, waiting for him, and several middle-aged executives had tried to pick her up.

Ted ordered a gin and tonic, and a Bloody Mary for her as soon as they sat down. He looked very serious in a suit and tie, and she saw a hint of the usual mischief in his eyes, but he was more subdued than she'd ever seen him before.

"So how's your job?" he asked her, and she was honest with him.

"Boring so far. I file and make coffee. They treat me like I don't have a brain. I guess it's inevitable fresh out of college. I love being there, but they act like I don't exist and have nothing to contribute."

He listened to what she had to say and took a long sip of his drink, and then avoided her eyes. She saw into him and through him, and he didn't want her to this time. She had the feeling that he was hiding something from her, or ashamed. "I just took a job myself," he said casually.

"Wow! With whom? Doing what?" She was happy to hear he had escaped his father's clutches. All through college, he had been pushing to have Ted work for him permanently. It was the one thing Ted always said he didn't want, and would never do.

"With my dad." Ted stunned her when he said it. "It's a pretty good opportunity at the bank. And the salary he offered is damn nice." He smiled at her, but when she looked at him more closely she could see that he was sad, as though he'd failed somehow, or something had gone wrong. But the gin gave him enough bravado to make it sound better than it was. He switched to tequila then, and she could see he was getting drunk.

"Is that what you really want?" She looked shocked by what he'd said.

"It wasn't," he said honestly. "But I've had some time to think about it. Working for my dad, I have the inside track, and can get ahead a lot faster than I would somewhere else. The money is good, and if I want to get married and start a family, I'm going to need a solid base and salary I can count on." She looked even more startled then. "I have job security with him," he said and then laughed. "At least I know he won't fire me."

"Since when are you planning to 'get married and start a family'? Did I miss something? Are you in love?"

"I've been seeing Emily again." He continued to avoid his friend's eyes. She knew him too well. She felt as though aliens had kidnapped him since she'd seen him at school.

"I thought you were through with her last summer, or the summer before, or wanted to be. What happened? Has she gotten more exciting since you graduated?" Meredith knew that she had hung on forever, with his family's encouragement, and Ted's own weakness for her when he went home. He was happy she was easy, willing, and right next door. She was familiar, and infatuated with him, but not much else. He'd always told Meredith he'd never been in love with her, and he still wasn't. According to Ted's descriptions of her, she had nothing to recommend her except cute girl-next-door looks and a family with a lot of money, like his own. And she wanted a husband and kids to complete the picture. Ted didn't. The thought of getting married panicked him and filled him with dread, but he didn't want to tell Merrie that.

"She's really a great girl, and she's crazy about me. And my parents think she'd make a terrific wife, and we'd be a perfect couple."

He gave Meredith the party line, but she wasn't buying it, at least not based on what she heard, and read between the lines.

"Why do you need a wife? You're twenty-three years old." It was a question she'd asked herself when her mother talked about her getting married. She felt too young, and there were so many other things she wanted to do, instead of getting tied down. They had a lifetime ahead of them, and a decade to find the right person, at the right time when they were older and had tasted more of life.

"My parents got married when they graduated," he said, as though that justified it, but it didn't to her.

"So did mine. I'd rather be single forever than have my mother's life, playing bridge three times a week and doing everything my father says. She never questions anything. I don't think she's had an independent thought in her entire life. She's like an appendage of my father's, like another arm. She went to college, for Chrissake. There must be more to her than that." But Meredith hadn't seen evidence of it in all the years she could remember.

"My parents think I'll have a better career if I'm married and settled down. Customers trust married bankers more than single ones. It's statistically proven."

"But you don't want to be a banker," she reminded him.

"Now I think I do. My father and I have talked about it a lot, and I think he's right. And I'd rather be in Greenwich at our bank than in the cutthroat banking world in New York." It was abundantly clear to Meredith, from everything Ted was saying, that he was taking the easy way out on every front. Working for his father at the family bank, living in Greenwich, Connecticut, in a sleepy bedroom community of rich people who had known their family for years, marrying a girl his parents approved of and had picked out for him as the perfect banker's wife. Their fathers were best friends and played golf together. Their mothers had gone to school together. And Emily hadn't even gone to college. Meredith wondered if she had a brain.

"Do you love her?" Meredith asked him, as he ordered a second tequila. Meredith was looking upset for him, as much so as he should have been himself, and running for his life.

"I think I do love her. She's awfully cute, and devoted to me."

"How long does 'cute' last?" she asked him, angry at his parents for brainwashing him, and at Ted for letting them.

"Long enough. My parents are still together. No one in my family has ever gotten divorced."

"Ted, don't rush into this. Think about it. You can work for your dad, you can always quit if you want to. But don't rush into marriage with a girl you always said you didn't love, and only 'think' you love now. You deserve so much better than that, like someone you're crazy about, and an exciting life. She may bore you to death in five or ten years, and then what will you do?"

"We want to have kids," he said firmly. She felt more than ever as though aliens had stolen her friend and replaced him with a robot that said everything he'd been programmed to, but didn't really feel.

"Now? We're kids ourselves. That's ridiculous. What's the hurry?"

"My parents were the age I am now when they had me," he said smugly, and Meredith wanted to scream.

"Stop that. That was them. This is you. The world has changed since the war, and it's changing faster than ever. It's 1958, not 1935, when they got married."

"Maybe change isn't a good thing. Maybe the old ways were best."

She groaned when he said it. "You sound like my father," she said, seriously unnerved as she finished her second drink and was feeling a little tipsy. She hated what he was saying, and about to do to his life.

"Not everyone's as brave as you are, Merrie. You're out there looking for challenges and mountains to climb. I'm not a mountain climber. I want an easier road than that," he said honestly.

"Don't sell your soul for that easier road, Ted. You'll pay a high price for it in the end. It may not be as easy as it looks," married to a woman he didn't love, working for his father in a job he hated.

"You may pay a higher price for the things you're willing to take on."

She knew that was true, but it was worth it to her. "It's what I want to do. I don't want to end up like my mother, without an independent thought in my head, living in the shadow of someone else, with nothing I can be proud of."

"Emily is a very pretty girl. I'll be proud to have her as my wife."

Meredith wanted to cry listening to him, and felt as though she had lost her friend. The funny, silly, scattered, disorganized guy who said he wanted a better life than his parents had and wanted to enjoy life. What he was describing did not sound like living to her. It sounded like death, at twenty-three.

"Well, don't rush into anything. Think about it. You can do anything you want."

"No, I can't," he said, looking somber for a moment, and more like himself. "My father will only help me financially if I work for him at the bank, and marry someone he approves of. And they like Emily a lot." His eyes looked like he was dreaming.

"Because she's convenient for them, but maybe not so convenient for you in the long run. I'm begging you, don't sell yourself short, and think about this seriously before you do anything crazy, or that you'll regret later on."

"I told you, I'm not as brave as you are. Sometimes you just have to do what makes the most sense. We're grown-ups now. It can't just be about fun." She could hear his father's voice. As he said it, he ordered another drink, but Meredith didn't. It was his third tequila after the gin and tonic. She'd had enough and felt overwhelmingly sad for him.

"Your happiness is what makes the most sense to me. You don't have to be brave. Just don't throw yourself off a cliff."

"I think she'll make me happy," he said, slurring his words a little, and then he laughed and looked at Meredith intently. "If you'd ever fallen for me, we wouldn't be having this conversation. I'd be following you around, doing all the crazy things you do."

But she realized now more than ever that he would never have been happy doing that. He didn't care about the same things she did. He wanted an easy life, in his familiar world, staying in the womb forever with the girl next door. Meredith was a revolutionary at heart, and a gladiator. She was no girl next door, which was why she and Ted had never wound up together, and it never would have worked. She saw that more than ever now. Ted was desperate to sell out and take no risks. But the path he was choosing was far more dangerous and intricate. He was willing to let Emily and his parents bury him alive.

"You'd have hated sharing my life," she told him honestly, "and your parents would never let you marry someone like me. And I don't want to get married anyway. I have too much else to do." She looked pensive as she said it. Fighting the good fight for the underprivileged and persecuted was not compatible with being married to a banker in Greenwich, trapped in the life his parents wanted for him. She felt suffocated just thinking about it.

"You'll probably marry some wild guy someday, that no one will approve of or understand." He was wistful as he said it.

"Maybe, or no one. Whichever suits me better."

"What's happening with Seth and Claudia, by the way?" He hadn't been in touch with Claudia since they left school two months before. He'd been busy at home, negotiating with his father and making plans. "Are they getting married?"

Meredith shook her head in answer, with a sad expression. "He broke up with her. His parents went crazy when he told them about her, so he ended it. She was devastated."

Ted looked shocked, he hadn't expected that to happen. "Why?" The obvious hadn't occurred to him.

"Because she's Jewish. They formally forbade him to marry her and said they'd never see him again. He didn't want to lose his family, so he dumped her."

"Is she okay?"

"No. But she will be. She's lost more than that before. But it was very hard on her. She really loved him. And probably will for a long time."

He looked sobered by what Meredith had told him. They ordered hamburgers for dinner. And afterward, he gazed at her seriously.

"Thank you for everything you said. You're the smartest woman I know. I just don't know if I have the balls you believe I do. What my dad is suggesting would be easy and makes a lot of sense." He was trying to justify it to himself. "As long as I don't think about it."

"It may be harder than you think."

They hugged outside P.J. Clarke's and promised to have dinner again soon. But she wondered if they would. If he sold out and did what his father wanted, she wasn't sure Ted would be able to face her again. After she left him, she hoped that something she had said had sunk in, and that wouldn't be the case. She didn't want to lose a friend, but she had a feeling that she already had.

She told Claudia about her dinner with Ted the next day when she called her on Long Island, and Claudia felt sorry for him too. Neither Ted nor Seth had the guts to stand up for themselves.

"That's what's going to happen to Seth. He'll wind up marrying some girl his parents pick for him, with a colonel or a general father, who'll be happy to have a husband who's career army and goes to church, just like them. I don't think Seth or Ted will be happy with those solutions, but it takes more courage than they've got to marry someone like me," Claudia said sadly. "Even if I'd converted, I wouldn't have been good enough for them."

Meredith suspected it might be true, although she knew Claudia genuinely loved him.

"Would you have married him if he asked you to convert?" Meredith asked, and Claudia thought about it for a minute.

"Probably not. I thought about it once or twice, but I couldn't do that to the memory of my parents, given the way they died. All I really wanted was for our children to be Jewish. I couldn't have deprived them of Jewish grandchildren, even if they're not here anymore."

"That might have been a deal breaker for him too."

"Maybe. But we never got that far with his parents."

They talked about Ted again then, and hoped he didn't marry Emily, since he didn't love her. But so many people they knew, particularly women, just followed in their parents' footsteps and assumed it would be enough. It wouldn't have been enough for Meredith, she was sure of that. And Claudia didn't think it would be either. She would prefer to marry someone Jewish, but she wanted more than her parents' staid and limited life. She expected more of herself. And she couldn't settle for someone she didn't love.

She said she hadn't heard back from any newspapers yet about a job, but it was too soon. She had been relaxing and spending time with her sisters on Long Island and trying not to think of Seth, which she did all the time, and wondered what he was doing and if he missed her. When the phone rang, she still hoped it was him, and her heart skipped a beat, she told Meredith. But she knew he would never call again. He was being the good son and doing what they wanted, even if it meant giving up the woman he loved forever. She was trying to make her peace with it, which was the hardest thing she'd ever done.

Meredith worked all summer, doing menial jobs at the ACLU. She was hungry to do real legal work, and relieved when Claudia came back at the end of August, so they could have dinner together and hang out on weekends. Claudia had had responses from two newspapers by then, and was excited about one of them. John Hay Whitney, the multimillionaire Wall Street investor, had bought the previously conservative *New York Herald Tribune* only months before. His declared intention was to turn it into a more modern news-paper, "without hypocrisy," as he put it, and he was looking for young people with fresh points of view to help turn it around.

Claudia had received a letter from a senior editor who wanted to see her right after Labor Day. She had been reading the *Herald Tribune* diligently ever since she'd heard from him, and liked every-thing she saw. They were taking bold positions and trying out new approaches to reporting the news, and it seemed like an exciting place to work. She could hardly wait for her interview, and Mere-dith was excited for her. It was a lot more interesting than her job at the ACLU, and she almost wondered if she should try to interview there too, but she didn't want to steal Claudia's thunder, or crowd her. Claudia had wanted to become a writer and journalist ever since they'd met. And Meredith was biding her time till law school. She was planning to apply for the following year.

Three days after Claudia got back to town, Governor Faubus was in the news in Little Rock again. In order to avoid desegregating the schools as he'd been ordered to, he closed all four public high schools in Little Rock, Arkansas, for the entire school year, pending a public vote for or against integration of the schools. In the meantime, high school students were left with no school to attend, and had to take correspondence classes or move elsewhere in the country to con-tinue their education. The hastily organized public vote supported his position against integration, and there was a huge outcry across the country over his stance, which was counter to the federal gov-ernment's ruling in favor of desegregation.

The *Herald Tribune* was still buzzing with it when Claudia went for her interview, and she almost jumped over the desk and kissed the senior editor when he hired her on the spot. He assigned her to cover minor society news for a start. She called Meredith as soon as she left the paper and got home, and Meredith was thrilled for her. Claudia sounded infused with new life and hope as soon as she got the job.

"Did you tell your parents yet?" Meredith asked. Things had been lively at the ACLU all week too, over the scandalous closing of the Little Rock high schools, but they still only had her doing filing in the New York office.

"No, I just got home five minutes ago."

Claudia told them at dinner that night, and their reaction was lukewarm. The *Herald Tribune* was a respectable paper, but more than anything, they still wished Claudia would give up the idea of working. She didn't need to work, and they were more than willing to indulge her and support her, as they did their other daughters. But Claudia felt she had to give something back to the world, and writing for a newspaper and honing her writing skills until she felt ready to write a book seemed the best way to do it. They didn't understand it, but by the end of the evening, they'd conceded, and her father teased her about being a newspaperwoman now.

She felt incredibly grown up when she reported for work two days later, in a navy blue suit her mother had bought her at Bergdorf's, with a small discreet hat, a white silk blouse, and navy high heels. She was assigned to the society desk as a junior editorial assistant, and given a tiny cubicle the size of a broom closet, but she loved every minute of it. Her career as a writer and journalist was on its way.

To counter the monotony of her own job at the ACLU, Meredith applied to Columbia Law School in October, for the following September. She told her father, who continued to growl about it, but he was relieved that she hadn't been sent on any revolutionary assignments for the ACLU. The job had proven to be tamer than Meredith had hoped, and less ominous than he'd feared. And she had a full year ahead of her to meet someone and get married, even if she was accepted by Columbia Law School for the following year.

But the person she met for dinner most often was Claudia, and they shared their dreams and thoughts about their budding careers, although they were both off to a slow start.

Meredith was nothing more than a low-level file clerk and errand girl at the ACLU, and Claudia had just covered a bridge tournament at the Colony Club, a staunch social club for blue-blooded society women. It was an event that no one wanted to cover, so she got the assignment. And three days later, she read in the *New York Times* society section that Ted was engaged to Emily. He had sold his soul to the devil after all. She called Meredith and told her. The news depressed them both.

Claudia was set to cover another bridge tournament two days later. And that time, she got a reprieve at the last minute when one of the assistant editors got sick. The ailing editor was supposed to cover a story for the Sunday magazine, not the newspaper, to interview a young movie producer who had recently made a documentary film about Hitler's Germany and the Holocaust that included interviews with survivors and real newsreel footage. The film had supposedly been very creatively done and was considered shocking, but had been well reviewed. It was one of those films that informed the public of important details and kept the memory of what had happened fresh and alive. She wanted to see the film before she met the producer, but had to finish another assignment that day and didn't have time. It was going to be her first interview, and she felt nervous and unprepared, and the subject of his film was not an easy one for her.

She was supposed to meet the producer at the bar of the Algonquin Hotel. Thaddeus Liebowitz was thirty-three years old, and he had been making documentaries for ten years. His credentials were excellent, and this new documentary had already won an award. Claudia felt out of her league interviewing him, but at least the subject was familiar to her, more than she wanted to admit. She felt a tremor every time she thought of the film.

She tried to look professional, in a black suit, a small hat, and a black Persian lamb coat that was a hand-me-down from her mother and a little too grown-up for her. She looked more like a young Park Avenue matron than a journalist, and she had worn her long blond hair in a neat bun that made her look serious.

She found Liebowitz easily at a table in the bar of the famous Algonquin, where the likes of Ernest Hemingway had hung out, and still did occasionally when he was in town. She asked the maître d' to point the producer out, and saw him in a back corner, smoking a cigar. He was wearing a tweed jacket and a black turtleneck sweater, and his hair was long. He smiled when she approached the table and identified herself, but he looked surprised to see her.

"I thought they'd send someone older," he said easily and invited her to sit down across from him. He looked "Bohemian," as her parents would have said, and intellectual. She could see that the cigar he was smoking was one of the best Cubans, since her father smoked the same brand occasionally, and when she was younger, he had always given her the paper rings to wear. After his opening comment, she just hoped he didn't guess it was her first interview.

"I'm sorry," she apologized immediately in answer to what he'd said. "The editor assigned to do the interview got sick." And then with a look of mischief, she said, "You spared me from covering an incredibly boring bridge tournament, my second one in a week. I'm usually assigned to the society desk." She looked apologetic as she said it. He laughed, she ordered a cup of tea and he a scotch on the rocks, and they got to work, talking about his movie. She was curious about him and why he'd made the film, so the questions came easily. And he was a cooperative subject, more than willing to share with her what had inspired him to make the film.

"It's been thirteen years since the camps were liberated," he said quietly. "People forget. I think they need to be reminded from time to time. And it was so disturbing when the news first came out. Some of the really gruesome footage was never shown. But I think people need to see that too. We know more since the trials in Nuremberg than we did at first. We need to really understand who Hitler was, and why he did it, so it never happens again."

It was easy to agree with what he said, as she took rapid notes. She hadn't even touched her tea yet, and it had long since grown cold, as she wrote down everything he said, and tried not to miss a word. She was diligent about it.

"I hope I haven't shocked you," he continued. "My film is very graphic, but I think that's what people need to make them aware. Particularly what they did to the children. Just about every Jewish child was shipped out of France. Many of them were hidden by members of the resistance, but an enormous number of French children were sent to labor camps and killed by the Germans. Not to mention the children in Germany who were more easily accessible, and throughout eastern Europe." He had excellent knowledge of the subject, and seemed to care about it deeply. "While we were sitting here, in the comfort and relative safety of the U.S., Jews all over Europe were decimated."

She nodded agreement and concentrated on what she was writing, so he didn't see how moved she was by it, and then she raised her eyes to meet his.

"They gassed all or most of the younger children as soon as they got to the camps. They only preserved those they thought were strong enough to work," she added and he looked at her with interest. He hadn't caught her last name or paid attention to it.

"You're interested in the subject?" he asked, eyeing her intently.

"Yes, I am," she admitted, not volunteering anything further about herself, which she thought would be unprofessional. "I know something about it," she added, and he nodded.

"Most people want to forget, now that the war is over. I think it's important not to let that happen."

"So do I," she agreed.

"It's the whole purpose of my film. How do you know that about the children, by the way?" He was intrigued by her. She was serious and diligent, despite her age. She didn't answer for a long moment and didn't know what to say.

"I just do" was all she said to him. After two hours, they both agreed that they had covered all the pertinent aspects of his documentary and the interview was over. She had never touched her tea, and he had finished his drink. They hadn't stopped talking for the entire two hours.

"Did you have friends or relatives who went to any of the camps?" he asked her, still curious about her, and why she knew about it.

She nodded gently. "Yes, I did."

"I had cousins who went to Bergen-Belsen. My father tried to get them out of Germany, but it was too late. And a whole branch of my mother's family died in the Warsaw ghetto." As they spoke for a few minutes after the interview, he thought he detected the faintest accent, although she spoke English perfectly. "Where are you from?" he asked.

"Here, now," she spoke in a soft voice. "And originally Germany. Berlin."

He didn't say anything then for a long moment, as he watched her intently. "Your family?" he asked in barely more than a whisper, and she decided to be honest with him. She felt she had no choice.

"Auschwitz," she said simply, and told the whole story with a single word, as a look of pain crossed his eyes, and compassion for her.

"How did you manage to escape that fate?" he asked, assuming that she had, and was shocked by her answer.

"I didn't. I was in Auschwitz from '42 to '45, until we were liberated by the Russians. I was the only one of my family who survived. I was ten when they freed us."

He looked like he was about to cry, and he felt terrible for not knowing it sooner. He wondered if his answers to her questions had been too harsh and unfeeling. This was not a film to her, it was her life.

"I'm so sorry. And I'm sorry if I was hard with my answers. I just feel that everyone should know what happened. But you already do. Did the magazine know when they sent you?"

She shook her head, looking shy and young, despite her grown-up clothes. "I don't usually talk about it, at least not with strangers. Or even friends. But it's good for other people to know, and for us to forget what we can."

He was moved beyond belief by this dignified young woman. And without saying a word then, she pulled up the sleeve of her jacket slightly and turned her arm, and he saw the tattoo that had identified her in the camp. She had been a number for three years, and not a human being.

"I'm truly sorry. I hope the interview wasn't too difficult for you." He felt guilty now for dragging her through it, but she looked calm and solid, and not flustered by what she'd heard. And she had to be a strong person to survive what she did. She knew the story, better than he did. He hadn't told her anything she didn't know.

"Don't be sorry. I knew what the interview was about. And I think you know the subject very well."

"I care a lot about it," he said with feeling.

"I can tell. I want to write a book about it one day."

"You should do it soon, before you forget the details."

"I won't forget." She smiled at him. "But I haven't felt ready. Maybe in a few years."

"You should push yourself to do it. The world needs those stories. Stories like yours, firsthand. It's not the same when another person tells it. How did you get here?"

"I was adopted by an American family, through a Jewish relief group. They've been wonderful to me."

"I wish I had known you when I made the movie. I interviewed a lot of people, but none of them had been in the camps as children." He didn't say that it had been hard to find many who had lived through it.

"Very few children survived. You had to work very hard for them to let you stay alive. I was on a rock-breaking crew my first year there. My father and brother were alive then too. They killed my mother and two small sisters immediately. Anyway, you know the stories. You must have heard it all before."

"Not from anyone who was so young. You must have a remarkable spirit."

"No more than anyone else. Who knows what keeps us alive? You can never predict who will be strong enough and who won't be. Many of the strongest people didn't make it, and some of the weaker ones did. It comes from within. I was seven when we arrived and the youngest one in my dormitory, but tall for my age." She wasn't a big woman now, and very slight, but stronger than she appeared. He looked at her then again with amazement and, without thinking, he reached out and gently touched her hand. She had turned her arm so the tattoo had disappeared again. She didn't like people to see it. It was a private thing now.

"Would you have dinner with me?" he asked, and she hesitated.

"I'm not sure if I'm supposed to."

"Let's just say the interview is over. It ended five minutes ago. Now we're just friends with things to talk about. Will you join me for dinner?" He repeated the invitation and she laughed at how he compartmentalized it. "I'd be honored," he added, and she was touched.

"All right, I will. That's very kind of you, Mr. Liebowitz."

"Thaddeus. And it's kind of you to dine with me. They actually have quite decent food here. Would this be all right?" It was bitter cold out and had snowed earlier, so the prospect of staying in the warm hotel was appealing to both of them.

He asked the maître d' in the bar to reserve a table for them in the dining room, and five minutes later, he escorted her into the restaurant, after they had checked her mother's coat. He was trying not to notice how pretty she was. He liked talking to her and didn't want to spoil it. This was not just about chasing a beautiful woman, but learning more about one who fascinated him and understood the subject of his movie even better than he did.

Over dinner, he told her about making movies in Hollywood, and how he had gotten into doing documentaries, not wanting to compete with his father, who was a famous Hollywood producer of feature films. He preferred more serious subjects to commercial films, although he had great respect for his father's work. They talked about a film Thaddeus had made in Italy and one in France, about artwork stolen by the Nazis, much of which had not been found yet. And he had recently made a documentary on Martin Luther King Jr., and had followed him for a month to do it. He said King was an extraordinary person, and Claudia was intrigued by how knowledgeable he was on a variety of subjects. She had a wonderful time listening to him, and was sorry when dinner was over.

"Could I see you again sometime?" he asked, sounding like a schoolboy when he helped her with her coat after dinner. She thought about it for a minute and then nodded. She wondered what her family would think of him. They didn't approve of people in show business, but he was very intellectual, knowledgeable, and well-read. And they would like the fact that he was Jewish.

"I'd like that," she answered his question. "I'll let you know when they're going to run the interview, and send you a copy of it before it comes out," she told him, being professional again. He walked her outside and put her in a taxi, and stood on the sidewalk in the cold, watching the cab until it disappeared. He felt like a bomb had hit him. Without even realizing she had, the graceful, gentle young woman had rocked his world.

Chapter Eight

C laudia began seeing Thaddeus for dinner from time to time in January. He was very pleased with the interview when it came out, and so was the magazine. They thought the piece had real merit and showed that she had journalistic talent. They started sending her on other interviews after that, with several important people. Claudia handled both the subjects and the writing efficiently and with obvious poise. And at Thaddeus's urging, she started making notes for the book she wanted to write. It was harder than she had expected, so she worked on it for a while, and then put it aside and came back to it. She was in no hurry to do it. It brought up so many painful memories for her.

She enjoyed the time they spent together immensely. She was fascinated by his films, and he by her life. After they had seen each other for a few months, she invited him home to dinner with her parents and sisters. He had shown up in a proper suit and tie. Predictably, they were ambivalent about him. The show-business side of his life didn't please them, no matter how famous his father was as a film maker, but he won them over rapidly with his intelligence, good manners, and kindness to their daughter, and there was no denying that he was a very interesting person. They thought that he was too old for Claudia, since she was ten years younger than he, but she insisted they were just friends, which was almost true but not quite. Thaddeus had been telling her that he was falling in love with her, and she had feelings for him, but after her experience with Seth, she was cautious, and told Thaddeus about that too.

Meredith was impressed that Claudia had taken him home to dinner. She had met Thaddeus and liked him a lot. They had spent an evening together, and she really enjoyed their conversations. Meredith thought that they were perfect for each other, but Claudia was still moving slowly. In April he went back to Hollywood to edit a film in his father's studio, and Claudia was relieved to have time to herself to think about it. He called her every day. He had respected her need not to rush, so far. He had kissed her before he left, but it had gone no further. Claudia wasn't ready, and he knew it. He could tell.

Later that month Meredith got the letter accepting her into Columbia Law School, and she told her father that night. He sighed when she handed it to him and asked again if she was sure, and she said she was. Alex wanted to go to law school one day too, and her father thought that was fine. He was only thirteen. He still had high school and college to get through, but her father thought the law was a suitable career for a man, and a tough one for a woman, and a huge sacrifice to make. He was convinced that being a lawyer was not compatible with being a wife and mother and that she'd have to choose one over the other.

Meredith and her father had found a new subject to disagree about, the Vietnam War. He thought it was right for the United States to be there and that the war would be good for the economy. Meredith was vehemently against it, all the reasons for it, and everything it stood for.

"Boys are going to start dying over there one of these days," she told him heatedly, and he insisted she was wrong.

"They're not there as soldiers, they're there as advisors."

"I don't care what they call them, they're military, and shots are going to be fired, and there will be young Americans coming back in body bags."

"You're always on some crusade, Meredith," he said, annoyed by the argument, "but you're wrong about this one. We're there on a peacekeeping mission."

"That's not true, Dad. The minute someone fires a shot, and you know that's going to happen, we're going to have a war on our hands. And I can tell you one thing, when we do, I don't want my brother in it," she said forcefully to her father.

"That will never happen. All you peaceniks, or doves, or whatever you call yourselves, or bleeding hearts, see danger everywhere. We have the situation in full control," he said confidently.

"So did the French," she reminded him, "and they lost their shirts there. Now we've got our neck on the line." It was one of those arguments that neither of them could ever win, but Meredith's grandfather agreed with her a hundred percent, and was terrified that the situation in Vietnam would escalate like a forest fire one of these days. Robert refused to believe it.

* * *

By the time Thaddeus came back from L.A. in June, Claudia had figured out that she was in love with him, and stopped resisting. She met him at the airport when he returned, and flew into his arms. She spent the night with him whenever she could get away with it, and Meredith covered for her. But she was twenty-four years old and knew what she wanted, and he treated her like a piece of spun glass. They had a wonderful time together. He encouraged her to work on her book whenever possible, and they had Meredith over to his apartment for dinner, and had intense conversations about de-segregation and the potential for real war in Vietnam, which terri-fied them all, except Meredith's father, who stubbornly insisted that American troops belonged there. Meredith had stopped even talk-ing to him about it. It was pointless.

Her job at the ACLU got a little more interesting before she left, but she was basically too low on the totem pole to get serious assign-ments. Her immediate supervisor encouraged her to come back once she had her law degree. She had been impressed by her, and they always needed attorneys. She left them at the end of June, was planning to spend July on Martha's Vineyard with her parents, and at the end of August she was starting law school. The past year had been a quiet one for her. Claudia was much busier with her job at the *Herald Tribune* and her relationship with Thaddeus, which she was still telling her parents was just a friendship and platonic, and they believed her.

Meredith was at the Vineyard with her family for the Fourth of July, and they gave a barbecue for friends as they did every year. It was a cozy homegrown event, with her father taking orders at the barbecue. He was always relaxed at the Vineyard.

Four days later, Meredith's predictions came true, when the first

American "advisor" was killed in Vietnam. It spawned a huge argument between them about what would come next.

"One day there will be a full-scale war over there, with American soldiers dying. How can you pretend that that won't happen?" Meredith said angrily to her father.

"One dead advisor is not indicative of a full-scale war coming," he insisted, and she looked at him with narrowed eyes.

"If that one dead advisor were Alex, you'd be looking at this very differently," she said. He didn't answer, and went back into the house. Afterward he told Janet that their daughter was crazy and she had a new crusade to rage about. It was always something with her. And he thought his father was as crazy as she was, since he agreed with her. Robert believed in the U.S. military presence in Vietnam, and he was even all for bombing the North Vietnamese *before* they created a serious problem, to scare them into line. But he didn't for a minute believe that there would be a full-scale war there, with the deaths of American boys. That just wasn't going to happen, in his opinion.

Meredith had lunch with her grandfather the day before she started law school. He was in New York on some personal business, and wanted to wish her well on her new adventure.

"You'll be changing the world after this," he said proudly. "Learn everything you can. Maybe you'll be on the Supreme Court one day. Or be president. You can do anything you set your mind to." He always flung open the doors for her, and the horizon was limitless the way he described it, unlike her parents, who wanted to keep her life small and disapproved of everything she wanted to try her hand at. They weren't thrilled about her going to law school, and were worried about where it would lead her. Certainly not in any of the directions they envisioned for her, straight into marriage and motherhood, where they were convinced she belonged. They were very old-school and still believed a woman's place was in the home. They thought she needed a husband to tame her, which sounded like a horrifying prospect to her. She didn't want to be tamed. She wanted to roam free, like a wild horse on the plains. Her grandfather understood that, and had been a wild horse all his life. It had worked well for him. But he was a man, and she was a young girl.

The classes at Columbia were harder than she'd expected, but she enjoyed them. She'd been there for two months when she got an invitation to Ted Jones's wedding in Greenwich to Miss Emily Margaret Barclay. She knew they'd gotten engaged a year before, but with no further news from him, she'd hoped he had come to his senses. Apparently he hadn't. He had gone to work at his father's bank, and was marrying the girl his parents wanted him to marry, the one he'd said bored him blind the whole time they were in college. Now they were getting married at twenty-four, and babies would be next. The thought of it made Meredith sad, because she knew he could have done so much better, and was settling for a life he didn't really want. He didn't have the courage to do otherwise. And Ted knew it too, however he justified it to himself.

She responded to the invitation with a heavy heart, and decided to go. Claudia was invited too, but she wasn't going. She had an interview to do that day, and was glad to miss it. Meredith had fantasies about standing up and objecting when the minister asked if anyone knew of a reason for the marriage not to go forward. "YES!" she wanted to scream. "He'll be miserable! And he doesn't love her!" She would then be dragged out of the wedding, and maybe even arrested by Emily's parents, while Ted would thank her and run away to freedom. But it wasn't going to happen that way. She was going to watch him put a noose around his neck and hang himself, or wish he had.

The wedding was the Saturday of Thanksgiving weekend. Meredith took the train to Greenwich in the outfit she was wearing to the black-tie wedding, complete with an old mink coat she had borrowed from her mother for the occasion. She was sorry she had never fallen in love with Ted. Even if she would have driven him crazy, he would have been happier than he was going to be with Emily for the rest of his life, or however long the marriage lasted. She hated to see him make a mistake like that. It was a big one.

She took a cab from the station to the house. The wedding was being held in the large, rambling home of Emily's parents, with a heated tent outside with chandeliers and a dance floor. The guests were already gathering in the part of the tent where the ceremony would be held with neat rows of gold chairs lined up. Meredith almost expected to see a hangman's noose dangling from the rafters of the tent. She recognized a few people from college, but most of the guests were friends of the parents and strangers to her. They were escorted to their seats, and a few minutes later the music began playing. Eight bridesmaids came down the aisle in pale pink velvet dresses and looked like Barbie dolls. The ushers all looked equally unreal. There was a surreal quality to all of it. Both sets of parents were seated in the front rows, with Ted's smiling grandmother, whom Meredith genuinely liked. Meredith was angry at Ted's parents for roping him into a marriage that felt like a fraud

Ted was waiting at the makeshift altar with the best man and the minister, and a moment later, Emily came down the aisle in white velvet trimmed in white fur, with a little white mink pillbox hat perched on top of her French twist. She looked like something in a bridal magazine. None of it felt like two people who genuinely loved each other, but Ted was beaming as he looked at her, and Meredith tried to tell herself that everything would be okay and maybe they really loved each other, at least for a few of the right reasons.

The crucial moment in the ceremony came and went and she didn't object or make a scene, and everyone cooed when he put the ring on Emily's finger and kissed her, and the minister declared them man and wife. Meredith noticed then that there were tears rolling down her cheeks, and she wasn't sure why. Ted was the first of her friends to get married, and she just hoped it would turn out all right for him. He looked happy. The lamb being led to slaughter, and willingly at that. Emily was gushing and squealing and kissing people and clapping her hands and showing off her diamond wedding ring and looked ridiculous to Meredith. She couldn't imagine anyone with a brain acting that way, even on her wedding day.

And then the champagne came out, poured lavishly, and the bar was open. Eventually dinner was served, and she found herself seated next to one of Ted's college roommates whom she hadn't seen in ages. They both had too much to drink and danced a lot. The bridal couple cut the wedding cake eventually, and Emily did a cute little thing where she smooshed it all over Ted's face and then he did it to her, which all made Meredith want to drink more. Ted's old roommate asked her if she wanted to go upstairs and have sex in one of the bedrooms, and she thought that it was a terrible idea, so he went with one of the bridesmaids instead a little later. She managed to hug Ted before he left on their honeymoon to Jamaica. She wasn't sure whether to say "Deepest sympathy" or "Condolences," but she said neither and just kissed him and wished him luck. He laughed at her when she did.

"You're shitfaced, McKenzie."

"That's a distinct possibility," she admitted. The champagne had been excellent. And she had just watched one of her best friends marry the wrong woman and get stuck in a dreary existence he would hate and bitterly regret for the rest of his life. "Have fun in Jamaica," she said, mellowed by the drinks she'd had. It was the only way she could get through the wedding.

"Watch out for Jason Leland, the guy sitting next to you," Ted warned her. Emily's mother had done the seating and didn't know Ted's friends.

"He's fine, I think he's upstairs with one of the bridesmaids."

She left a few minutes after the bridal couple, in one of the cabs Emily's parents had provided for departing guests, and she caught the train back to New York. She was sad, thinking about him. She had just watched someone she loved ruin his life. And with that, she fell asleep and slept all the way to Pennsylvania Station in New York. As she left the train and made her way to the taxis, she realized that she was going to have one hell of a headache the next day. But it was nothing compared to the headache Ted would have when he woke up next to Emily for the rest of his life. It seemed like a terrible waste of a good guy to her.

Chapter Nine

O ne of the most exciting things to happen to Meredith in her first year of law school was the prospect of John Fitzgerald Kennedy running for president. Like most people of her generation, she was crazy about him. But he was more than just a solid, complete liberal candidate for the presidency. He was a dashing, handsome example of American royalty, filled with charisma, and everything about him and around him was magical. His beautiful wife, her fabulous clothes, her beauty, their adorable little girl, the way they lived, the eloquence of his speeches, the promises he made the nation. He was the American dream personified and captured everyone's imagination. Meredith was carried along on the tidal wave of his limitless charm, and she volunteered to work on his campaign early on. She wanted desperately for him to win. The country needed him to pull them out of the doldrums of the Eisenhower administration. She thought Richard Nixon, as the Republican candidate, was a grim alternative, whom her father preferred, of course. And as a Democratic appointee to the Supreme Court, her grandfather supported Kennedy wholeheartedly.

Working on his campaign as early as January was fun for Meredith. The young people already supporting him were enthusiastic and dynamic. She met lots of people of all ages who were as excited about him as she was. She volunteered at least two nights a week, and planned to spend more time later in the campaign if he won the nomination.

And after considerable thought, she decided to spend her spring break from law school in Greensboro, North Carolina. She signed up through the ACLU to join a protest organized by four young black college students from North Carolina Agricultural and Technical College. They had singled out the Woolworth's lunch counter, where only whites were served, and on a rotating basis, they had black and white volunteers sit at the counter to protest that blacks were not served. It was relatively peaceful and had caught the attention of the country as a further step in the ongoing protests against segregation. It didn't scare Meredith, who had told her parents she was going to Florida with friends from law school for spring break, which seemed fine to them. Meredith was planning to spend a week in Greensboro, and take the shifts she was assigned to sit at the counter for several hours.

Everything was fine until her father turned on the news one night before dinner, saw the filmed reports of the protests at Woolworth's in North Carolina, and spotted his daughter sitting at the counter. He had no way to reach her, but he was livid as soon as he saw her. He called his father in Washington to find out if he knew anything about it.

"No, I didn't. But are you really surprised?" Bill McKenzie asked his son. "That's who she is, Robert, right now, anyway. She'll be fine," he said soothingly, which only enraged his son further.

"What if she gets arrested?"

"If she does, she'll call you, and you can bail her out." Bill sounded calm about it. They couldn't reach her to stop her anyway, and her grandfather thought joining the protest in Greensboro was brave of her. You never knew how those things would go, or if they'd get out of hand. He worried about her too, but he had faith in her ability to make good decisions and take care of herself in most circumstances. She was a sensible girl.

As it turned out, things happened just the way her grandfather said they might. On Meredith's third day in North Carolina, after four hours at the lunch counter, someone got in an argument with the Woolworth's employees, who were stressed and angry about the protest, and Meredith and five other protestors were arrested and taken to jail. Feeling somewhat sheepish, she called her father, told him where she was, and asked him to pay her bail.

"I know where you are," he said, furious with her. Fortunately, it was a Saturday and he was at home to get the call. "I saw you on television. Your mother and I have been worried sick about you."

"I'm fine, Dad, but they won't let me stay on the phone. Can you do something about posting bail for me?"

"I will if you swear to me you'll get on the next bus or train home. I want you out of there, Meredith, as fast as you can."

She hesitated for a second. "I was planning to stay here for a week."

"You lied to us, you said you'd be in Florida," he said sternly. "You heard me. I'll post bail if you come straight home. If you're going to hang around down there, you can stay in jail. You're safer there."

"Fine, I'll come home," she said, sounding like a surly child, and hung up.

Robert called a judge he knew in Raleigh that he'd gone to law school with, explained the situation to him, and asked if he could arrange for bail, and Robert would send him a check immediately to reimburse him. The judge guffawed for a minute. "I don't like this thing any better than you do, Bob. I think one of my boys is there too. He may have gotten arrested with her, he just called me from jail. I'll take care of it right away." Robert thanked him profusely and was somewhat reassured. And two hours later, Meredith called him from the bus station. She was on her way home.

"Thanks, Dad," she said, sounding slightly mollified. It was the first time she'd been arrested, and it was terrifying, but the police had been relatively nice because she was white. Her colored fellow protestors hadn't fared as well. The police told her to go home and forget Negro problems, when they let her out of jail. Let the police take care of it, they said.

"I want to talk to you as soon as you get home," her father said harshly, and she could imagine what he was going to say. She could tell that he was livid. "You risked your life down there, Meredith. You could be hurt or killed by one of the locals, or get caught in a riot. This isn't your battle. Stay out of it."

"I have to catch the bus, Dad," she said to cut him off. "See you later." He hung up, and told her mother that she was on her way home.

She walked into the apartment at six in the morning after a seventeen-hour bus ride, and her father was waiting for her. He gave her all the stern warnings she expected. "You're an embarrassment to me. Do you understand that?" She was shocked when he said it to her. "I don't ever want you doing something like this again." She nodded but didn't promise, because she believed in what she was doing, even if he didn't.

Her mother cried when she saw her later that morning, and Meredith called Claudia and told her what had happened. She was nervous for her too. Meredith was fearless, but that wasn't entirely a good thing, and Claudia could just imagine how angry the McKenzies were. Her own parents would have been irate if she'd gotten arrested for a protest.

After Meredith went back to law school a week later, her father had good news for them when he came home one night. He was being appointed a federal judge by President Eisenhower. Meredith realized it was probably his last chance to be a Republican appointee, if there was a Democrat in the White House after the next election. And she hoped there would be, if it was John Fitzgerald Kennedy. But she was happy and excited for her father. It was a big step up for him. So they had a federal judge in the family now and a Supreme Court justice. And as her grandfather told her at her father's swearing-in, "Now it's up to you, Merrie." She hoped he was right.

A month later, the army sent more military advisors to Vietnam. They were beefing up for something, but no one knew what, and Meredith got into more arguments with her father about the growing threat in Vietnam, none of which he believed, no matter how often she and her grandfather said it to him. He remained a devoted hawk.

The only real fun in Meredith's life at the moment was the campaign work she did for John Kennedy. She stepped up the time she committed to it in the spring. And she was either in the library, studying for school, or at campaign headquarters, doing whatever tasks she was assigned. She was willing to do anything to help.

It all paid off in July when Kennedy won the Democratic nomination. And two weeks later, Richard Nixon won the Republican nomination. He was still Robert's preferred candidate, of course.

As things got busier over the summer, Meredith found herself working side by side with a third-year Harvard law student, Adam Thompson, who was as dedicated to Kennedy's campaign as she was, and they went out for a drink afterward several times. They were both in love with the idea of Kennedy in the White House and everything it would mean to the nation. It seemed like America's time had come, they had found their prince, and everyone's dreams would come true.

Meredith liked Kennedy's position on civil rights, and she enjoyed going out with Adam. They had fun together, grousing about law school and how much work it was. He was spending the whole summer working on the campaign, and other than a week on Martha's Vineyard, so did she. She even got her little brother to hand out flyers and leaflets with her, and he was excited about Kennedy too. Neither of them thought Nixon was an appealing prospect, and she hoped he wouldn't win. Her father was staunchly wearing a Nixon button on his lapel every day. And every time she and her brother put up Kennedy posters or banners in the house, he took them down.

Adam, her Harvard law student friend, was good company. He told her that he'd recently broken up with a Radcliffe senior named Wendy at the beginning of the summer and admitted that he wasn't completely over her yet. So they went on outings, but Merrie wouldn't sleep with him, although he tried. They took a blazing hot day off and went to Jones Beach together. She introduced him to Claudia and Thaddeus, and they liked him. Claudia and Thaddeus were fairly serious by then. She was working on her book with his encouragement, and making slow but steady progress, recording her childhood memories of the war, her family, and the camp.

Meredith hated to take time off from the campaign when she went back to law school for her second year. But every weekend, she turned up at campaign headquarters for at least one day and Adam came down from Boston to volunteer and see her. He could have worked on the campaign in Boston, but he liked spending time with her. They hadn't decided if they were really dating or just fooling around. The campaign was the glue that held them together, and everything was secondary to that. They decided to figure it out later. They had too much to do now, keeping up with law school and helping Kennedy's cause.

By the beginning of October, Meredith was at campaign head-quarters every night, Claudia and Thaddeus had decided to join her several nights a week, and Adam continued to come down from Cambridge every weekend. The rooms were crowded constantly with devoted hopeful Democrats, who were desperate for their candidate to win. Every speech he made, every appearance, made more people fall in love with him. He handled each situation with ease. He was the kind of man they wanted running the country, and despite Nixon's political experience, his stuffy awkward style held no appeal for Meredith and her friends. There was even something very touching about seeing a pregnant Jackie campaigning for her husband. They were real people, with a family and unlimited charm.

And John Kennedy had big dreams for the country, and solutions to their problems. He seemed to be the answer to their prayers.

In the final weeks before the election, Meredith had never put so much energy into anything in her life. She was willing him to win, and every conversation with her father ended in an argument, so she stopped discussing it with him.

The night of the election, Claudia, Thaddeus, and Adam were with her at campaign headquarters. They'd all voted, and all eyes were glued to the televisions set up in every room. There were TV cameras standing by to film all of them throughout the evening, and in case their man won.

Meredith smiled at Claudia in a quiet moment. "It's exciting, isn't it?" Thaddeus and Adam had gone outside for a smoke. Thaddeus loved his Cuban cigars, and Claudia liked the pungent smell of them now.

"It is exciting. What's with you and Adam? I can never figure out if you two are an item or just friends." Meredith always seemed to keep her distance. Her causes were more important to her than her men.

"Neither can we." She laughed in answer. "We can't decide if it's campaign fever or true love. We both have law school to finish, and he's in Cambridge and I'm here. We'll both have a lot of catching up to do for school when this is over. My professors have been pretty good about it, but I'll have to make up the work I missed by the end of the semester. And so will he. He just broke up with some girl at Radcliffe a few months ago. It doesn't sound like it's over yet. My heart isn't deeply engaged here. We're just having fun together."

"Your heart is never deeply engaged," Claudia commented, "except in the causes you care about. Don't you want more romance in your life?" She was so happy with Thaddeus, and wished Meredith would meet someone like him. But he was older and more mature than the boys Meredith dated.

She thought about it seriously before she answered. "Not now. I think a serious romance would slow me down. I'm not ready. I don't want someone telling me what to do, that I can't go to a protest or a march, or telling me something is too dangerous. It would be like dating my father. I hear enough of that from him. I have some battles to engage in first. I need to do that on my own."

"Don't wait too long," Claudia said gently. "When the right man comes along, grab him. It doesn't happen every day."

"I don't think Adam is that guy, for me anyway," Meredith said honestly. She'd been considering it lately, as the election drew closer. "We have a good time together, but that's not really enough. I have fun doing a lot of things. If I fall for someone, I want it to be someone really special. Maybe that's a once-in-a-lifetime thing, and it hasn't showed up in my life yet."

"It will someday," Claudia reassured her.

"What about you and Thaddeus? Are you thinking of getting married?" she asked, and Claudia looked pensive when she answered.

"Not for now, and maybe never. I'm not sure he's the kind of guy who'd want to get married." It had already been almost two years and they steered carefully around the subject. The only thing that Claudia would have liked about it was being able to live together openly, instead of sneaking around for whatever nights they could steal or lie about, or having someone cover for her, the way Meredith did. Living with him would have been wonderful, but marriage seemed like a lot to take on, and Claudia wasn't ready either. She wanted to finish her book first, and she knew her parents wouldn't be thrilled if she married him. He was Jewish, but they wanted her to marry some nice conservative doctor or lawyer from Temple Emanu-El, and Claudia had never met anyone there she liked. Thaddeus was much more interesting than that and suited her better, but she didn't want to upset her parents.

The boys came back from their smoke then, and they all went back to watching the television sets that were starting to announce the results of the election. The tension was mounting, as the voting stations closed across the country and the results were tallied. It looked like it was going to be a close race, and Meredith was sure her parents were watching at home, cheering for Nixon.

The New York Times declared Kennedy the winner shortly before midnight. The results were confusing at first, because Nixon had won more states but Kennedy had carried the electoral and popular votes. And the tally was extremely close. America had a new president, and it was John Fitzgerald Kennedy, the youngest president America had ever elected to office at forty-three. And the First Lady, at thirty, was only six years older than Meredith but seemed infinitely more sophisticated. Nixon made a speech at 3 A.M., implying defeat, but not officially conceding yet. There was jubilation around the country, especially in Washington, and the campaign workers went crazy at Kennedy headquarters.

Adam kissed Meredith firmly on the mouth as soon as they saw the results on the screen and heard the news. They had worked hard for this together, along with so many others. And at the McKenzies' apartment, Alex was doing a little jig in his bedroom, while his father turned the TV off in the living room and looked unhappily at his wife.

"Well, we have a Democrat in the White House. God help us." He was doubly grateful for his appointment to the bench only months before. It wouldn't have happened with a Democratic president, since he was known to be a staunch Republican, but he was firmly entrenched on the federal bench now, and pleased to be there.

Adam and Meredith went to Thaddeus's apartment in Greenwich Village with Claudia and had a drink to celebrate. None of them could remember this kind of excitement when Eisenhower was elected. And they hadn't had a Democratic president since Truman, and Franklin Roosevelt before him. They were happy to have the Democrats back, and so was most of the country.

After they all relaxed and talked about it for a while, they left and headed uptown. Claudia had to go home that night. Adam and Meredith shared a cab, and she dropped him off at Penn Station. He was going back to Boston, but he had said a few days before that he'd come to New York again soon. Things seemed different tonight, as she looked at him and he kissed her.

"Something happened, didn't it?" She could see it in his eyes. "Is it the election?"

He shook his head. "It's Wendy. I saw her last week. She wants to give it another try, and I feel like I should. We had two years together. It's hard to walk away from that, and she says she's willing to make some changes."

Meredith nodded. She understood, and it didn't surprise her. She figured something like that would happen. He had admitted right in the beginning that he wasn't totally over Wendy, and she had had that sense about him. Her instincts had been right, and she had protected herself in case this happened. She was disappointed but not crushed or heartbroken. And she was glad she hadn't slept with him. He hadn't pushed it because of Wendy. "I'm sorry, Merrie."

"It's okay. We had fun during the campaign." He kissed her one last time and got out of the cab with a look over his shoulder.

"You're an amazing woman, Meredith McKenzie, and don't let anyone tell you otherwise. When you're ready, the right guy will come along. I don't think you have a lot of room for one right now."

"No, I don't." She smiled ruefully at him. "Tell Wendy to treat you right, or I'll come to Cambridge and beat her up." She waved at him and the cab pulled away, and for a moment she was sad on the way home, and then she thought about the election. They had a new president that night, and he was going to be a great one. She'd lost a boyfriend she never really had anyway, but they had a hero in the White House. On balance, it was not too bad.

Alex was asleep on her bed when she got home, and he woke up when he heard her. "We won!" he said ecstatically, and threw his arms around her.

"We sure did! How pissed is Dad?" she asked, smiling.

"Very." He grinned.

"I figured. The good times are coming, Alex. For us all." She walked him to his bedroom, he kissed her good night sleepily, and she went back to her own room, smiling. She was going to miss Adam, but not too much. It had been a moment. That was enough. And now they both had to get on with their lives. She knew he had made the right decision to go back to Wendy. She wasn't going to be ready for a serious relationship for a long, long time.

Chapter Ten

The morning after the election, Meredith's grandfather called her from Washington.

"How sweet is that?" he said when she came to the phone. He had offered his sympathy to Robert first, who was in deep mourning about a Democrat in the White House.

"It's very sweet, Grampa." She was smiling as she said it.

"I called to find out what you're doing on January twentieth."

"I don't know. Why?" The date didn't ring any bells.

"As a justice of the Supreme Court, I happen to have two tickets to the inauguration, and two tickets to the inaugural balls. Your grandma says she doesn't feel up to going, with all the standing around and the crowds. Her hip is bothering her, and I wonder if you would do me the honor of going with me."

"Grampa!" She squealed into the phone, unable to believe her good luck and the opportunity. She couldn't think of anything more wonderful than seeing those historical occasions and going with him. It was a dream come true. "I'd love it!"

"Then you're on, young lady. Buy yourself a dress for each occasion and charge them to me. Nothing too sassy for the balls, or the newspaper will say I was out with my girlfriend. . . . On the other hand, maybe that's not such a bad thing. Buy whatever you want. I think we're going to have a lot of fun together." She could hardly wait.

It felt like a great day when she left for school, and she stayed late at the library that night to catch up on work. She thought about Adam for a few minutes and knew he had done the right thing for both of them. She had always suspected he'd probably go back to Wendy, who really wanted him, and Meredith was never totally sure she did. Something about him always made her hesitate, possibly the specter of Wendy.

When she got home that night, she found an announcement from Ted and Emily on her bed. They'd had a baby boy on the first of November, eleven months after they got married. They hadn't wasted any time. Now they were a family. For a minute, she felt sorry for him again. He was twenty-five years old with a wife and child, and he was a banker, which was everything he had never wanted and didn't feel ready for. But he had done it to himself. She hoped that the baby solidified his marriage.

It was weird to think about as she brushed her teeth and got ready for bed. Ted was her goofiest friend and now he was a father. She wondered what that felt like, and if she'd ever know. She could never visualize herself with children. Alex had been her baby when he was born when she was ten. She had experienced it with him, and that seemed like enough. She wasn't looking to do it again with kids of her own, and he was even more fun now that he was a teen-ager. He was about to turn fifteen, and such a nice boy. She loved spending time with him, although their age difference made it difficult. She'd left for Vassar when he was eight, and in the six years since, she was either working, in law school, or pursuing her causes. And now he was in high school and busy with other school sports and activities of his own. Even living at home, she hardly saw him.

She put Ted's baby announcement on her desk, so she'd remember to send them a present, and was glad it wasn't her.

The swearing-in of John Fitzgerald Kennedy, the thirty-fifth president of the United States, on January 20, 1961, was the most amazing event Meredith had ever been to. There was snow on the ground and the city looked magical. Kennedy wore a black top hat and full gray morning dress, and removed his top hat and overcoat for the swearing-in despite freezing weather. And his beautiful First Lady, Jackie, wore a fawn-colored dress and matching coat with sable collar, a sable muff and fur-trimmed boots, and a sable pillbox hat. Mrs. Kennedy had recently given birth to a baby boy, John-John, and looked stylish and spectacular. The president's parents and family were there.

Robert Frost read a poem, a first at an inaugural ceremony. Marian Anderson sang the national anthem. And Lyndon Johnson was sworn in as vice president. Eleanor Roosevelt was there, and important members of the arts, including Ernest Hemingway, Carl Sandburg, and John Steinbeck.

It was an unforgettable moment in history. And Kennedy's speech after he was sworn in was deeply moving. The words "Ask not what your country can do for you—ask what you can do for your country," rang in her ears for hours afterward, and felt like a message spoken directly to her. It was the question she had been asking herself all her life. What could she do for her country and her countrymen, the disadvantaged, the unfortunate, the persecuted, those who were discriminated against? They were the people she wanted to serve and find answers for. They were why she was in law school, and had gone to North Carolina to sit at the counter at Woolworth's.

It looked like the happiest day of Jackie Kennedy's life, and it was certainly one of the best days of Meredith's. Her grandfather could have chosen to sit on the platform, but since Merrie couldn't, he sat in front-row seats with her so they could enjoy the events together.

She clung to her grandfather's arm and kept smiling up at him and thanking him for bringing her. There were five inaugural balls that night, and Merrie and her grandfather attended the one at the Mayflower Hotel and stopped briefly at the one at the National Guard Armory on the way home. Meredith wore a new black velvet gown and long white gloves and looked spectacular herself. As always, her grandfather was immensely proud of her. The balls finally ended at three A.M., and Merrie and her grandfather went home, happy and exhausted. He tucked her hand under his arm, and he looked handsome in white tie and tails. Jackie had worn a magnificent white satin evening gown made for her by Bergdorf Goodman. And there was something so dazzlingly handsome and aristocratic about the new president as he appeared at each ball with Mrs. Kennedy in her white gown covered with brilliants, and a matching floor-length cape. Meredith had never seen anything so beautiful. The First Lady looked like a queen.

They got back to her grandfather's house just after three in the morning. He said he'd had a fantastic time and made a date with her for all subsequent inaugurations. They both hoped there would be another Kennedy inauguration in four years.

Meredith drifted up the stairs to the guest bedroom as she delicately peeled off her long white kid gloves, and her grandfather smiled as he caught a last glimpse of her. She was a beautiful young woman, and he'd had such a good time with her. It was an evening that he knew they would never forget, and even more so because they'd been together, and they shared a very special relationship. He was her mentor and her inspiration and role model as well as her grandfather.

She hated to go back to New York the next day and said that she felt like Cinderella after the ball. The coach had turned into a pumpkin and the coachman into white mice. She had to clean the castle again and there was no sign of the handsome prince. But the handsome prince was in the White House now, and would be for the next four years. It was good news for all of them.

Meredith sat dreamily on the train all the way back to New York, and told her family about it that night at dinner. She had called Claudia as soon as she got back. It had really been a magical night.

"That's why people voted for him, because he's good-looking and he has a pretty wife," her father said grumpily at dinner. "Nixon would have been a much better president. He's got more experience."

"And he's a Republican," Meredith teased him.

Everyone watched closely as Kennedy settled into the White House, to see what political steps he'd take and his position about Vietnam.

The Kennedys gave spectacular, elegant state dinners, and heads of state came from all over the world to pay their respects and meet both of them.

In May, Vice President Johnson went to visit South Vietnam, after the political fiasco of the Bay of Pigs invasion of Cuba a month before.

In June, Meredith finished her second year of law school. Classes had ended only a few days before when she got a call from the ACLU. They told her that CORE, the Congress of Racial Equality, had been organizing bus and train rides throughout the South and needed volunteers, to attempt to desegregate all public transportation. They called them Freedom Rides, and wanted to know if she'd sign up. She thought about it for about two minutes and agreed.

She debated telling her parents and decided not to, and told Claudia instead.

"Do you think you should? You got arrested the last time you did something like that. Your father will have a fit if it happens again."

"I'm twenty-five years old. I have a right to make my own decisions. And this sounds pretty tame. It's just a couple of bus and train rides. There's nothing dangerous about it." But they both knew that when integration was involved, anything could happen, and they'd be traveling in the Deep South.

She left on the Fourth of July, the day after her parents and Alex left for Martha's Vineyard. She had said that she was spending the Fourth of July weekend on Long Island. In fact, she was going to be away for two weeks.

She was planning to call her parents at the Vineyard without telling them where she was. But she promised Claudia she'd let her know.

She'd been assigned several bus trips and train rides. It was very well organized, and Martin Luther King Jr. was involved, as usual. The first week of her assigned rides went smoothly and everything happened according to plan. It was a little dicier on the Fourth of July weekend, and several people objected when her integrated group of black and white people got on the train. But eventually they calmed down and the Freedom Riders got off at their destination without incident.

But two days later on a train from Atlanta to Birmingham, the conductor spoke to the men riding the train but they refused to move. State troopers were called, the Freedom Riders were dragged off the train, and Meredith was back in jail again, with no way to pay bail and no one to call but her father. He was outraged when he heard where she was and what she'd been doing, and threatened to leave her in jail this time. For a minute it sounded like he'd do it, but in the end, he rescued her again. She was tempted to stay with the Freedom Riders once she got out, but she'd already been there for a week, and she knew she couldn't defy her father, who had demanded that she come to Martha's Vineyard immediately. She was taking a train to Boston, and from there to Newport, Rhode Island, to get the ferry to the Vineyard. She spent the night on a bench at the dock, and took the first ferry in the morning. Her parents and Alex were having breakfast when she walked in.

"Don't even speak to me," her father said with a look of fury. "You may want to spend your life as a jailbird, but I'm a federal judge now. This is unthinkable. I don't know what you think you're doing, Meredith, but I won't bail you out again. Next time you can rot in jail," he said, slamming a fist down on the table, as Alex looked worried. He had never seen his father so angry, nor had Merrie. And he looked as though he meant it. "I don't know what's driving you to behave this way, but it's sick."

"Someone has to do it," she said in a quiet, respectful voice. She didn't want to argue with him, and it was upsetting for all of them. Alex looked shaken this time too. Bad people went to jail. So what was his sister doing there?

She had called Claudia from the station when she changed trains and she said Meredith's trips for the ACLU made her nervous too. She was afraid Meredith was going to get injured one of these times, or trapped in the midst of a riot and killed.

"Let someone else do it," her father said, still angry at her. "Women from your background don't do things like this." And her mother looked like she'd been crying. She kept wondering how they'd failed, that Meredith was turning out to be such a rebel. "You're going to get yourself killed one of these days," her father went on. "And for what? So a Negro can ride a bus in Montgomery, or a train in Mississippi, or have lunch at Woolworth's in North Carolina? The victories are too small, and the risks too huge. You don't belong down there. This isn't your battle," her father said, looking fierce.

"Yes, it is our battle. And the victories add up. The laws are changing. Look at Little Rock. Black kids can go to high school there now. These aren't small victories."

"Well, let someone else win them," he said again. "And you're not leaving this house all summer. I want you here until you go back to school." She nodded and went to her room. But at least she had made a small contribution, and had done what she could.

Her two-month house arrest on Martha's Vineyard was not unpleasant. She went fishing with her brother, swam in the ocean, and went sailing with friends, and eventually her father stopped being angry at her. On Labor Day they went back to New York, and the next day she started her third year of law school at Columbia.

The Freedom Riders had been in the news all summer. Many of them were arrested, but no one had been killed, which was an even bigger victory than the precedents they were establishing and the freedoms they were winning.

She had lunch with Claudia right after school started and she told Merrie she had finished her book over the summer and was looking for a publisher for it. Thaddeus was going to help her find one, he had the connections she needed to get published. She had just sent the book to two editors he knew, and was excited about it.

A week after she started back to school, Meredith got another announcement from Ted. They'd had another baby boy, ten months after the last one. At twenty-six, he was married and had two kids. She called him and teased him about it, and he said he was happy and the boys were adorable, and Emily was really good with them. But Meredith wondered if she was good with him too. They were just two kids themselves, and now they had two sons.

"And what are you up to? Still going to protests and getting arrested?" He sounded affectionate as he said it, and said he missed her. But they never came into the city anymore. Emily didn't like to leave their babies. It didn't sound like much fun to Merrie.

"I haven't gotten arrested in at least two months. My father locked me up on the Vineyard this summer, after I got arrested on the Freedom Rides in July."

"You're incurable. Just don't get yourself murdered," he said seriously. It was what everyone said to her.

159

They promised to have lunch if he ever came to the city, but it didn't sound like he did. And he didn't invite her to Connecticut. He said Emily would be busy with the new baby, and he was working hard for his dad. It was nice talking to him, but their lives had gone in totally separate directions. She was glad she saw Claudia as much as she did. She would have been lonely without her.

She was busy at school for the next three months, and in December, three days before Christmas, the nation was shocked when the first U.S. combat death occurred in Vietnam. So it was happening now. They weren't just advisors anymore, they were combat troops, and one of them had been killed. Unfortunately, it proved her right, she said to her father when they switched off the TV. American boys were going to die there. It had already started.

"It's just one," her father argued the point with her.

"That's one too many," she insisted, reminding him again that it could be Alex, and he stormed out of the room. He didn't want to hear it. It was too close to the truth.

Chapter Eleven

The second publisher who saw Claudia's book bought it a week after she read it, and seven months later, in April, Claudia had a book signing at a little bookstore in her parents' neighborhood on the Upper West Side, near West End Avenue. It was a respectable publisher, and she had called the book *Point of No Return*. It was nonfiction, her story of the war, and there was a photograph on the cover taken by a soldier of a few emaciated children standing behind the barbed wire at Auschwitz when the camp was liberated. The photograph could have been of Claudia, but it wasn't.

It was a powerful book and she had already gotten two good reviews, but you had to have a strong stomach to read it. She had told the unvarnished truth. Her mother had read it and sobbed all the way through. Claudia had never even told her those stories. She was too traumatized when she arrived, and afterward she didn't want to talk about it, and her mother had discouraged her from clinging to the memories. But it had been healing for Claudia to write the book.

Her whole family came to the book signing, and so did Meredith, Claudia's work friends from the *Herald Tribune,* several of Thaddeus's friends, and the customers of the bookstore.

With the money the publisher had paid her, she had told her parents she was going to rent a small apartment in Greenwich Village. She was very excited about it, and they didn't know it, but Thaddeus was planning to move in with her. They had been together for three years. Her parents had finally stopped pushing her to meet someone else and get married. They had accepted him at last, despite his successful Hollywood father whom Claudia had met and liked. But she and Thaddeus had no plans to marry. The relationship worked well as it was.

Her mother wondered now if the tragic experiences she'd been through in Germany made it harder for her to make a commitment. Maybe she was afraid to lose the people she loved again. But whatever the reason, she seemed to have no interest in marriage or children.

Her mother never knew about him, but it had more to do with Seth Ballard, who had disappointed her so severely. She had never heard from him again. And one of her sisters was getting married that summer, to an investment banker who was the son of friends of her parents. So her mother was busy planning the wedding. Her sister was the same age as Meredith, who had no interest in marriage either. Sometimes her mother thought that the two close friends were too modern in their thinking and a bad influence on each other.

The book had opened Claudia's eyes to new avenues for her writing. She loved her job and also wanted to do some freelance pieces. Thaddeus wanted her to work on a documentary with him, and at twenty-seven, she was already working on a second book, a novel about an independent young woman in New York. Her career as a writer was off and running.

The book signing went well. More people came than expected, and Claudia was beaming as she signed the books. It was an important moment for her, the culmination of a lifetime goal, and she had finally achieved it. And this was only the beginning.

Three weeks later, in May, Claudia and Thaddeus joined the McKenzies at Meredith's Columbia Law School graduation. Her grandfather was there, smiling broadly, and so were her parents. Meredith was worried about her father. He seemed angry and negative and increasingly vocal in favor of the war in Vietnam, which added tension to Merrie's relationship with him. As far as he was concerned, people didn't understand the benefits of the conflict and should support it, instead of criticizing it all the time. There were eleven thousand "military advisors" there now, and they had the right to bear arms and fire them as needed, so American military personnel were slowly slipping from an advisory role to a combat capacity, which terrified Merrie, and she remained convinced that things were going to get worse before they got better.

It upset her too that as a federal judge, her father was in a position to sentence conscientious objectors to prison instead of to alternative service in hospitals and other medical facilities. He hadn't had to make that decision yet, but she knew he might. And if he did so, she knew it would strain their relationship even more than it already was. They seemed to disagree about everything. Her goals and ideals made no sense to him. He wasn't even pleased by her finishing law school. He was afraid that she was going to use her degree to benefit the causes she espoused.

She was going back to work at the ACLU until she took the bar exam in a few months. As a lawyer, they would give her more interesting projects than the ones she'd had before. But it was only a stopgap measure for her until she passed the bar. She was looking for a position in a law firm. She wanted to work for one that handled discrimination cases, which she hadn't told her father yet. He had made her an offer to join the family law firm, and was still angry that she had turned it down. Wall Street didn't interest her. She wanted to do the most good, not make the most money. Money and personal gain had never been the motivator for her. She had far more in common with her eighty-year-old grandfather, who had a younger person's view of the world than her cantankerous father, who was constantly resisting change.

Alex was having trouble relating to Robert too. He worshipped his father but was saddened by his rigid, antiquated ideas. Alex had just turned sixteen and looked like a beanpole. He was a handsome boy, and already thinking about college. He wanted to go to Harvard or Yale, and Harvard Law one day, and Meredith was sure he would since he was bright and had relatively good grades.

Her father had taken over the private room at 21 again, as he had after her graduation from Vassar, and Meredith wanted Adelaide invited this time. She was part of the family, but her father objected and said it would make everyone uncomfortable.

"Why would that make anyone uncomfortable?" Meredith asked, looking startled. She and Addie had long talks every day, and she had been with them for all of Merrie's life. She had a right to share in the celebration, but her father was adamant and her mother agreed, as she always did with everything he said. "That's ridiculous. Besides, I want her there. She practically brought me and Alex up except when we were in Germany." And they still got Christmas cards from Anna, who had four children now and sent them a card every year with their picture.

"Bottom line, Meredith," her father said tersely, "you don't invite the maid to a fancy dinner. It just doesn't make sense. I'm sure she wouldn't want to be there either. She knows it's not her place."

"It's what I ride around on trains and buses for in Alabama and Mississippi, and get arrested for, so Addie can come to dinner wherever she wants, and is wanted."

"Your mother and I don't want her there," he said clearly. "She doesn't belong with our family and friends. Just like you didn't belong at her church. We can't lose our boundaries just because nine kids integrated Central High School in Little Rock. Those are legal technicalities. This is real life."

"No," Meredith said quietly, "they're one and the same. And she's too important to leave out this time. I wanted to ask her last time, but I forgot."

"Well, don't ask her this time. You can have dinner with her in the kitchen sometime, if you want to."

"Dad, that's disgusting," Meredith objected, but he didn't give an inch. And shortly after that, he went upstairs to his room. In his mind, the subject was closed. It shocked and saddened Meredith to realize how prejudiced some people still were, even in big cities in the North, educated people like her own father, a judge. In the end, most of them didn't want to have dinner with Negroes. And Meredith realized she was fighting for the right for something that many people she knew didn't want, and maybe never would. It was horrifying to her. She lived and breathed her ideals.

In the end, she forced it on them, and invited Adelaide herself.

She sat at the end of the table at 21 next to Alex, but at least she was there. She had cried when Meredith asked her, and worn her best dress to dinner. It was a bright red satin dress and she had worn a small red hat with a veil, and shiny black shoes. Meredith thought she looked terrific and was thrilled to have her there. And Addie said she'd never forget it. She knew how her employers felt and was proud of Merrie for being different.

Adelaide thanked her especially for it the next day. She knew it must have taken a lot to get her there. She thought Meredith was wrong for some of the things she did—messing around with buses in Alabama, lunch counters in North Carolina, and getting arrested— and she didn't want her to get hurt. But she really appreciated being invited to dinner, and she wanted to thank Merrie and her parents for taking a big step forward. Meredith gave her a hug and then left the kitchen. She had to get to work. She couldn't wait to start at a law firm, but for now she was pleased to be working for the ACLU. This time they were going to include her in projects and meetings.

She was surprised when the subject of a major protest came up at work that morning. James Meredith was a black student who had applied for admission to the University of Mississippi the previous September and had been denied due to his race, although he was an Air Force veteran. He had just filed suit to support his application. It was likely to evolve into an explosive situation by the fall, and they spent the entire morning trying to anticipate what could happen next if his suit against the university was upheld. It was a potentially serious situation.

"We don't want to be facing Little Rock all over again," one of the members of the advance planning team said.

"It sounds like we're heading there," someone added. The South was a bastion of segregated education. They finally decided that they had time to see where things went and didn't need to panic yet, but this was definitely liable to be their next hot spot and proving ground in the next four months. Merrie listened to the discussions with interest and agreed that the situation could rapidly get out of hand.

She had interviews that week with two law firms that she was interested in. Both specialized in discrimination suits, and she would have been happy with a job from either one.

She told her father about it that night, and he looked unhappy. After dinner he came to her room. She was studying for the bar exam, and thought longingly of Claudia's new apartment. She would have loved to have her own place, where she could have peace and the freedom to do whatever she wanted. But she knew her parents would never agree to her moving to her own apartment. They still believed that only bad girls had their own apartments, and she couldn't afford it without their help. She had to live at home.

When he walked into her room, she invited her father to sit down. He had come to improve his offer to join the family firm. He said he didn't want her joining one of the "troublemaking" firms she was interviewing with, but they were exactly what she wanted. She wasn't interested in tax law and she thought that their family firm's ideas were too antiquated.

"I hate to think of you going to work for one of those fly-by-night firms that handle discrimination suits. They're all disreputable. I'd rather you work with us." She was touched by his insistence but couldn't do it, no matter what they'd pay her. She hadn't gone to law school for that, and his frequent accusations that she was a crusader weren't wrong.

"It really means a lot to me, Dad, that you want me," she said gently, "but I can't. I need to do what I've been trying to do since college. I want to help make it a better world."

"It was a better world before things started to change ever since the war," he said sadly. She wondered at what point he'd given up and become so rigid and hostile to any kind of change. This wasn't the father she'd grown up with who'd gone to Nuremberg for the war crime trials, and it made her sad for him. He seemed like an old man now, even older than his father. Robert couldn't stem the tides or stop progress, no matter how tightly he closed his eyes. The world would pry them open to the realities of all that needed to change now. His own father and daughter were the torchbearers of the future, trying to shine light into the darkness, while he was choosing to be left behind. They stood looking at each other for a long moment, across the distance that separated them, and he nodded and left her room without another word. In his own mind, he had lost her, and they both knew they would never be on the same side again. Everything he represented and believed in was what Merrie was dedicating her life to alter, and he was fighting just as hard to stop it from happening. The pull of the future was too strong for him. And she could almost see him weakening physically as the walls of his world were crumbling around him.

She called Claudia afterward to talk to her about it, and she agreed with Meredith about not joining the family law firm. It wasn't even a remote possibility for her.

For the rest of the week, the ACLU was trying to figure out how to stave off the dangers and limit the damage in Mississippi if James Meredith enrolled at Ole Miss in September. It was going to be a long summer worrying about it.

She took the bar exam in July and waited anxiously for the results while working at her job at the ACLU, and continued to send her résumé to various law firms, looking for a job in the fall.

It was a quiet summer. Claudia moved into her new apartment, with a locked closet for Thaddeus's things that her mother didn't comment on when she visited the apartment. Claudia was trying to furnish it from secondhand stores because she wanted to pay for it herself. And unbeknownst to her mother, Thaddeus helped. He went back and forth to Los Angeles a lot that summer, working on a new documentary about discrimination and using his father's editing facilities. His frequent trips gave the two girls time to spend together, and when they could, they went to Jones Beach for the day on the weekends, and Meredith spent the Fourth of July weekend with the Steinbergs on Long Island. Claudia's mother was frantic getting ready for the wedding in August. They had replanted the gardens, and everything was going to happen in a series of enormous tents on the grounds. They were expecting three hundred guests, and their plans sounded lavish for their first daughter to be married.

By August, the ACLU office in New York was getting daily bulletins about James Meredith's situation in Mississippi. Meredith listened to them intently and offered suggestions whenever she could. He was determined to be the first black student to attend Ole Miss. Governor Ross Barnett of Mississippi had flatly refused to obey the integration laws that applied, and said that as long as he was governor, there would be no Negroes at the university or any other university in the state. James Meredith, although qualified, had already been denied admission twice and had been applying for a year when he filed his suit in May.

The situation got heated in September when the court of appeals found the governor in civil contempt, and ordered him to be arrested and pay a $10,000 per day fine for each day he refused James Meredith's admission to the university. The lieutenant governor was also arrested, and fined $5,000 per day under the same condition.

The president made a speech urging all educational institutions and citizens to follow the laws of integration. And his brother, Attorney General Robert Kennedy, intervened and convinced Governor Barnett to allow James Meredith to enroll. Everyone who worked for the ACLU was on the edge of their seats by then, and Merrie among them. The attorney general ordered five hundred federal marshals to accompany James Meredith when he arrived at the university to enroll. They had long discussions at the ACLU office late into the night about whether or not to be on site when James Meredith entered the university, and on September 25, they asked Merrie her position on it. She only gave it a moment's thought and then nodded.

"I'm in," she said, knowing full well how her father would react if he knew about it. But these were life choices she was making for herself, whether he understood that or not. She left for Mississippi the next day and checked into a motel with several other members of the ACLU who had come from other cities to lend their support. She didn't tell her parents where she was going, and said she was going to Chicago for an interview. Her father was in court the morning she left, and she was vague with her mother, who never questioned her as closely, and said she'd be back in a few days and would call then, since she didn't know where she was staying. Chicago seemed like a benign destination to use as a cover. She didn't even tell Claudia this time, who was working on her novel, and an article for the *Herald Tribune* Sunday magazine. She knew Claudia would say that she was crazy to go. But just as Claudia needed to carry the banners of the past that were meaningful to her, Meredith had to carry the flag of the future with just as much determination. She had taken very seriously the president's message from his inaugural speech a year and a half before. This was what she could do for her country.

On the night of September 29, state senator George Yarbrough called off the state highway police, who were working to contain crowds of protestors, and riots broke out. The National Guard was called in swiftly to bring things back into control. Two men were killed, many injured, university property was damaged, and rocks were thrown at the riot police. Merrie was on the campus that night, along with a dozen other ACLU workers, two from the New York office. She got hit on her temple with a rock thrown by a student, and subsequently clubbed by a member of the National Guard in the melee. She was removed from the campus while still unconscious and woke up in jail, with the side of her head caked with blood and a blinding headache. She struggled to her feet and asked what had happened, and was told by others in the holding pen that two men had died.

She remained in jail and didn't call her father this time. She had brought the little money she had saved so she could pay her own bail if something went awry. And to resounding cheers as they watched it on TV in jail, on October 1, troops took control and James Meredith enrolled in the University of Mississippi and became its first black student, after battling his way through the legal system for a year and a half to achieve it. Merrie had tears running down her cheeks as she watched it on TV. The legal system of the United

States had functioned, and the University of Mississippi had been integrated. Not easily and not without bloodshed, and the victory had been hard won, but she had no doubt whatsoever that it was worth it.

She paid her bail the next day after she was charged with disorderly conduct and resisting arrest, neither of which she had committed, but she didn't oppose it. And she headed back to New York, after seeing a doctor at a local hospital emergency room. No one asked her how the bruises on her face had happened, and she assumed they knew. They refrained from comment, and told her she had a mild concussion and to take it easy for a week. They put a gauze bandage on the superficial wound. She had a black eye, but the headache was better. As she left the emergency room, a nurse said under her breath, just loud enough for Merrie to hear her, "Nigger lover." Meredith didn't react, and left. She knew better than to argue with her. She had been trained not to respond or react during sit-ins and protests, and she was used to the insults of those wanting to uphold segregation. None of it mattered to her. They had won an important battle in the war. James Meredith was officially enrolled as a student at Ole Miss.

She took the train back to New York with four of her colleagues. Members of the ACLU had come from cities throughout the East. One of the others had a broken arm, and another had stitches on his head. But they were alive, they had survived it, and despite considerable damage to property, two deaths, and many minor injuries, they all knew it could have been a lot worse. Martin Luther King Jr. had made an impassioned speech about the rightness of what they'd done, and the bravery of all those who had supported James Meredith, including the attorney general and the president of the United States. He compared JFK to Abraham Lincoln.

The five ACLU workers who took the train back to New York slept most of the way. They were exhausted after what they'd seen and been through, the tension of many days, and the chaos in jail. A lot of others hadn't been released yet. Merrie was exhausted when she caught a cab outside Penn Station and headed home to their Park Avenue apartment. She was grateful that only Adelaide was home when she got there. She had carefully removed the bandage, and let her hair fall over the wound on her face, and tried to cover her black eye with some powder she had in her purse. She looked ragtag and disheveled when she walked into the apartment, and wanted to take a bath before she saw her parents.

"My God, child, what happened to you? You look like you got hit by a train," Addie said, and then she fell silent and stared at Merrie in anger and fear. "You were there, weren't you? I've been watching on TV." There was no point denying it. Adelaide knew her well enough to guess instantly, and she looked deeply upset as she pulled Merrie's hair back and scrutinized the wound on her temple. It was sensitive when she touched it and a nasty scrape and bruise. "You're crazy. You're gonna get yourself killed. This isn't your fight, you know. Let Reverend King and his friends fight those battles. You're from up here, you're not southern, you're not black, you don't belong there."

"Yes, I do," Meredith said quietly and sat down at the kitchen table. She still had a headache, and now that she was home, she realized how exhausted she was, and Addie could see it.

"I thought you were in Chicago," she said, dismayed, and sat down across from her. "If they don't want to ride on the back of the bus, let them come up north. They don't have to burn down the world and kill people to get a seat on the bus. They just troublemakers," she said in stern disapproval. Meredith already knew that a lot of older Negroes didn't believe in the disruption the new generation was creating for change. They thought it was just going to get everyone mad at them, which was a situation they didn't want or need, or even approve of.

"Everyone has a right to an education, Addie," Merrie said gently. "If your kids want to go to Ole Miss or any other school, they have to be allowed to. Don't you want that for them?"

"They can get a good education at a black school. They don't have to fight their way into a school where they're not wanted and get people killed to do it. They don't need to be uppity. All they need is a good education."

"Wherever they want," Meredith emphasized, and Adelaide looked chagrined.

"I can tell you one thing. It's not worth you getting killed for. That boy would get his sorry ass into Ole Miss, if that's what he wants to do, without you getting a black eye for him, or shot, or clubbed to death. He don't need your help, and you're gonna break your parents' heart, and your brother's, if you die for him. Did you go to jail?" she asked, and Merrie nodded. "I didn't bring you up to be no jailbird, Meredith McKenzie," she said sternly, which was her parents' position too. "Are you going to tell them?" She looked worried.

"I haven't decided," but Meredith hadn't called her father for bail money this time. She had taken care of it herself.

"Your daddy is going to be *maaaddddd*," she said, and Meredith smiled. There was no question about that. She went to clean up then, thinking about Adelaide's position. Meredith knew that elder members of the black community, particularly in the North where they didn't have the same constraints, didn't want the boat rocked, or to suffer retaliation for it, which they were afraid of. Adelaide didn't see the value of what Meredith and the others were doing, fighting for the rights of blacks throughout the country. She just saw it as foolhardy and reckless and troublemaking. It wasn't the first time Meredith had heard it. There were blacks in the South who felt that way too. They didn't want to live with the fallout of riots and sit-ins, and the Ku Klux Klan seeking revenge and killing their children. There was a lot at stake here, on all sides.

Meredith managed to cover her injuries artfully before she saw her parents that evening at dinner. She used makeup to conceal them, and her hair was hanging down to cover her temple. Addie frowned severely as she served dinner. Meredith's mother asked her how Chicago was, and Meredith dodged her with a bland answer. Her father was unusually silent but as they left the dining room he took her aside.

"I don't know where you've been, Meredith, but I can guess, and it wasn't Chicago. And I don't want to know where you were or what you did there. You've embarked on a path that I don't understand. And you have no reason to. It's not your world or your problem, although you don't see it that way. I can't stop you. I see that now."

He looked defeated as he said it, and she felt sorry for him. She knew that she would have been unhappy in his shoes too, with a daughter he didn't understand, whom he could no longer control or subdue, who put herself in harm's way for a cause she believed in.

"Just be careful. That's all I ask. Your mother and I will be devastated if anything happens to you."

She nodded, kissed him on the cheek, and went back to her room then. It marked a turning point in their relationship, and a hard one for him. But he had finally understood that he couldn't stop her or change her, and she would never be the kind of woman he wanted her to be. She was a very different one. And no matter how much they loved her, she would never be her mother. She had to be who she was, whatever it cost her, and whatever it took. Robert McKenzie had finally understood it. She had come back alive from Mississippi. He had been praying for her safe return as he watched the riots on the news, and had sensed instantly that she was there. And even though she had come home in one piece, he understood fully now that he had lost her and they could no longer protect her. She had no idea what it had cost him to accept that. And as he went to his own room, there were tears rolling down his cheeks.

Chapter Twelve

After the riots at the University of Mississippi, Meredith learned that she had passed the bar exam. She was free to practice law in the state of New York, and in November, she accepted one of the jobs she'd been offered, in the most radical of the various firms she had applied to. They had other clients, though not many, but their specialty was discrimination suits of all kinds: race, color, gender, religion. They did a lot of pro bono work, and the salary they offered her was lower than some of the other firms, but it was exactly the kind of law she wanted to practice and it fit in with her ideals.

She had already given notice at the ACLU when her father called her early one morning. She could tell instantly from his voice that something grave had happened. Her grandmother had been failing from a serious heart condition, and she had died in her sleep during the night. She had gone peacefully and it wasn't entirely unexpected, but it was a loss anyway. She had been a quiet, mild, unobtrusive woman, without strong opinions or beliefs, but she had been the perfect mate for her powerful, determined husband and an important support system for him, and a loving mother and grandmother. Her grandchildren Meredith and Alex were going to miss her, and Robert sounded stricken on the phone. It was a week before Thanksgiving and they were going to make the arrangements for the funeral in the next few days.

Merrie called her grandfather as soon as she hung up, he was crying when he answered the phone. The funeral home had just taken her away. They were sending her body to New York for burial there, and he sounded distraught.

"I don't know what I'm going to do without her, Merrie." They had been married for sixty years. He couldn't imagine his life without her, and for the first time, he suddenly sounded old. He was flying to New York that night, and Merrie was worried about him when she hung up.

Merrie took three days off from work to be with her family and do whatever she could to help. She stayed close to her grandfather. The funeral was dignified and well attended by their many friends and supporters from the various phases of Bill's career, as attorney, judge, and now justice of the Supreme Court. They came to show their sympathy and respect for him and his loss of the woman that most of them barely knew. She had always been a behind-the-scenes person while he was the star of the show. It occurred to Meredith after the funeral that her father had married a woman very much like his mother and had expected the same quietly supportive, discreet presence from her, and her mother had filled that role for him. It was why Meredith was such a shock for him. She was the first woman in their family who had strong opinions and her own voice. Her grandfather had encouraged her to be that way.

She went back to work the day after the funeral, but only for a few days to wrap up.

She left the ACLU after Thanksgiving and planned to start at the firm on the first of the year. Her father knew that even when she left the ACLU, she was liable to volunteer for something anytime they asked her to, if she thought it was important and they needed her. She was on the list of volunteers they could count on, and frequently did.

The senior partner of the firm that hired her was a Harvard graduate and a revolutionary in his own way. Jock Hayden was from a wealthy family in Boston, and had grown up with the Kennedys. His political positions were more extreme than theirs, but he was an ardent supporter, and he liked Meredith's CV as soon as he saw it. She was right up his alley and fit in perfectly, and she'd been part of some very important demonstrations: Greensboro, the Freedom Riders, and Mississippi, and a number of smaller ones in border states. Her arrest record didn't bother him, it was a badge of honor, and he was impressed that her father was a federal judge and her grandfather a justice of the Supreme Court.

The week after Thanksgiving, she went to Washington to check on her grandfather since he had gone back to work. She told him about the new job, and he approved, but she was distressed to find him seeming frail and looking tired since her grandmother's death. It was still recent, but he seemed to be floundering without her. Although he had always been the stronger of the two, he had counted on her to keep him organized and on track. She had been his silent cheering team for the sixty years that they were married. He knew he always had her approval and support, whatever he did.

Meredith was upset to see him looking disheveled. His tie was slightly askew, and his collar was sticking up, his hair not as neatly brushed as usual. He had talked about retiring once in a while in the past two years, but was still brilliant and sharp. But understandably, he seemed sad now, and the fire had dimmed in his eyes. He was turning eighty-one on his next birthday, and was the second oldest justice on the Supreme Court. Although justices were appointed for life, the oldest was planning to retire in June and had just announced it.

But he perked up when talking to Merrie about her new job. He liked the sound of the law firm she had signed on with, although he didn't know them.

"I'm glad you didn't let your father talk you into joining the firm." It had been her grandfather's firm once too, but not since his first judicial appointment, and he felt no bond with it anymore. He considered it Robert's firm now, although he had started it himself. And they had a competent managing partner. "You would have been wasted there," he said of the family firm. "I can't see you ever doing tax law and estate planning." He smiled at her, and she admitted that neither could she. They both laughed at the thought.

"I think Dad's feelings were hurt, but I would have hated it, and they would have hated me. I'm glad I held out for the offer I got."

"You would have been a huge pain in their ass." Her grandfather guffawed and looked more like himself, and she laughed. "Although it might have done them some good. Your father gets more conservative every year," he said, looking puzzled. "You'd think he'd mellow with age, but it's just the opposite." Her grandfather got more liberal and modern in his thinking year by year. He was innovative and creative, always wanting to stretch the envelope further and move forward with the times. It was a particular talent to remain that open-minded, and she hoped that she would be that way too at his age. He was her hero, and always had been, and a remarkable man. A true legend.

"I can't talk to him about Vietnam anymore," she admitted. "He's such a rabid hawk, we just get into arguments. He can't see any other point of view, or where they're headed. They keep sending more troops there, and I don't care what they call them, we're in for a real war," she said seriously, and Bill nodded.

"I completely agree with you. I said the same thing about World War II, while Roosevelt was promising everyone we'd never get into it, and Hitler was running amok all over Europe. Sooner or later, you have to fight back whether you want to or not. People say Vietnam is not our fight, which is true in theory, but if they're sending our boys there, we'll have to support them, or they'll be slaughtered." She nodded agreement, and after lunch, she walked him back to his chambers. He seemed more cheerful after her visit, and she was glad she'd come. He was going to spend Christmas with them, and it would do him good to be with the family after his wife's recent death.

When her grandfather got to New York for the holidays, Meredith spent a lot of time with him, and Alex talked to him about college. He was going to apply to Harvard in the fall as his first choice, and his grandfather told him he better keep his grades up. He was applying to Princeton and Yale too, and some backup schools. But he had a good shot at Harvard, although his school performance had sometimes been erratic, with occasional dips when he got distracted by other things, usually sports or girls, and lately more the latter. He was a good-looking boy, and girls were crazy about him.

After the holidays, Claudia startled Meredith by telling her that she and Thaddeus were going to get married. After four years to-gether, they had decided that they wanted to have children. Her youngest sister had just gotten married in December, to a Reform rabbi, in a small ceremony. She didn't want a big wedding, after her other sister's major event. And after the second wedding, she and Thaddeus had talked about it and made the decision. She hadn't told her parents yet, but was going to soon. They weren't in a hurry and were talking about getting married in May or June. She was twenty-eight years old, and it felt like the right time. Meredith was happy for her, but was afraid it might change things between them, especially if she and Thaddeus had children, but Claudia promised that her being married or having babies wouldn't change anything. They were best friends forever.

Once she got pregnant, they were going to look for a house in the country. She was planning to quit her job when they had kids, write freelance articles from home, and work on her books. Thaddeus worked from home too, on his documentaries. She didn't intend to stop writing, she saw it as her lifetime career. Quitting her job to write and have children felt like a major life decision to Meredith, even before they'd done it. Change was in the air. It was hard to imagine Claudia living in the country, married, and having babies. They both loved their jobs and living in the city.

And as though to underline it further, she got an announcement from Ted that they had just had twin boys. So now he had four chil-dren, and he and Claudia were the same age. He had sent a moving notice too, with a note on it, that with the arrival of the twins, they had to move to a bigger house, still in Greenwich, and he was still working for his father. "Trying to create my own baseball team while working at the bank. If all else fails, we can become a circus act. Greetings from your most conservative friend, father of four, living in the 'burbs. Love you, Ted."

He didn't say if he was happy or not, but that was beside the point. He had gone the most traditional possible route, and with a wife and four children, he couldn't afford to stray off that path. She hoped his income was growing as fast as his family. It was a responsibility she couldn't imagine taking on, with four kids to feed and house, and educate one day. But his family could afford it, luckily for him, as long as he continued working for them. There was no deviation possible there. She hadn't talked to him in a year and never saw him, but their baby announcements kept them in touch. She wondered if he'd have more or if this was it.

She wondered how many children Claudia would have too. When they'd met she'd always said she didn't want to have children, in case the world went crazy again one day and the same thing happened. She didn't want to risk exposing a child to a holocaust like the one she'd lived through, but in her years with Thaddeus, her faith in the future seemed to have been restored, and he was wonderful to her.

And Meredith was loving her new job. It kept her busy, and they had given her a number of small cases right from the beginning, mostly women who'd been passed over for promotions or were being paid less than their male counterparts. A man who had been persecuted because he was Jewish, and a very bright college-educated black man who was discriminated against. Meredith felt respected and supported by her boss. The firm was small but busy, and she won her first case in court in May, for a Hispanic woman who was fired as a maid at a hotel. Her clients were mostly women, but some were men.

She was the maid of honor at Claudia's wedding in May, at their

Long Island home. It was beautiful and discreet, just the way the couple wanted. His parents had hoped they'd get married in L.A., but there was no question of it. Claudia had reported that the meeting between the parents had gone surprisingly well. His father was undeniably in show business, but they were loving parents and respectable people, and the two mothers got along. The Steinbergs had come to respect Thaddeus's talent and work and loved how good he was to Claudia. At the wedding the couple was married by Claudia's brother-in-law under a canopy of flowers. Both the bride and groom cried when they exchanged their vows, and cheers went up when the groom broke the glass and they were man and wife.

The ceremony was very traditional, and everyone was happy for them. It was the culmination of eighteen years of the Steinbergs' love for Claudia, after they rescued her from the horrors of what she'd suffered in the war. They were wonderful parents and were happy to see her settle down with a good man, even if he was slightly different from what they'd hoped for her. But Thaddeus's deep love for her was obvious, and she was marrying into a family that loved her too. One could only be happy for her, and Meredith was certain that she was going to be much happier and better cared for than she would ever have been with Seth, although she didn't say it to Claudia, not wanting to raise old ghosts. He had totally faded from her life, and was a dim memory now, five years, almost to the day, from when he had broken her heart. She was ready for a good life now with the man she loved. The wedding had a joyous, ebullient feeling that touched them all. And Thaddeus's father's speech was so eloquent and moving, welcoming her into their family and honoring her, that it made everyone cry.

Thaddeus had wanted to take her to Paris for the honeymoon, but Claudia didn't want to go to Europe, and they were going to Mexico instead. The assembled company waved them off in a shower of rose petals, as Meredith wiped the tears from her eyes. It had been everything a wedding should be, and everyone was happy for them and wished them well. Claudia had been a radiant bride, and Meredith knew she deserved it all. She was sure they would have an interesting and happy life.

They were still on their honeymoon when Meredith watched President Kennedy's speech proposing the Civil Rights Act on the night of June 11. She got a call from one of her old ACLU coworkers early the next morning to tell her that civil rights activist Medgar Evers had been shot in the back and killed in Mississippi hours after the speech. The violence and tragedies were continuing. Meredith was deeply saddened by it when she went to work the next morning. They still had so far to go.

But Claudia's good news raised her spirits. They were trying to get pregnant and started looking at houses after they got back from Mexico. They bought an old farm in Sharon, Connecticut, not too far from the city. And in July, Claudia told Merrie she was pregnant. She was ecstatic, and so was Meredith for her.

Meredith helped them move on Labor Day, and Claudia had already designated a guest room for her. She wanted Meredith to spend weekends with them, she said she had told Thaddeus that Meredith was part of the deal when they got married, and he'd laughed and said he had no objection to it, and considered her an additional sister-in-law.

After that, Meredith spent several weeks helping Alex with his college applications at night. He was growing into manhood, and was a truly great kid, with good values and a kind heart. He wasn't quite as liberal as his sister, but he was light-years removed from his parents' ultraconservative Republican politics. More than anything, he was worried about Vietnam.

"I don't want to end up there, Merrie," he told her with a terrified look.

"I don't want you there either. Just make sure you keep your grades up." They were not drafting men into the army for Vietnam, but it had been the subject of political discussion, and if they started to, young men Alex's age, once he turned eighteen in a few months, were likely to be among the first to go. Meredith remained convinced that the war in Vietnam, whatever they called it, was a disaster waiting to happen, and she didn't want her brother to become a victim of it.

They had already finished two of his applications before Thanksgiving, still had four to do before Christmas vacation, and Alex was grateful for her help. In one of his applications he had written an essay about his grandfather, which Meredith thought was a knockout and told him so. He was very proud of it, and wanted to use it as a school paper too.

He had left with it that morning, while Adelaide talked at breakfast about what she was making for Thanksgiving dinner. Meredith was meeting with a new client that day, a woman who had been fired from her job for being pregnant. She was in her office listening to what the woman had to say when the senior partner, Jock Hayden, came running into her office and shouted at her and her client. "You've got to come in my office. . . . Kennedy has just been shot in Dallas!" He was scheduled to speak at a luncheon that day with the First Lady, and at first Meredith didn't understand.

"What do you mean 'shot'?" It made no sense as she and her client ran down the hall and pressed into the crowd watching the scene on Jock's TV. They showed a photo of the president waving in the motorcade, with the First Lady next to him, another of the president hit by the shots seconds later and slumping over as Secret Service men ran toward them, leapt into the car, and all hell broke loose. The anchorman reporting it said the president's condition was grave and they were waiting for news from spokesmen at Parkland Hospital in Dallas. Everyone in the room stared at each other, and many were crying. From the photos and the reports, the president had appeared so severely injured that there seemed to be no way he could have survived it. The entire world was watching their television sets by then. Business had come to a halt, classrooms had emptied, people were standing in the street watching televisions in stores. People around the world were crying and didn't stop for many days.

The announcement of John Fitzgerald Kennedy's death was made by Walter Cronkite on TV at 2:38 P.M. eastern time as the nation mourned him, joined by the entire world. Within hours, images of Mrs. Kennedy, now the president's widow, in her blood-stained pink suit, accompanying the casket, were splashed all over the TV. Young people were crying, old people, foreigners, Americans. He had been the most beloved president America had ever known or shared with the world. He was the youngest president to hold the office, and he had a beautiful young wife and two small children. In three short years, he had barely had time to accomplish what he wanted to, but he had left his mark indelibly on important issues.

Meredith's client grabbed her coat and bag and left crying. Her father adjourned his courtroom at the federal courthouse after making an announcement as soon as the bailiff told him what had happened. Adelaide sat in their living room watching TV and sobbing.

Her mother huddled with her bridge partners as they cried, watching Mrs. Kennedy. The entire city and country had come to a standstill.

Not since the assassination of Abraham Lincoln had the nation been so shocked and devastated over a president. Everything about John Kennedy had been the stuff that won the hearts of all those who saw him, as husband, president, father, brother, son.

Meredith went home to her parents' apartment after it was clear that the president had died, and she sat next to Addie, both of them crying, until Alex and her parents came home. And at 3:38 P.M. eastern time, they saw photos and heard Vice President Lyndon Johnson sworn in on Air Force One with his wife and Mrs. Kennedy, still in the same blood-stained suit, beside him. It was the first time a female judge had sworn in a president. The only activity anyone engaged in for the next five days was to watch their television sets, to see the president lying in state in the Capitol rotunda, Mrs. Kennedy beneath a heavy black veil visiting her husband's casket with her children beside her, images of mourners everywhere, the funeral, his three-year-old son saluting him, the riderless horse tethered behind as his casket was taken to Arlington Cemetery. Each image was more heart-wrenching than the last, and then the additional shock of a lone gunman, Jack Ruby, breaking from a crowd in a basement garage to kill the killer who had gunned down the president, with no reason or explanation known yet, but countless theories being explored. It was one more blow to a national psyche that had been stretched to its emotional limits for days.

Everyone was in deep mourning. The dream had ended all too quickly. For many, it was the death of hope, as President Johnson attempted to rally the nation's spirits. It was a shocking experience for all, the world over. A week later, Americans were still subdued and struggling to understand what had happened, as citizens of other countries around the world sent messages of sympathy to the American people and the late president's family. It was a moment in time and an event Meredith knew she would never forget and would be etched in her mind in its most minute detail forever, when Jock had run into her office to tell her the president had been shot, and the days that had come after. It was beyond unforgettable. Everything else, even in one's own life, paled in comparison and seemed insignificant.

Thanksgiving was a mournful event after that, and even Christmas. Meredith's grandfather was deeply shaken by the assassination of the president. He couldn't imagine it happening in this country. The combination of losing his wife and the president's murder had left him quieter than Meredith had ever seen him. He seemed suddenly smaller, and subdued.

The only cheering note in Meredith's own life was Claudia's pregnancy, which was going well. The baby was due in February. She and Thaddeus were beside themselves with excitement, and had painted the nursery yellow, which she showed Merrie proudly when she came to visit. And she had put decals on the walls, of storybook characters, that would be suitable for either sex.

But at the end of January, Meredith lost another hero. Her grandfather caught a bad flu in Washington, which rapidly turned to pneumonia. He insisted it was nothing, just a cold, but Robert went to Washington to see him and admitted him to the hospital. He told Meredith that the doctors were confident he would recover, but just to be conservative they had preferred to admit him. His condition continued to worsen for the next three days, and early one morning she heard the phone ring, and her mother answered it in her bedroom. Meredith appeared in the doorway a few minutes later and saw the look on her mother's face.

"Grampa?" But she knew before her mother told her. Janet nodded and got out of bed to put her arms around her daughter. He was just weeks shy of his eighty-second birthday, and had served the nation well for many years in the Supreme Court and the landmark decisions he made and upheld with his peers. A bright light had been extinguished. The loss of his wife had dimmed him, and the recent shock of the Kennedy assassination had discouraged him as nothing else ever had. Meredith was glad that he hadn't been sick for a long time or physically diminished, or lost the acute sharpness of his mind. But time had finally caught up with him, and Meredith knew that the world would never be the same for her without him. He had been her role model and inspiration ever since she was a little girl.

Her father stayed in Washington to arrange the funeral, and Meredith and Alex and their mother flew down that night. The naval band played at his funeral, and President Johnson attended it, with all the other justices of the Supreme Court. As she stood there, missing him unbearably, she thought of going to John Kennedy's inauguration with him, and the balls, and both men were gone now. One so much too early, and her beloved grandfather at a more fitting time, but to be mourned forever. He had made history on more than one occasion, and helped her be all that she was. It was the saddest day of her life.

They returned to New York the day after the funeral, and a few days later, her father asked her to come to his study, with a serious expression. He handed her a copy of a document and told her it was her grandfather's will. He had only one son, and two grandchildren. He wasn't a rich man, but he had made many wise investments over the years and lived carefully and very comfortably. And he had been a generous man in life. Despite her modesty, his wife had inherited a considerable fortune, which she left him when she died, to be distributed at his death. Robert explained to Meredith that William had left him, Alex, and Meredith each a third of his fortune, to be divided equally, and the house in Washington, which they would be selling. Her father estimated the global amount he'd left her, and she was stunned. She had never thought about what he and Grandma had or what he would leave her, and didn't care. She loved him. It was enough for her to buy a home one day, if she wished to, and start her own law practice, and live well forever if she was cautious with it. But above all, she could have the kind of legal practice she wanted, without working for someone else, and she could support the causes that were important to her. Her father reminded her to guard it judiciously and make sensible, conservative investments. But he was not surprised to hear her say that she wanted to start a legal practice of her own. He had suspected she would.

He gave her a copy of the will to study carefully, and she thanked him and went back to her room to think about it. Once again, with this final gift, and all his encouragement, her grandfather had given her freedom and the wings she needed to fly. Her life had suddenly taken a huge leap ahead. She really was a free woman, thanks to her grandfather. She could hear him in her head telling her to fight the good fight. And with his blessings, it was full steam ahead. Nothing could stop her now.

Chapter Thirteen

As soon as Meredith had absorbed the change in her situation, she advised Jock Hayden that she'd be leaving the firm to open her own office. She was prepared to give them decent notice, but she had wanted to warn him early. He said he was deeply sorry to lose her.

"You're a damn fine attorney, Meredith," he said to her sincerely. "I wish we could have kept you," but he knew he couldn't stand in her way, and he didn't try to.

She said she would start to get organized in the next few weeks, and was giving him a month's notice. By early March she wanted to open the doors of her own practice. She got busy immediately, looking at office space, and she needed to hire a paralegal to assist her since she would be a sole practitioner and the only attorney in the office, and would need administrative help. She was going to put the word out with other attorneys she knew, so they would recommend her for small discrimination cases, and one day, once she'd proven herself, hopefully big ones.

She had just found an office space she liked downtown, and was thinking about renting an apartment near it, in Gramercy Park, when Claudia called and invited her to come out for the weekend. She was in the final days of her pregnancy and said she felt like an elephant and could hardly move. She was bored and wanted to see Merrie. Everything was done and ready, and she had nothing to do. She had finished her last article assignment and had completed her novel.

Meredith promised to come out that weekend. She brought Claudia some books and magazines to distract her, and she laughed when she saw her. She looked like a little round ball. She had gotten much bigger since Meredith had last seen her a few weeks before, and said she felt huge.

They went for a long walk together on the first day when Meredith got there, but it snowed that night and they were stuck indoors after that. They sat by the fire and talked, while Thaddeus kept busy with his writing for his latest documentary and came in to check on Claudia every half hour to ask if she needed anything. She was two days overdue by then, but there was no sign of anything happening. Her mother and sisters had come out to see her that week, and the oldest of her sisters was pregnant too, but the baby wasn't due for several months.

Meredith told her all about the office she was opening and the location she'd found. And now she wanted to find an apartment. Her grandfather had given her great freedom with what he'd left her. And she was anxious to get started with her practice. Claudia was delighted for her.

The three of them cooked dinner together that night, but Claudia said she wasn't hungry. She had no room with the baby pressing on everything, and she lay on the couch afterward, looking peaceful while Thaddeus glanced at her adoringly. She had shown Meredith the nursery, and all the little clothes folded and put away. Everything was ready.

"I never thought anything like this would happen to me," she admitted to Meredith.

"Having a baby?" She was surprised. It didn't seem so unimaginable to her for Claudia, especially now that she was married.

"No, all of it," Claudia said seriously. "When I look back at my life . . . and the time in the camp . . . I stopped believing that good things could ever happen to me. And now I'm so happy and Thad is so wonderful to me." They were loving to each other, which Meredith liked to see. And a baby would be a happy addition to their lives. They both seemed ready, and were genuinely excited.

They made an early night of it, because Claudia was tired, and the next day she said her back hurt and she could hardly get out of bed. She joined them for breakfast and lunch, and then said she was going back to bed. Meredith left them and went back to New York, and Claudia called her at midnight that night, sounding exhausted but ecstatic. They had gone to the hospital when her water broke two hours after Meredith left, and the baby came at ten o'clock. It was a girl. She said it had been hard at the end but was worth every bit of it, and they'd both cried when she was born.

"She looks so much like my mother," Claudia said, sounding deeply moved. She had expected her to look like Thaddeus or herself, and it touched her that the baby was so similar to the mother she had lost.

"What are you calling her?" Meredith asked with tears in her eyes, happy for her friend.

"We're naming her after my mother and sisters," she said softly, and Meredith knew she meant her German family, and in Jewish tradition they named children after relatives who had died. "Sarah Rachel Rose."

"That's beautiful," Meredith said and promised to come to see her in a few days. They were planning to stay in the hospital for four or five days, and her mother had hired a baby nurse to help her for a few weeks. And Thaddeus's mother was coming to visit. She was the first grandchild on their side too. Claudia would have a houseful for a while, but Meredith wanted to see her in her new role of motherhood. She sounded peaceful and calm and happy.

For the next several days, Meredith raced everywhere. She signed the lease for her office space in a small commercial building that already had several lawyers in it, in Murray Hill. And she found an apartment she liked in Gramercy Park. She could walk to work in decent weather. She bought the office furniture she needed. And she interviewed three possible paralegals, one of them male, and two female. One of the women was in her late fifties, and said she wanted to retire in five years. The other had too little experience. The man was businesslike and efficient, seemed organized at the interview, and had excellent references. Charlie was thirty-two years old, and Meredith liked him and hired him. He was free and able to start the following week.

By the time she went to see Claudia and meet little Sarah, she had everything in order for her new office and was planning to open her doors in two weeks.

Thaddeus was holding the baby when she got there, and Claudia was her old bouncy, lively self, beaming at the baby and looking at Thaddeus as though they had found the Holy Grail. And it struck Meredith that they were no longer just two people who loved each other. They were a family now. The baby was exquisite and perfectly formed, peaceful at her mother's breast. The baby nurse was bustling around looking officious in a white uniform. Claudia was breastfeeding, which the nurse had told her was no longer in fashion and that she should really do bottles, but she had been firm about it. Meredith watched with wonder as she nursed, and the beautiful infant dozed off in her arms.

"You make it all look so easy," Meredith said suspiciously.

"It is." Claudia laughed at her. "You should try it someday."

"I'm not sure I'd be good at it," Meredith said honestly. She had never felt maternal or wanted babies. "Besides, I'd have to have a man in my life, and I don't have time for one."

"Wait a few years," Claudia said calmly, as Thaddeus gently took the baby from her to put her back in her crib after he changed her. He had become an instant father, and Meredith was impressed. Claudia said she was too. They couldn't wait for the nurse to leave. She was in the way more than helpful, and was kind of a battle-ax.

Meredith didn't see Claudia for several weeks after that. She was busy setting up her office and sending out notices to attorneys she knew, advising them of her practice. A month after Sarah was born, Alex got accepted to Harvard, and the whole family was thrilled about it. Robert had been talking to Alex about joining the Army Reserves when he turned eighteen. He said that that way if he ever got drafted, he would go as an officer and not an infantryman, which he thought was a good idea. And the reserves were not likely to be called into active service, in his opinion.

"How about he doesn't go at all?" Meredith had interrupted her father when he brought it up at dinner. "I think joining the Reserves would be a dangerous thing to do."

"It might be good for him," Robert insisted. "He's a student, so he won't get drafted. And they're not going to call up the reserves for Vietnam."

"I'm not so sure," she said, worried about her brother. She didn't want their father to influence him to join the military in any form.

"He'd have a student deferral anyway. And the situation in Vietnam will be over by the time he graduates."

"And if he drops out? Or it's not over?"

Her father looked annoyed and changed the subject, but Meredith sensed they hadn't heard the last of it, and she whispered to her brother later not to enlist in anything. She spoke about her new office then, and her father came to visit her a few days later, and said he was impressed. She had done a nice job of it. And he approved of Charles, her paralegal, who seemed to be a businesslike young man. Her office appeared very professional, and he commented that her grandfather would have been proud of her and so was he, which warmed her heart. It was rare praise from him, given their frequent differences of opinion, which created friction between them.

All eyes were on the news again in June, when three young men, two white and one black, CORE civil rights volunteers, working to register black voters in Meridian, Mississippi, disappeared. After a federal investigation, their bodies were found murdered and buried in a local swamp. The nation was outraged. Another racial tragedy had occurred. Meredith felt heartsick when she read about it. There was still so much to do.

Meredith alternated between Claudia in Connecticut and her parents at the Vineyard for weekends that summer, and she was with Claudia when the United States bombed North Vietnam for the first time, which heightened all her fears about what would happen. When she was at the Vineyard she noticed that Alex was going a little wild in his last days before college, and got drunk several times while she was there. She mentioned it to her parents, and her father said to let him have his fun. He'd have to settle down at school soon enough. But Meredith lectured him like a big sister anyway, and he promised to behave.

She went with her parents when they settled him in Cambridge over Labor Day. He had a room with two other boys in Stoughton Hall, and couldn't wait for his family to leave. One of the boys was from California, and the other from Chicago, and they all seemed to get along, as they set up their stereos and tossed their clothes into their respective closets, and didn't bother decorating the room.

Meredith smiled thinking about how different they were from when she went to Vassar. They were only interested in meeting their classmates and dorm mates, checking out the campus, and eventually meeting the Radcliffe girls. And she suspected that the girls were less determined to find husbands than they had been ten years before. Times had changed. Everyone had more freedom now, and the creation of the birth control pill had started a sexual revolution that allowed girls to be as freewheeling as boys. It was a *major* change.

They hardly heard from Alex once he started college, and when he came home for Christmas, Meredith suspected why. He was out every night with friends, drinking a lot, and had two girlfriends simultaneously. Boston was a paradise for students, and their father wasn't happy when he got his grades.

"He's screwing up," he said grimly.

"Freshman-itis," Meredith said, feeling more like a parent than a sister, but angry with him nonetheless. He had had three Cs, a D, and an F in subjects that had always been easy for him, and where he had previously gotten As in high school.

"They'll kick him out if he's not careful," her father said, and they both talked to Alex separately. He wasn't on drugs, he wasn't a bad kid, he was just having too much fun away from parental supervision.

"If you get kicked out, you could get drafted, and then you're screwed. Do you understand that?" Meredith said to him seriously, and he looked unimpressed.

"Dad says if I join the reserves, they'll never get called up, even if there is a draft. I'll be an officer, and I won't wind up in Vietnam. They don't send the reserves into combat," Alex said confidently.

"I don't know what dream world he's living in, but everyone your age not in school can wind up drafted and up shit creek, and I don't want that to be you. There are two hundred thousand troops in Vietnam now. They're gearing up for some serious combat," she warned him.

"If they have that many guys there now, they won't need me," he said with the blindness of youth.

She talked to her father again about not pushing him into the reserves.

"He'd be much better off as an officer in the reserves than drafted as an infantryman," he argued with her. "And when do they ever deploy the reserves except in a world war? He can do ROTC, or just join the Army Reserves." She felt like she was talking to a wall with him, as usual.

When she wasn't worrying about her brother, her new law office was doing well. She was so busy with that, she had no time to date. Her practice had gotten off to a slow start, but she had three discrimination cases at the moment, and had her hands full. Charles, her paralegal, had turned out to be pure gold. He was the perfect assistant and the soul of efficiency. But she was worried about her brother now, not her business. And Claudia told her at Christmas that she was pregnant again and due in August. They were hoping for a boy this time, but didn't really care which sex it was.

The news from Vietnam was increasingly alarming after the first of the year. In February, the Vietcong attacked a U.S. Air Force base in Pleiku, South Vietnam. A month later, in March, Operation Rolling Thunder began to bomb key targets in North Vietnam, and within weeks, U.S. combat units began arriving in Vietnam. They were signs that some serious combat missions were coming up, all of which pointed to more boys getting drafted eventually. But for once her father had seen the handwriting on the wall too.

Her brother came home for a weekend during spring break, and he and her father announced that Alex had enlisted in the reserves, which her father remained convinced would protect him from winding up in Vietnam as a foot soldier, or at all, but now the army owned him for the next four years, and if there was trouble, he could be one of the first to go, not the last. And if he didn't graduate from college, he wouldn't be an officer anyway.

She went pale when they said it at the dinner table, and she talked to her father alone afterward.

"Do you realize how dangerous this is?" she asked, and he dismissed it.

"He's a student, he's safe. They're not going to call up the reserves, and if they do, wouldn't you rather have him there as an officer than an infantryman?"

"No," she said angrily. "He's my brother and he's a baby. I'd rather have him in frilly pink underwear claiming to be gay and sitting it out in Canada. I don't want him to go to war." She was nearly in tears, and cried when she heard what they'd done.

"Neither do I. But they're unlikely to ever send the reserves. They never do."

She wanted to scream, but her father was certain that what he'd done was the right thing, and it was too late now anyway. Alex had signed up for the reserves, with his father's blessing. At his insistence, in fact.

A month later, they got a letter from Harvard. Alex had three Ds, an F, and an incomplete, all in required courses, and while they acknowledged that his high school grades had qualified him for admission to Harvard, he clearly was not mature enough to handle it. Rather than expelling him totally, they were "releasing" him for a year until the following spring semester, when he would be welcome to return and try again, on academic probation. Until then he was no longer enrolled in Harvard University. They hoped that he would benefit from a year off. Her father was shaking as he read the letter, and handed it to Meredith when she next had dinner with them. She came home for dinner two or three times a week, even though she had her own apartment, so they didn't feel as though she had abandoned them.

"Shit," she said when she read the letter. "Now what?" she asked her father.

"He should get a job. There's no point sending him to another school for a year. He's obviously not ready for college."

"But he also won't get a student deferment if they call anyone up," Merrie said clearly, and her father knew it too.

"We're covered with the reserves now," Robert said, but she didn't believe him. He called his son that night and told him to get his ass back to New York immediately. The party was over. Alex sounded heartbroken at the news. He'd been having so much fun, and had so many friends at school. He didn't want to come home and get a job.

He took his time getting back to New York and arrived on the weekend. Meredith had dinner with her family, so she could talk to him too. He was deeply apologetic when his father scolded him, and said he hadn't realized he was doing so poorly.

"Did you ever go to class?" Meredith asked, and his answer was noncommittal, which told her he didn't. The biggest part of the problem was that he was immature. She had known boys like him in college, who just couldn't function without being policed constantly, and they all wound up flunking out.

His father told him he had to get a job, and he agreed to it. But three weeks later none of them were prepared for the letter he got in May. It advised him that a single unit of the reserves had been chosen to join the advisors and combat troops in Vietnam. He was to report to Fort Dix, New Jersey, the following Monday, for a two-week preliminary training period and then he was shipping out to Vietnam for additional training. He had lost his student deferral, and since he hadn't graduated he was going to Vietnam as a private, not an officer after all. Meredith was stunned. It was exactly what she had warned her father could happen. According to the letter, he would be on a flight to Vietnam on June 1. She couldn't believe it, and her father had tears in his eyes as he stared at her.

"They can't do this," he said in a choked voice.

"Yes, they can," Meredith answered him. "Can you pull any strings to get him out of it?" Her grandfather probably could have, if he were willing to, but he was gone. But her father was a federal judge. "Can you claim some kind of physical or psychological problem? Whatever works."

Her mother had been silent until then, listening to them, and then asked if it was a good idea to have Alex saddled with a diagnosis of psychological problems that could trail him forever. She had a point, but it was worth the risk, and her father agreed with Meredith. He had to get him out of it, if he could.

"It doesn't matter, Mom. The alternative is worse," Meredith explained to her mother about the psychiatric diagnosis.

Her father stayed home for two days, and canceled his court calendar. He called everyone he could think of, but they all told him the same thing. Once accepted by the reserves, which Alex had been, he was stuck, and it was too late to get him off the hook. They would have had better luck with a draft board, possibly, than a contract he had willingly signed.

Alex burst into tears when they told him, and he accused his father of lying to him. "You said they'd never call me up."

"They shouldn't have, but apparently this is an unusual occurrence. It's the only reserve unit they're calling up. They needed another battalion, and they're taking it from the reserves." It was, in effect, the whole purpose of the reserves, to fill in when they didn't have enough regular troops.

"Can I go to Canada?" Alex asked, looking desperate, but Robert shook his head.

"You'll never be able to get back in this country. That's too big a chance to take."

Meredith liked the idea, but Robert didn't want his son to be an outcast forever from his homeland, and a criminal for desertion.

"So is dying in Vietnam," Alex said angrily, in tears.

There was nothing they could do, and Alex reported to Fort Dix the following Monday, for a speedy preliminary basic training before he shipped out. He was terrified. In part, it was his own fault for screwing around and getting sent home from Harvard, and his father had given him bad advice about the military. There was nothing they could do to stop it now. And on June 1, after spending the night with them following his brief training, he left for Fort Dix at 5 A.M. and was put on a military transport plane and flown to Guam, and from there to Saigon to Tan Son Nhut for intensive combat training. Meredith and her parents looked devastated after he left. They had all gotten up that morning to say goodbye.

He called from Guam to say he had arrived safely, but they never heard from him in Saigon. He had been taken straight to a base for combat training. And no one cared that he said he was in the reserves, didn't mean it when he signed up, and didn't want to be there. Neither did anyone else.

It was five weeks before he called them on the Fourth of July. He said he was miserable. The heat was unbearable, he'd had dysentery since he arrived, and the training was brutal. All he wanted was for them to find a way to bring him home. He'd turned nineteen while he was there, and Meredith felt sick every time she thought of him, and she could see that her parents did too. She never said a word to her father about it being his fault for talking Alex into joining the reserves. It had been a terrible idea, but it was too late now, and she could see how horrible her father felt about it. No one had expected this to happen, or not this fast.

They were at the Vineyard when he called them. All Alex's friends were there, and asked for him, and they had to explain that he was in Vietnam. They were all shocked, and thought he'd been at Harvard, having fun. He'd had too much fun, and was now paying a heavy price.

Meredith was in her office after the weekend, when her mother called her and asked her to come home immediately. It was four in the afternoon, and she had just seen her last client. "What's wrong, Mom?"

"Just come home," Janet said in a strangled voice and hung up.

She took a cab uptown and let herself into the apartment with her keys. The lights were off, and she could see Adelaide in the kitchen crying. She found her father in his study, in the dark, with the shades drawn. He looked at her blindly and handed her a telegram. "I killed him" was all he said, and then her mother walked into the room and started to sob.

The telegram told them that Alex had died on July 5 in a skirmish with the Vietcong. He had been felled by a sniper bullet, while defending himself and his unit honorably. The United States Army extended their deepest sympathy and commended him for dying a hero's death. And then further went on to say that they would be contacted and notified as to when their son's body would be shipped home so they could make the appropriate arrangements. He had died one month and four days after he had flown to Vietnam.

"Oh my God," Meredith said, as she felt her legs turn to Jell-O underneath her, and sat down next to her father and took his hand in hers.

"It's not your fault, Dad," she said in a desperate voice. "You didn't know this could happen. He flunked out of school. It was a series of bad circumstances. It was fate," she said and put her arms around her father as he was convulsed with sobs.

"I killed my son. I killed my son," he kept saying over and over, and then Meredith pulled her mother into the embrace with them. As terrible as she felt herself, she couldn't imagine how they felt losing a child, with her father convinced it was his fault.

Adelaide came in and was crying as hard as they were. "I'm so sorry. . . . I'm so sorry. . . . He was my boy."

Meredith couldn't even imagine never seeing him again. He was her baby, and so ridiculously young and immature to be sent to war. It was such a waste and a travesty. She didn't know what to do, except to keep hugging her parents. They were inconsolable. And finally she put them both to bed.

She went to her own room then and called Claudia, and broke down in sobs the moment she answered the phone.

"Oh my God . . . what happened?" Claudia started crying too as soon as she told her. "He was such a sweet kid. Your father must feel responsible for pushing him into the reserves." Meredith had complained about it to her several times.

"I'm not sure he'll ever recover from it, or my mother. I just put them to bed. Oh my God, how do things like this happen? How did a sweet boy like him get sent to a hellhole like Vietnam and get killed in a month? He would have been better off in Canada for the rest of his life."

"There are some things we just can't explain," Claudia said sadly. She knew it better than anyone, and had lost her own brother twenty years before, and all the others. But now she had Thaddeus and Sarah, so sometimes life compensated for the cruelties one couldn't understand. "What can I do for you?" she asked.

"Nothing. They're going to send his body home, but they didn't say when. I don't know how my parents are going to survive this." Meredith sounded desperate as she said it.

"I'll come in tomorrow," Claudia promised.

Thaddeus drove her so she didn't have to take the train eight months pregnant, and they both extended their deepest condolences to the McKenzies, and spent some time alone with Meredith afterward. They thought her parents were still in shock, which was easy to understand. It was hard to know what to say to them. They had sat in the living room like zombies with Claudia and Thaddeus.

Claudia hugged Meredith hard before she left. "Call me if you need me," she said softly.

Meredith and her father both took a week off from work, and then they had to go back to their respective jobs. The agony continued when they were notified that Alex's body had been sent to Fort Dix and was waiting for them there.

Robert didn't want Janet to go through it, so he went with Meredith. They had made all the arrangements at Frank E. Campbell, who sent a hearse for them.

"I'll never forgive myself," her father said to her in the car on the way home.

"You have to, for Mom's sake," she said quietly. "She needs you. You didn't know this would happen. It's not your fault. We just have to live with it now."

"I don't know how," he said sadly, as tears poured down his cheeks and she held his hand.

"We'll get through it together, one day at a time."

The funeral was another intolerable agony. They put the obituary in *The New York Times,* and a surprising number of Alex's school friends showed up, in spite of it being August and many people being away. The Steinbergs came too, and Claudia came in from Connecticut again. She could hardly walk, she was so big and so far along.

After that, they had to learn to live with the loss. When people asked about Alex, and how he was liking Harvard, they had to say he had died in Vietnam, and then see how shocked people were. It would be a long time before everybody knew and stopped asking.

Meredith hated to leave her parents, but she had her own grief to deal with, and she needed a break. She was trying to do everything she could for them when she wasn't working, and her mother was like a child. She was totally lost. They went through his room together, and framed some photographs and awards that were loose on his desk. Janet folded his clothes lovingly as though he were coming back. She didn't want to throw anything away, and Meredith didn't push her. They had to learn to live with this however they could.

She went to spend a weekend with Claudia after the funeral. The apartment was so oppressive she couldn't stand it anymore. It was a relief to be with Claudia and Thaddeus and hold Sarah in her arms. She was a happy child. And Claudia's baby was due any minute.

As it turned out, she had it while Meredith was there. It went very quickly, and Claudia asked Merrie to stay in the labor room with them.

"Are you sure?" Meredith looked scared. She'd never seen anyone give birth.

"If I scream too loud you can leave," Claudia said, grimacing through the pains. She'd done it naturally with Sarah and wanted to try again.

Meredith and Thaddeus were at her head, encouraging her and telling her to push, while the doctor and nurse were at her feet, watching the baby's progress. Meredith winced when Claudia cried out in pain and then pushed again. It looked brutal to her, but an hour after they got there, she gave one big push, with Thaddeus holding her shoulders and a nurse holding each leg, and a tiny face appeared between her legs screaming loudly. Claudia shouted with delight, and they waited to find out what they had, as the doctor gently eased the baby's body out of her.

"It's a boy!" he said, Thaddeus was already crying, and so was Merrie. She had never seen anything so moving in her life. And suddenly she realized that life came full circle. Her beautiful little brother had died, and now this wonder of a child was born, from a woman who had almost died herself as a child, and only been spared by some kind of miracle after the atrocities she'd been through.

Claudia lay peacefully with the baby in her arms after they cleaned him up and wrapped him in a blue blanket. She smiled at

Meredith with tears in her eyes. "We're going to call him Alex. Thaddeus and I decided before he was born. Alexander Johann Friedrich, for my father and brother and your Alex, if that's all right with you." Meredith couldn't even speak, she was so touched. She could only nod as she sobbed. They hugged each other, and their tears mingled as they cried for the boy who had died, and the one whose life had just begun. Meredith prayed that he would be blessed and lead a long, happy life.

Chapter Fourteen

The rest of the summer was difficult for all of the McKenzies. It was impossible to understand that Alex was never coming back. That his room would forever be empty, his clothes would never be worn. He wouldn't be going back to Harvard to redeem himself, his friends would never visit again. He was gone. Meredith had trouble with the idea too. And her father had guilt weighing on him with the loss. He looked like he had aged a dozen years overnight. At sixty, he wasn't old, but he suddenly appeared to be an old man. And her mother just hung around the house, wandering in and out of Alex's room, smoothing the bedspread, opening the curtains, closing them again so nothing would fade, straightening his trophies, just standing in the doorway staring, or sitting on the bed. Meredith didn't know what to do to turn the tides of grief for them. She was desperately sad, but she was angry too. She hated the war in Vietnam, and the hypocrisy of it, and wanted it stopped.

There were mass demonstrations against the war now, in front of government buildings and in public places. The voice of the doves was growing louder. And after losing his son, Robert was no longer a hawk. He was a grieving parent whose boy had been killed by a Vietcong sniper in a war they shouldn't have been fighting.

Meredith went to rallies and protests regularly, but never told her parents. They'd been through enough, and she didn't want them to worry about her. She had been told about a demonstration on a Saturday night in October, she dressed warmly for it, and left from her apartment in Gramercy Park. It was to be held in front of the Federal Building downtown, and she got there as the crowd was gathering, each one holding a candle for the boys who had already died in the war.

They sang the songs that were familiar to her from protests in the South, including "We Shall Overcome," and at one point the crowd sang "God Bless America," and everyone had tears in their eyes or on their cheeks.

They linked arms and stood together, holding up signs against the war, and she saw the riot police arriving and didn't care. She'd been to jail before, in tougher crowds than this.

She was bracing herself to make sure that the force of the crowd didn't knock her down, and turned to see what the police on horseback were doing so she didn't get trampled, and farther back in the crowd she saw a familiar face with a determined look. He was crying, and he had locked arms with two women who were crying too. It was her father, and she was stunned that he was there. She pushed her way backward into the crowd until she reached him, and looked into his eyes. He looked better and more alive than he had since July.

"You should go, Dad," she shouted so he could hear her, and he shook his head. "They're going to start arresting people." She could see the riot police closing in on the crowd.

"I know," he said again.

"You're a judge," she shouted, and he smiled.

"I lost my son," he shouted back. "Fuck this war. Bring our boys home!" She started to laugh looking at him. Her father, the militant Republican hawk, was marching for peace.

"I love you," she mouthed to him.

"I love you too," he shouted at her. "See you in jail."

"I'll bail you out," she promised, and he grinned. And a few minutes later, the riot squads plunged into the crowd and started dragging them away and putting them in paddy wagons. She could smell marijuana in the air, and hoped her father didn't get arrested for drugs. That wouldn't sit well for a judge, but neither would an anti-war protest. She wondered if he'd get kicked off the bench, but he didn't seem to care.

They were put in separate wagons, and she was taken to the women's jail. She'd brought enough money to pay bail for herself, since she doubted they'd be charged with more than disturbing the peace. Once she was released, shortly after midnight, she went to the men's jail to find her father, and wondered if he'd already gone home. She asked for him by name, and was told he was probably still in a holding cell with the others, but they didn't have his name on any lists. She found an officer and asked if he could inquire, and said she was worried about her father, and she gave him his name. He came back a few minutes later and drew her aside.

"There's a guy back there who says he's Robert McKenzie." And then he whispered to her, "Is he the judge?" She nodded and the policeman looked unnerved.

"My brother was killed in Vietnam in July. He was nineteen." She didn't know what else to say, and he told her to wait. He came out with her father a few minutes later, and Robert was smiling.

"I forgot my wallet at home and no one believed who I was," he said when he got to his daughter. "Everyone was very nice."

She laughed at him, and the policeman ushered them to a side door and said there were no charges against her father, and they should leave quickly. They hailed a cab as soon as they got outside. "They didn't even arrest me," her father complained.

"Of course not, you're a judge." She grinned at him in the back seat of the cab, and he leaned over and kissed her.

"I'm glad I went," he said proudly.

"So am I."

"Let's do it again sometime," he said, and she laughed as he put an arm around her and hugged her close, smiling for the first time in months.

Her father was better after the peace march, although he still had hard moments, and so did her mother, and Meredith herself. They missed Alex terribly. She had a photograph of him on her desk now, of him laughing on Martha's Vineyard the summer before, after he caught a big fish.

She was making notes for one of her clients, in a discrimination case about an unlawful termination, when Claudia dropped by to see her. She was in the city to have lunch with her mother, and said there was something she wanted to ask Meredith. She seemed hesitant about it, and embarrassed. But her eyes looked serious.

"I want to do something for my children," she said quietly. "I don't know where to start."

"Do you want to set up a trust for them?" Meredith asked her. They obviously didn't need a discrimination lawyer at their age. "My father can help you do that. He'll send you to the right person. I can probably figure it out, but I'm not very good at it."

"That's not what I had in mind. And I don't want to tell my parents, they'd be upset. I want to open a restitution claim against the Federal Republic of Germany. I know that other people have done it. I always said I didn't want to, but it's different now, with my children. It's the only thing my parents can give them, and I think they'd want to. They had wonderful houses, important art. My mother had lovely jewelry that I still remember. I met some people a long time ago who knew my parents and grandparents in Berlin, and they were talking about how beautiful their house was and how much art they had. I never asked for anything back. And I think there's a very small limit for what they give. Maybe nothing even. But I'd like to at least try. I don't have any photographs or any kind of proof, but there must be some record of it somewhere, or what was taken from them, where they lived, the house, something. I was too young to try to get anything after the war. But whatever I get, I'd like to give to my children, as a gift from their grandparents and a symbol of the life I lost."

Meredith assumed that the Steinbergs would leave Claudia something one day. They were fair people and very wealthy, and Thaddeus's family had done extremely well. Her children would never lack, but Meredith understood instantly what it meant to her, from the look on her face, and it went straight to her heart. It was the first time she had ever asked for something back from the people who had tried to kill her, and successfully destroyed everyone she loved.

"We both speak German, so I thought we could figure it out," Claudia said.

"I'll make inquiries right away," Meredith told her. "The consulate must have information, or forms. I'm sure a lot of people ask for restitution."

"The war ended twenty years ago," she reminded her. "It may be too late."

"I'll bet it isn't. Let's find out."

"Will you help me, Merrie?"

"Of course." Meredith smiled at her. "I'd love to. Let's get the bad guys and make them pay," she said, and Claudia laughed. "I don't know yet. But we might have to go to Germany to appear in court there. Would that be okay?"

Claudia looked shocked and shook her head. "No, no . . . I couldn't. I can't go back. I don't want to see any of it again. You'd have to go." She went pale at the thought. It would be like returning to the camp again. It was unthinkable for her.

"Let's see how it works before you get upset. Does Thaddeus know you're doing this, by the way?"

Claudia shook her head. "No. I just wanted to talk to you. If it's not possible, I don't need to tell him. He might think it's weird."

"I doubt that," Meredith said quietly. "I think he'd understand. You had a whole life there, and a heritage and a family that were taken from you. That's a lot to lose."

"I know. That's why I want to do it. Thank you," she said and stood up. She had to go to lunch.

"I'll call you as soon as I know something."

Claudia hugged her then and left a few minutes later, as Meredith sat at her desk, thinking about it. It sounded like a challenging project to her, and just the kind she liked. Claudia was the epitome of the Jews who had lost everything, and she deserved to get something back.

Meredith waited until after lunchtime and then called the German consulate. They gave her the runaround and acted like they didn't know what she was talking about, even in German. So she hung up and called the embassy in Washington, and wished her grandfather were still alive, to impress them.

But at the embassy, they were shining examples of Germanic organization and efficiency, and said that previously there was an entire section for requests such as hers. They said it was no longer fully active, but there was a New York office of the Claims Conference, and a Herr Gross would be able to answer her questions. They gave her the phone number, and Meredith got through to him immediately. He told her that requests for restitution had to be submitted in writing with all details available, names, addresses, bank statements, receipts where possible, testimonials, photographs. She listened to the list until he wore himself out.

"I don't think most camp survivors were able to travel with those documents, Herr Gross," she reminded him and there was silence at the other end.

"You are calling for a camp survivor?" He sounded nervous as he said the words.

"I am."

"Which camp?" Did it matter?

217

"Auschwitz. Her entire family died there. All of their property was seized by the Nazis, and restitution was never made."

"Has she requested it previously?"

"No, she has not."

"We only make restitution when requested. We cannot track everyone down," he said, sounding defensive and annoyed.

"No, I suppose you can't. That would be a lot of people. She'll have very little of the documentation you're asking for, because she left Europe straight from the camp, but there must be public records of their houses, addresses, bank accounts. It was a prominent family. They were not unknown."

"Jewish, I assume," he said drily.

"Obviously."

"Well, send me what you have. If the claim appears to be valid, I will send it on to Germany. It must be submitted to the Claims Conference in West Berlin, and then she will have to make an appearance to substantiate her claim, and be interviewed by the committee. There are different departments. Real estate, banking, art."

"What if she's not able to appear?" Meredith was testing the waters.

"It could disqualify her. Is she physically disabled? We would have to have extensive medical documentation to prove it."

She didn't want to tell him she was traumatized and too scared to go back. "She's not disabled," Meredith said quietly.

"Send me your request. In German. I will pass it on." She had been speaking to him in German, so he knew it wasn't a problem. And she was exhilarated after their conversation. It didn't sound easy, but it was entirely possible. And he hadn't said it was too late.

She called Claudia at her mother's apartment and reached her just before she left. "This is very exciting. I spoke to the embassy in Washington. They were useless here. The embassy in Washington referred me to a claims office in New York. I spoke to them. You have to make a request in writing, in German, listing whatever you lost, with any proof you have. I told him there was none. He sends it to a committee in Germany, and they evaluate the claim. If they feel it's bona fide, then we have to appear before them so they can interview you. I know you don't want to go, Claudia. But this is for your kids. Don't blow it because you won't go back. I want you to think about it. You don't have to decide now. And I want you to write a letter, describing everything you lost. Everything, houses, art, cars, describe everything and your family too. Get to work."

"I'm not going."

"I get that. Just shut up and give me the list, and make it long!" She was excited by the project and wanted to help her, and she wanted to go back to Germany with her. It would be incredible if they could actually get something out of them. Claudia had never thought of it before, and since the Steinbergs had wanted her to sever all ties with Germany and her past, they had never suggested it either.

"I'm not sure if I love you or hate you," she said, and Meredith smiled.

"Either one will do. I'll come out and work on it with you this weekend if you want."

"That's perfect. Thaddeus is going to L.A. to interview some subjects for a film. He won't be here."

"You can't keep this a secret forever," Meredith chided her.

"For a while. *Auf wiedersehen,* goodbye," she said, and then hung up.

* * *

As promised, Meredith took the train to Connecticut to see Claudia that weekend. She had fun playing with Sarah and Alex until Claudia put them to bed. They were the only children Meredith ever saw. And she loved them like a niece and nephew. She couldn't imagine herself with children of her own. Her clients and cases were her babies. It was a choice she had made. Work was always a comfort to her, especially since Alex's death. She had brought legal pads and files, and once the children were asleep, Claudia brought out the list she'd been working on all week.

"I'm impressed!" Meredith said to her friend. "I figured you were going to tell me you didn't have time."

"I'm not lazy," she said, looking insulted, and handed her list to Meredith, who sat staring at it for a long time. There were three houses listed: one in Berlin in the Wannsee district, which Meredith knew was the best residential part of town, where all the really important houses were, a country house near Werneuchen, and a schloss in southern Germany near Munich. She had included them all, approximate size, name, location, and mentioned that the schloss had been in her family since the fifteenth century. She had put down as many of the cars as she remembered. And she said that all three houses were filled with art. She recalled some of the names of the artists, like Renoir, and her father liked Picasso and had several of them, although she had always thought they were crazy looking.

She mentioned her mother's jewelry, and a boat they kept on a lake near the schloss. She listed a great deal of silver in the home, and chandeliers in every room. Meredith could imagine the committee, and Herr Gross before that, shocked at the magnitude of her claim. She was describing *very* important homes, and everything in them worth a great deal of money. And then she described her family and the people she had lost in a way that tore Meredith's heart out. She had told about each one and what they meant to her. The whole picture was there. She had written it in her very poignant, touching way, without exaggeration, but the facts alone were powerful, particularly the description of the family she had lost.

"Do you think I should change anything?" she asked Meredith, who said not a word. Merrie had her write it out longhand, which seemed more personal and human, and she was going to take it with her when she left on Sunday, so she could make copies for the file, Herr Gross at the Claims Conference in New York, and the committee in Germany. And then she suddenly thought of something she had never asked Claudia before.

"Wait a minute. You listed your name as adopted by the Steinbergs. You have to put your original name on here. What was your name before they adopted you?"

Claudia hesitated for a moment. She hadn't even spoken the name in twenty years. "I have no identification in that name," she said, hesitating.

"Are you kidding? They have a record of every crust of bread they served in the camps, on what day and to whom, you think they won't have a record of a whole family they killed, and a child who survived there for three years?"

Claudia looked at her and said the name in barely more than a whisper as Meredith stared at her. It was a name like Rockefeller or Astor, except among German Jews. Even she had heard the name as part of Germany's history of wealthy families. "That's you?" Meredith looked shocked. "Are you serious? They wiped out your whole family and took everything?"

"They did it to a lot of people like us."

"Oh my God, Claudia, they must owe you millions. I doubt they'll pay you what they owe, but they're going to faint when they see that name on the documents."

"I've never said that name since the Steinbergs adopted me. I thought it would be disloyal to them since they saved me. I would love to recover some of the art, but I was too young, and I don't know enough about it. I could never give them a reliable list they could verify. My mother had beautiful Degases and Renoirs in her boudoir, and my father loved Monet. He used to explain the paintings to me and tell me about the artists." It was surreal listening to her remember, but what she had listed was substantial enough. "I'll take whatever they give my children," she said meekly, and Meredith stopped her.

"Not so fast. These people owe you millions and damn near killed you, and killed your entire family. They owe you whatever we can get from them."

Claudia nodded, and they hugged tightly when Meredith left to take the train back to New York on Sunday. Meredith wanted her to get everything she could.

The next day in the office, she got all of Claudia's paperwork in order, in duplicate and triplicate, with the correct maiden name on it, as well as her married name. But it was her original name that was the showstopper.

Charlie, her assistant, had the package for the Claims Conference ready to take to the post office, when a very attractive tall young black woman walked in, and asked for Meredith.

"Is she expecting you?" he asked coolly.

"No, she isn't," she admitted, and he was about to tell her to leave her name, when Meredith walked out of the office to remind him of something else, and she smiled at the woman.

"Hello. Can I help you?" Meredith offered, and the young woman smiled at her.

"I hope so. I'm sorry, I don't have an appointment, I just took a chance and dropped by."

"I've got a few minutes," Meredith said, and indicated the way into her office. The young woman sat down and got down to business, so as not to waste Merrie's time.

"My name is Angela Taylor. I'm a lawyer." She mentioned her school, and it was one of the better schools for black women and had a law school Merrie had heard of. "I got a job at Elkins, Stein and Hammersmith, and they promised me a partnership in five years, a junior partnership in three, advances and raises no different from anyone else's. And none of that was true. I didn't get a raise or a promotion in three years. They passed me over for everything, never gave me the good cases, and treated me like slave labor. They let me go and replaced me with a recent graduate with no experience, who's someone's niece, and pay her more than they were paying me after three years, and I did a good job on the cases they gave me."

"Do you have any proof? Messages? Letters? Memos?"

Angela shook her head. "Nothing I could prove. They're too smart for that, but they know what they've been doing. I want to nail them."

Meredith nodded. The woman sounded angry and bitter.

"I was a lingerie model when I was in school, to pay the bills. I'm thirty-two and single. Basically, they lied to me and never gave me what they promised."

Meredith listened carefully and made notes. She heard it from women all the time, white and black. "I'd like to go after them with guns blazing for discrimination, both race and gender, and scare the shit out of them. And then settle the case for you for a nice chunk of money," Meredith said calmly. "It usually works."

"And what do you get?" Angela asked with interest.

"An hourly fee. I don't do contingency. I'm not an ambulance chaser. You get a nice settlement, and I get a reputation for doing a good job for my clients, and my fee. That works for me."

She told her the hourly rate and Angela didn't find it exorbitant. She stuck out a hand to shake Merrie's. She wasn't a warm person, but businesslike and clear about what she wanted. Money. As much as she could get. "You've got a deal, counselor."

"Thank you." Meredith smiled at her. "Let's meet tomorrow and go over the details. I can file the suit by the end of the week, and then we can watch them dance a little. See you tomorrow. Ten-thirty?" she said.

Angela nodded and left a few minutes later. Meredith thought she would be a solid client. She was smart, direct, and seemed honest. At least she hoped she was. It sounded like they had a good case. With her case and Claudia's she would have her hands full, and she had a few others percolating at the moment. Her practice was going well. She described the case to Charlie when he came back from the post office.

"She looks tough," he commented, "and ambitious."

"She'd have to be, to be a black female lawyer on Wall Street."

Angela came back the next day, and they spent two hours together building her case. She was efficient and intelligent, and somewhat ruthless, but Meredith didn't mind. What she had said to Charlie was accurate. Angela had to be tough in her shoes.

True to her word, Meredith filed the lawsuit on Friday. And the press had picked it up by Monday. It was a good story, especially since Angela was represented by the granddaughter of a previous and greatly respected Supreme Court justice and the daughter of a sitting federal judge. Her name had resonated immediately as the attorney on the complaint and caught the attention of the press.

Angela called and said she was very pleased. Her previous employer had called her and left messages pleading for her to reconsider, but she wasn't taking their calls.

"Let them sit for a while," Meredith warned her.

When Meredith got back to her apartment that night, her father called her. He chatted inanely for a while, which wasn't like him, and then said he had a favor to ask.

"Sure, Dad, what?" She was closer to him now since her brother's death, and their war protest together.

"I think you took on a case recently. The plaintiff is a young black woman. The defendants are Elkins, Stein and Hammersmith. Larry Elkins and Bert Hammersmith are old friends of mine. And they'd like you to do them a favor."

"They want to pay us a big settlement so we drop the case? We'd love it," she said playfully.

"Actually, to be honest, they'd like you to get off the case. I think they're afraid you'll do too good a job, and your being attached to it excites the press."

"Very flattering, but I'm not ditching my client."

"This could be embarrassing for me. They asked me to call you and convince you, if I could."

"I don't do favors like that, Dad. I'm an attorney, not a bookie. She's my client and she has a good case."

"That's what they're worried about. It seems she slipped through the cracks. It's a big firm and they passed over her a number of times, unintentionally of course."

"They should have thought of that before they let her go and replaced her with someone's white niece and paid her more money than my client got after three years. It's a clear-cut discrimination case, Dad. They're in the wrong here."

"This could be very awkward because of her color."

"Precisely. We'll be happy to accept a big settlement and all will be forgiven. It's what my client deserves. Now what else can I do for you?"

He sounded flustered and a few minutes later asked her when she was coming for dinner. And the next morning, the settlement offers started rolling in.

It took her six weeks to get a final settlement for Angela. She got the equivalent of a year's wages and an apology, so she didn't report them to the NAACP for the press value, which Meredith had threatened to do. Angela was very happy with the result, but Meredith had another idea. She had liked working with her. Angela was smart and to the point, businesslike, and professional. She was well educated too.

"How would you like to work with me? I'm thinking of taking on an associate and another paralegal or assistant. What do you think?

No Wall Street politics or games. I'm a straight shooter and I think you are too. Does that appeal to you at all?"

"Yeah, actually it does. People are going to be afraid to hire me now after I threatened a lawsuit. I need to let things cool for a while."

"I hope you stay. With me, what you see is what you get," Meredith said openly.

"That works."

Meredith quoted her a fair salary and Angela said she liked it. Half an hour later, she left Merrie's office. She had a new job and a nice fat settlement, and Merrie had a new associate. She had to hire a second paralegal, but thought that would be easy. And she loved Charlie. He proved his worth every day, and she trusted him completely. He made excellent decisions, and suggestions about her cases.

Her father called her that afternoon and told her she had done a good job with Angela's case.

"We got a good settlement." She was pleased.

"They were afraid of worse. What you asked for was fair."

"Damn, I should have asked for more," she teased him. But she wanted to be respected, not hated. She was satisfied. And Angela was too.

The second paralegal she hired wasn't as impressive as Charles, and she was a little unsure of herself, but Meredith had the feeling she'd try hard. Her name was Peggy. She was in her late forties, and very anxious to please.

Meredith split her backlog of smaller cases with Angela once she started working.

Then Meredith got what she'd been waiting for. She smiled when she opened the letter.

"You look like you just won the lottery," Charlie said to her when he walked into her office to ask a question.

"I think I did. I'm going to Germany on a restitution case in January," she said, waving the letter.

"Will you need a translator?" He was curious.

"Nope. I'm fluent in German, and so is my client. I spent four years there as a kid."

"Impressive." Angela had walked in and heard what Meredith said. She admired her a lot. She was working on two small termination cases Meredith had given her. Meredith liked her better and better. She was just what she needed, and she was a hard worker.

She could hardly wait to tell Claudia that the committee in West Berlin had agreed to meet with them there on their turf. Whether Claudia wanted to or not, as far as Meredith was concerned, come hell or high water, they were going.

Chapter Fifteen

Claudia and Meredith's plane to Geneva took off from New York in January right after New Year. Both women had decided to treat themselves to first class seats since they were taking the night flight and had to take a second flight from Geneva to West Berlin. They had to meet with the Restitution Committee in West Berlin the same afternoon. Claudia didn't want to be away from the children for too long, and she was still nervous about being in Germany. She had no idea how it would feel to be back after almost twenty-one years. Her last glimpse of Germany had been from the plane on her way to America, after being liberated from Auschwitz. She had been a terrified child then, an orphan, on her way to a family to adopt her. Now she was a grown woman, with a husband and children of her own.

As they flew over Berlin, they could see the ominous Berlin Wall snaking its way through the city, separating east from west, and surrounding West Berlin. When they landed at Berlin Tegel Airport, a car was waiting for them. Meredith had arranged everything. She wanted to make the trip as easy as possible for her friend. She knew how much Claudia didn't want to be there, and how traumatic it was for her. Claudia was silent on the way into the city, and they were staying at the Kempinski Hotel Bristol. Claudia sat looking out the window at the remaining familiar landmarks of her childhood, and remembered them all. The Restitution Committee was at the Rathaus Schöneberg, the city hall for West Berlin, which had been handling the restitution cases since the war. Most claims were either about architecture or art, when houses were involved. And financial issues were handled by the Bundesbank, where they had kept careful records of the Jewish bank accounts that were seized, many of which were still being held because they belonged to people who had died during the war. What hadn't been stolen by the Nazis had been frozen ever since. There were similar accounts in Switzerland that had never been claimed.

Meredith was planning to hand over a copy of their entire file, and discuss with them what they were willing to validate. Meredith had managed to find photographs of Claudia's parents' homes. One was a hotel now, another was a museum, and the third one, the schloss, was privately owned by a Bavarian prince.

"Are you okay?" she asked Claudia, who nodded. She followed Meredith silently as they walked into the Kempinski Hotel. She couldn't speak, she was so unnerved just being in Berlin.

They had agreed to share a room, since they had splurged on the air tickets, and Claudia was happy not to be alone. It had seemed strange listening to everyone speak German around her, and she and Meredith lapsed into English as they walked into the room.

They ordered breakfast and afterward decided to go for a walk. They walked down the Kurfürstendamm and glanced at the shops, and Claudia remembered shopping there with her mother as a child. She was six when she was hidden by friends, and seven when she was sent to the camps, so all her memories were from before that, as a very young child. But they were vivid even now. And she felt like a child again as she walked along, steeped in memories with Meredith at her side. And then unable to resist it, drawn to it inexorably, they hired a car and asked the driver to take them past Claudia's family house. She got out and stood staring up at it for a long time, with all her memories, and then got back in the car with an anguished expression. Seeing the house had been hard.

"Does it look the way you remembered?" Meredith asked her gently. She could tell how moved Claudia was. This was a pilgrimage for her into the past.

"Only a little smaller," she said, referring to the house, which looked enormous to Merrie. They had lunch at a beer garden before going to the appointment with the committee.

A woman came out to greet them when they arrived. She looked stiff and stern, introduced herself as Frau Hoffmann, and asked them to follow her. There were five people in the room she led them to, sitting around a table, and all of them looked intently at Claudia as she and Meredith walked in and Frau Hoffmann invited them to sit down.

"Thank you for coming," Frau Hoffmann said. They started out politely and Meredith could see a little shiver go down Claudia's spine. Claudia was trying to remind herself that they weren't going to hurt her, she wasn't going to prison, and no one was going to kill her. They weren't Nazis and she wasn't a child. But the echoes of the past were very loud in her head as she tried to focus on what they were saying, and she reached for Meredith's hand and held it tight.

"I'm sorry, but this is very difficult for me," she said in a small, tense voice. "I didn't want to come, but Miss McKenzie said that you would not validate my claim if I didn't come in person. I never wanted to come back to Germany again," she said, shaking visibly and speaking carefully to them. She didn't want to offend them.

"We understand," Frau Hoffmann said, and pulled the file toward her, looking serious and official, sitting up very straight. She leafed through it carefully, stopping at the photographs of her parents' houses. She had seen parts of the file before. "And you wish restitution for all of this?" she asked Claudia, who didn't answer for a minute. "Why did you wait so long?" Her eyes met Claudia's directly.

"At first, I didn't know that I could get restitution. Now I only want what is right for my children. I realize that much of it will never be recovered, and can't be proven now. I was a child then and there is no record of what we had. But the homes were ours, that's a known fact, and many important paintings, and my mother's jewelry that's hard to trace, and all the money they had. The Nazis took everything from us, and killed my two sisters, my brother and my parents, and my grandparents. I don't even know how I will explain it to my children one day, that something like that could happen."

"It was a terrible time for Germany," Frau Hoffmann said drily, as though it absolved them.

"And for us," Claudia corrected her. "Have others been able to get restitution?" Claudia asked. She knew they had, but not in what amounts.

"Some," the woman said honestly. "But not many. And not on this scale. So much was lost during and after the war."

"And so many people during the war," Claudia persisted.

"It's a miracle that you lived through it," one of the men said more gently. "You were so young." Claudia nodded. He looked sympathetic and sad for her.

"I was seven when they sent me to Auschwitz, and ten when the Russians liberated the camp."

And then they went through the file looking at the pictures, the houses, the art, the schloss, and some photographs that Meredith had found of Claudia's mother in German newspapers. She had been a very beautiful woman, and her father very handsome.

Each member of the committee looked at it carefully page by page without comment. They also asked her countless questions about her time in Auschwitz, and the death of her parents and siblings, and after they had been there for three hours, Frau Hoffmann stood up and thanked them for coming, indicating that the interview was over, and led them out of the room again.

Claudia looked shell-shocked when they were back on the sidewalk, and she stared at Meredith.

"That's it?"

"That's it," Meredith said. "They should tell us in a few months what they're willing to give you, and we'll probably have to appeal many times in the next few years. This is just the beginning. But for now, it's all over."

Claudia was visibly relieved, and they went back to the hotel and she lay down on the bed. They were going back to New York in the morning and she didn't want to leave the hotel room. She was drained.

"Do you want to go out to dinner tonight?" Meredith asked, and Claudia shook her head.

"I don't think I can. I would fall over." Instead she lay there and fell asleep and woke up several hours later. She wondered if it was crazy to have come. But it couldn't do any harm. They couldn't hurt her or take her away again. She had been terrified the whole time she spoke to the committee, and they had awakened all the memories she wanted to forget.

She hadn't told the Steinbergs she was coming and was glad she hadn't. It would have seemed disloyal to them after all they had done for her.

She didn't speak to Meredith for the rest of the night, and in the morning they dressed and went to the airport. Claudia could only speak again when they were back on the plane. She was shaken but glad she'd come. It felt right, no matter how hard it was.

"I thought they were going to take me away again," she said in a shaking voice after they took off.

"No one's going to take you away again," Meredith said gently.

"It didn't feel that way in that room. Do you think they'll give me anything?" she asked. "It would be nice for my children."

"It doesn't matter. You were very brave, and you came, that's all that counts." Claudia nodded and fell asleep until they landed in New York. She was absolutely exhausted. Thaddeus was there to meet her with Alex and Sarah in a stroller, and she smiled when she saw them.

"How was it?" he asked her as soon as they came through customs, and she threw herself into his arms and kissed her babies.

"Hard. It brought a lot of memories back I thought I had forgotten, and wish I had."

Meredith left them at the entrance of the garage and took a cab into the city. The trip had been short but rugged. There had been nothing easy about it, which they had expected.

She went to Connecticut to talk to Claudia about it that weekend, to make sure she was all right, and was startled to find she had a guest. He was a friend of Thaddeus, and he said he traveled a great deal for work. He was German, in his early forties, and said he spent time in Brazil, Argentina, Uruguay, and Germany. He had stopped in New York to talk to Thaddeus about a film about it. His name was Gunther Weiss, and he was interesting to talk to. He had a mane of dark hair and piercing blue eyes.

"What sort of work do you do?" Meredith asked him, trying to guess but she couldn't. He was quiet and serious. He said he hunted criminals, which startled her.

"A bounty hunter?"

"Not really. I bring Nazis in hiding to justice. It takes a long time to find them, all over the world. Many have been hidden, with new identities, since the war." Meredith didn't know what to say at first. It was a noble task. "I really have no home base," he said simply. "I travel all the time."

She told him about her father being part of the Nuremberg war trials, and he was impressed.

"That was just the beginning. Now we must keep going until we find them all, or learn what happened to them, if they died." It sounded difficult and challenging, and he was fascinating to talk to during dinner. He was knowledgeable on many subjects.

He asked Meredith if she was Jewish and she said she wasn't. She said that she was a discrimination lawyer, mostly for integration issues, or gender or religious matters. He was on his way to Brazil after the weekend, and said he spent a lot of time there. He and Thaddeus had been friends for years, and he liked Claudia and their children. She wanted to know more about him. But he was a man of mystery, and said very little about himself.

"I was in the camps too," he said to her quietly after the others went upstairs that night. "I lost everyone, just like Claudia. We're a small club, the survivors of the camps. Some of us recover, and others never do." She wondered which one he was, or if she'd ever find out. She wanted to know more about him but doubted she ever would, or even see him again. "I've made it my life's mission to find the men who did it to us." He wasn't married, had no children, and seemed to have no home, just as he said.

And in the morning, when they got up, he was gone. Back to Brazil.

"That's the way he is," Claudia said. "He's caught some very important Nazis," she said admiringly. "It's all he thinks about and lives for." Meredith could see that. He had given his whole life to his beliefs. She thought he was the most intriguing man she'd ever met.

"Don't go falling in love with him," Claudia warned her.

"Don't be ridiculous," Meredith said to her friend. "He's just very interesting to talk to," she said casually.

"That's what women always say, and then they fall madly in love with him, because they can't have him. He never gets attached to anyone. The only thing he cares about is finding the next Nazi and bringing him in. He lives for that. I think he had a girlfriend in the camps who died in his arms. Some people never recover. I was lucky I was young."

Meredith thought about what she'd said on the train ride back to New York, and, in spite of herself, hoped their paths would cross again. The men she met in her life paled in comparison to him.

* * *

They didn't hear anything further about Claudia's restitution case for the rest of the year, which seemed like a long time to Meredith. She checked on it regularly, and they told her the Claims Conference had not come to a final decision yet.

Her practice was thriving, and she continued to have a regular flow of small discrimination cases, referred to her by other attorneys. She and Angela worked well together, and Meredith thought about offering her a partnership, but it was too soon. But she definitely had it in mind. At the end of the year, Angela said she had a new boyfriend. She mentioned that he was white, and a partner in an important Wall Street firm. She was out with him every night, but still worked hard. She was unfailingly professional about her job.

And when Meredith had spare time, she went to protests and demonstrations against the Vietnam War. Her father hadn't gone again, but he approved of her position. There were almost five hundred thousand U.S. combat troops in Vietnam by then. And when Martin Luther King Jr. spoke at a massive demonstration against the war in April 1967, Meredith went, and to the march on the Pentagon in October. She was walking down the street in Georgetown afterward when she saw a man who looked vaguely familiar, and realized it was Claudia and Thaddeus's friend, the Nazi hunter, Gunther Weiss. He recognized her too, walked across the street to talk to her, and looked pleased to see her. It had been almost two years since she'd seen him.

"What are you doing here?" he asked her.

"Trying to get arrested," she said easily, and he laughed.

"I'm here to see friends, I'm going back to Germany tonight. Do you want to have dinner? I'm on a late flight." It sounded appealing to her, and they walked around the city for a while and then went to her hotel for a drink. And she noticed again what a striking man he was.

"How are you doing on Claudia's restitution case?" he asked her over their drinks.

"We haven't heard a word since we went. Maybe they're going to just ignore us forever. If they start to pay for everything they lost, even just the houses, it will cost them a fortune."

"They won't pay that much," he said firmly, "but they should pay something. They always take a long time."

"What are you doing now?"

"Same as always." He smiled at her. "Looking for Nazis and dragging them back to be prosecuted." He'd had a major find the year before, in Uruguay. Meredith remembered Claudia telling her about it. "What you and I do is not so different. We are always making people accountable for the bad things they do to other people, because they're black or Jewish or women. It's a good thing to do."

"What I do is a lot tamer," she said, though not always. "And what you do is dangerous. I can't imagine that the Nazis you find go back willingly."

"True. I've killed a few who tried to shoot me. Mostly they just try to buy me off. A lot of them still have a great deal of the money they stole hidden away. They're not leading bad lives. Until I find them." He looked hard as he said it, and his mentioning that he had killed some of them didn't go unnoticed. There was something disconnected and intensely cold about him, and yet she had seen how gentle he was with Claudia's children. But he looked like he could take care of himself in any situation. He seemed fearless, even ruthless.

"I like your values," he said to her over dinner. "We give up a lot for lives like ours," he continued thoughtfully. He seemed to have no regrets for the life he led. "We pay a high price for it, but I think it's worth it."

"So do I," she said honestly. "I knew when I went to law school that I was making a choice. I'd probably never be married or have children. My grandfather taught me to be a fighter for what I believe in. My parents weren't too happy about it."

"And now?" He was curious about her, and had been when they met. There was an unmistakable attaction between them. They were both warriors, who fought to defend others.

She smiled. "I think they've given up. I'm turning thirty-one. I think it's a little late for the kind of life they wanted me to have. And I have an arrest record a mile long, from protests, marches, demonstrations. I think most men would have a little trouble with that," she said, and they both laughed. She hadn't had a date in a year, and didn't think about it, until she met someone like him. Her independence alone scared off most men.

"It only makes you more interesting," he said easily about her arrest record, which seemed insignificant to him.

"Not to the people I know. I'm a renegade. So was my grandfather. He was the one who convinced me to go after what I believe in."

"And have you?" He was curious about her, and his blue eyes were mesmerizing.

"Pretty much. I have my own law practice and live by my beliefs. There will always be another battle to fight, for the underdog and the underprivileged, and people who don't get a fair chance because of the color of their skin, or their religion, or because they're women.

I can't let those kinds of things go," she admitted. "I never have, and probably never will."

"What does your father do?"

"He's a federal judge, and way more conservative and respectable than I am." She smiled.

"Who are your heroes?" he asked, and she thought about it for a minute, but not for long.

"Martin Luther King. John Kennedy. My grandfather. You, maybe, for what you do."

"I'm not a hero," Gunther said firmly. "I'm a bad guy with a good excuse. There's a difference." It was an intriguing thought. "I'm an angry person with a fire that will never go out until I catch and kill them all."

"I don't want to kill anybody," she said thoughtfully. "I just want to make them do the right thing."

"Sometimes it's easier to kill them," he said honestly. "Some people will never do the right thing."

"We have to try."

"What you do is harder. I take them by force."

"You can't always do that," she said quietly, and he nodded.

He looked at his watch at the end of dinner. "I have to go. I have to pick up my bags on the way to the airport. I hope we meet again one day," he said, smiling at her.

"Call me if you ever come to New York," she said, wishing he would, and remembering Claudia's warning that women fell for him constantly and he never got attached. There was something frightening about him and appealing at the same time. He was as tough as the men he hunted. Maybe tougher. For a good cause.

"I will," he said, and sounded as though he meant it. Just talking to him seemed a little dangerous or even a lot. She sensed that one could get badly hurt if one loved him. "You can take me to a protest march one day. I hate the Vietnam War too. Such needless death."

"I lost my brother there two years ago."

"I'm sorry," he said gently, and they left the restaurant. He hailed a taxi to go to his friends' home to pick up his bag, and just before he got in the cab, he turned to Meredith and bent to kiss her. He barely touched her lips with his, but the impression was searing, he was so intense. He put a gentle finger to her cheek for an instant with a serious expression, and got into the cab, as she stood watching while it drove away, and then she walked back into her hotel. He was everything Claudia had said. Dangerous, unattainable, exciting, alluring, mysterious, both gentle and fierce, untamed and untamable, and she sensed clearly that even if by chance she did see him again, she would never have him. It was probably just as well. There was something broken deep inside him that only killing Nazis would satisfy. The rest of his life, and the people in it, meant little to him. He was too damaged to even love again. Revenge was all he had left. He was the ultimate freedom fighter, and he was both frightening and appealing all at once.

Chapter Sixteen

Meredith tried not to think of Gunther Weiss after she ran into him in Washington, but he came to mind more than she would have liked. There was something mesmerizing about him. He was the ultimate unattainable man, fighting his wars, hunting down criminals, honoring the past. There was something sexy and romantic about it, but she had a sense now too of how brutal and dangerous he was. It was tempting to want to tame him, but no one ever would. He was too wounded deep within. But spending even an hour with him was tantalizing.

She put him out of mind and forgot him eventually, and when her father took her to lunch a month later, he stunned her with an announcement. He said he was tired, and they both knew that Alex's death two years before had made him question his values and belief system. Nothing seemed solid in his world anymore. The government was clearly lying to people about the war in Vietnam, with five hundred thousand troops on the ground. Robert wasn't old, he was turning sixty-three, but he told her he had decided to retire at the end of the year. Her grandfather had been strong and vital at his age, but he hadn't lost a son either, and Robert was a very different man. Losing Alex had taken everything out of him. He had aged a dozen years in two, and her mother suddenly seemed much older as well. Meredith was very sorry to hear about his plans.

"You're too young to retire, Dad," she insisted, trying to convince him. "You make a difference on the bench. What'll you do if you retire?"

"Play golf," he said, smiling at her. "Travel with your mother. Relax. See friends." He was describing an old man's life, and she felt he wasn't there yet, or didn't want him to be. But by the end of lunch, she could see that he was determined, and it saddened her, thinking about it on her way back to the office. She could tell that whatever he said, he had given up on life, and had no fight left in him. Meredith was thinking about it as she walked back to her office and smiled when she saw Charlie and Angela laughing and talking.

Angela was glowing and held out her left hand. She had gotten engaged the night before to her important law firm boyfriend. And the ring was a good size. She was thrilled.

"You're not giving up practicing law to be a lady of leisure, are you?" Meredith teased her, and Angela said of course not. The wedding was in August and she said she had lots to plan. They were going to spend their honeymoon in Paris. She mentioned that her future parents-in-law weren't a hundred percent sold on their son's marriage to a woman of color, but her fiancé was standing firm, and Angela thought they'd come around. Meredith hoped that was true. It made her think of Claudia with Seth after graduation, when he just didn't have the courage to stand up to his family and marry a

Jewish girl. But Angela was thirty-six, and her fiancé, Brady Collins, was thirty-nine. They were adults and knew what they wanted and weren't dependent on anyone, unlike Claudia and Seth at the time, fresh out of college.

For the next several weeks, Meredith was worried about her father's retirement. She had asked if he'd be working at the family law firm after he left the bench, but he said he didn't want to, and they'd been managing fine without him, so he was just going to take life easy and stay home. Meredith was sad that her mother had agreed to the plan. It didn't sound like a good idea to Merrie, and she was concerned that her father would sink into a depression at home. It didn't seem healthy to her. He had years of life left in him, but losing Alex had changed all that. Some vital part of him had died with his son.

She was trying not to think about it when Charlie put a thick envelope forwarded by the German embassy in Washington on her desk. She sat staring at it, afraid to open it. Claudia's answer was inside. It had taken almost two years to get it, an inordinate amount of time. And whatever the Claims Conference offered or didn't, they planned to appeal the decision, because Meredith was sure that it would be inadequate. She took a deep breath and opened the envelope carefully.

Their response was in German, as all of her correspondence with them had been. And there was a long paragraph of greetings, apologies for the time it had taken, and formal salutations in archaic German. She raced ahead to the next paragraph where they said that much of what Meredith had listed was impossible to evaluate and was listed through the eyes of a child at the time. And making restitution for artwork, jewels, and possessions in the lifestyle of her family was beyond the conference's means. But they agreed there was no dispute about the three family homes in Berlin, the countryside, and Bavaria, which were known to have belonged to her family and been seized by the Nazis. Since there was no one to claim them at the end of the war, and Claudia's parents' deaths in Auschwitz had been confirmed, when she left the country at the age of ten, they had all been sold for the benefit of the government, in most cases well below their actual value, even at the time. Germany had been up for grabs after the war, with properties sold for very little money, abandoned by families who had fled or been killed, Jews who had been deported and never returned.

They also said that it was impossible to put a value on the relatives Mrs. Liebowitz had lost, the childhood that had been stolen from her, and her terrible suffering in the camp. There was no way to measure it or put a financial value on it. But they were fully cognizant of and deeply regretted the pain and losses she had suffered. In light of that, however, in acknowledgment of the homes that had been taken from them, her becoming an orphan, and the three years she had spent at Auschwitz, they were prepared to offer her the following amount. Meredith read it in deutsche marks then made a rapid conversion, and realized she had calculated it wrong. She did it again, and saw that there was an additional zero on the figure from what she'd originally seen and did the math again.

"Holy *shit!*" she shouted through her open office doorway, and Charlie came running from his desk, followed by Peggy more slowly.

"What's wrong?" he asked her immediately, and she grinned at him.

"Not wrong, Charlie. Very, very right." They had offered her the equivalent of three million dollars, which was a fraction of what her family had lost, but it was a very healthy amount, probably one of the largest they'd given, and one day would make a significant difference to Claudia's children when they grew up and went to college. "Oh my God." She did a little jig and danced around the room. She couldn't wait to tell Claudia. She had been so right to apply for restitution. It had been a long wait, but was well worth it. She called her a few minutes later. She wanted to tell her in person. "What are you doing tonight?"

"Nothing. Thaddeus left for L.A. this morning. He's wrapping up a film. He'll be back Sunday night. Why?"

"I'm bored in the city, and I thought I'd come out and have dinner with you."

"Just like that?" Claudia sounded touched and surprised. Meredith normally only visited on weekends. She worked hard during the week and stayed late in her office.

"Sure. Why not? My love life is at a dead standstill, it's ancient history, and I haven't been to a protest in two months," she said lightly, and Claudia laughed.

"We have to find you a boyfriend."

"I saw Gunther in Washington two months ago. We had dinner."

"That'll never get you anywhere. He lives with his passport and an airline ticket in his teeth."

Meredith tried not to think of the kiss, but it had been memorable. "True, but he's good to talk to. So can I come out?"

"Sure."

Meredith left the office early and was at Claudia's tidy little farmhouse in Sharon at seven-thirty. They made small talk for a few minutes and Meredith helped her put the children to bed and read Sarah a story and then they came back to the kitchen to scrounge something for dinner. And before Claudia could start cooking, Meredith took the envelope from Germany out of her purse and handed it to her.

"What's that?" Claudia looked puzzled. She had assumed their silence meant that she had been declined, and had stopped waiting for a response.

"Open it and take a look," Meredith said, her eyes glowing as she watched her friend take it in shaking hands. It was like going back to Germany all over again, holding the envelope and knowing the answer was in it.

"Did they turn us down?"

Meredith refused to answer, and Claudia took the letter out of the envelope and began reading. Suddenly her eyes flew to Merrie's and opened wide. "Marks?" she said in German. "That's insane!"

"Are you crazy?" Meredith corrected her. "Do you realize what your parents' estate was worth, the art and the houses alone, not to mention the money and all the rest? That's peanuts, but very nice peanuts in the scheme of restitution, and they took your pain and suffering into account. We did it!" Meredith said and threw her arms around her, and they danced around crying and laughing. And then Claudia got serious again.

"We're not going to appeal it, are we? I don't think we should."

"I suspect this is one of the largest amounts they've given anyone and we shouldn't push our luck," Meredith confirmed.

"I totally agree." They sat at the kitchen table then, talking about it, and how glad Claudia was that she had filed the claim. It was only right.

Meredith spent the night in Connecticut with her and went back to the city in the morning. She helped Claudia give the children breakfast, and when she left to go to work, Claudia gave her an enormous hug.

"You're my hero, Merrie," she said with tears in her eyes.

"Merry Christmas . . . or Happy Chanukah. You deserve every bit of it and more."

"Thank you," Claudia whispered, and they hugged again.

Meredith rode back to New York on the train smiling the whole way. It didn't make up for what had happened to Claudia, but Meredith had the satisfaction of knowing it was a job well done for a friend she cared about deeply.

After the unbridled joy of Claudia's restitution award, which she had told Thaddeus about and he was stunned, 1968 got off to a bad start. In January, the Tet Offensive shocked everyone with their eyes on Vietnam. Seventy thousand North Vietnamese and Vietcong launched a simultaneous attack on 126 towns and villages in South Vietnam, and ultimately the North claimed it as a victory.

Claudia called Meredith a week later.

"Did you see *The New York Times* today?" She sounded shaken and like she'd been crying.

"Not yet. I've had a busy day at the office, and the news is so depressing."

"Seth was killed at the Battle of Hue in the Tet Offensive. He was married and had three children," and had apparently followed the military career his parents had wanted him to. And now he was dead at thirty-three. They both fell silent for a minute thinking about him. Claudia was sad, even though she hadn't seen or heard from him in ten years.

And a month later, My Lai was even more horrifying, when U.S. soldiers took revenge and murdered civilians, mostly women and children and elderly people, in an attack on the local population that was beyond comprehension. The world was out of control.

But the most painful blow of all in Meredith's eyes came on April 4, when Martin Luther King Jr., one of Meredith's heroes, was killed in Memphis, Tennessee. Claudia called her immediately when she heard, and Meredith was devastated. She couldn't imagine a world without him. She had gone to his marches, sit-ins, protests, and demonstrations and believed in what he stood for. She went to Atlanta for the funeral, and mourned and cried with all of those who loved him. She was shattered by his death.

She hadn't even begun to recover from it when John F. Kennedy's brother Robert, the senator, was gunned down in California two months later. All of their shining heroes were being killed.

Meredith was still reeling from all the bad news when Angela, her associate, dealt her another blow. She walked quietly into Meredith's office a week after Robert Kennedy was killed and told her she was leaving. Her future husband had used his connections and found her a fantastic job at a distinguished Wall Street law firm.

"You're quitting?" Meredith looked stunned. She had come to rely on her, loved working with her, respected her, and had been planning to offer Angela a partnership in her firm. There had been no sign that she was unhappy. "Why?" Meredith asked, feeling betrayed, and Angela was honest with her, which was one of the things Merrie liked about her.

"Are you serious? I've been offered an opportunity I can't pass up. It's a major career move for me, and let's face it, this isn't. I love working with you. You're an amazing woman, but we have different goals. All my life I've dreamed of making it in the white man's world. That's why I went to Wall Street in the first place. I didn't go there for my health. I want to be a big deal one day, a senior partner, a managing partner in a big firm, and the first woman to do it, the first *black* woman to do it. And I want to make a shitload of money. I can only do it in a white man's world. I'm every bit as good and smart as they are, and I want to prove it. I want every guy on Wall Street to know my name.

"I'm not like you. You're a purist and some kind of saint. You care about causes and wars and Negroes on buses and getting them the vote. I admire you like crazy for it. Martin Luther King is your hero, and Medgar Evers. J. P. Morgan and John D. Rockefeller are mine. You care about the underdog, you really are a saint, Merrie. I care about my pay. I grew up dirt poor and I learned that no one was ever going to get me out of there but me. I don't think you care about how much money you make. I do. We all make choices in life. I know what mine are. It affects who I marry, what I do, where I work. And I'm never going to set the world on fire sitting here." She was brutally honest, and Charlie had been right about her in the beginning. Angela was ambitious, and driven by it. The two women sat looking at each other for a long moment, and Meredith didn't know what to say.

"When are you leaving?" was all that came to mind.

"I'm giving you two weeks' notice. They want me to start right away."

Meredith nodded.

"You can leave sooner if you want." There was no point hanging on, and she'd have to take over her workload anyway.

"Thank you, Merrie," Angela said quietly and stood up and left her office. There was no sentiment to her. She was smart but all she really cared about was herself. Meredith had been a stepping stone for her, and never really a friend. Meredith sat there feeling betrayed and overwhelmed. She was disappointed that Angela didn't have the same ideals she did. She realized that she had been naïve and had assumed she did, just because she was black. Angela hadn't lied to her, but Meredith assumed they had the same goals, and never saw it coming, or suspected she might leave.

She went for a walk after that to clear her head and think about it. She wasn't heartbroken or angry, but she felt let down that Angela wanted to quit. She thought that Angela was better than that, but she was an opportunist and a shrewd woman. It reminded Meredith of something her grandfather had said, that fighting for other people's freedom could be a lonely life at times, without allies or friends, but it was worth doing anyway. She had no regrets about the life she had chosen, and few illusions. She had given up having a husband and children to fight the good fight and other people's wars. Her grandfather was right. It was lonely at times, but it was the only life she wanted.

When she went back to the office, Charlie told her that Angela had packed up her things and left at lunchtime, and said she wasn't coming back. She hadn't stayed to say goodbye or left Meredith a note to thank her. She had moved on, and put a stack of files with her cases on Merrie's desk.

That was just the way it worked sometimes, she told herself as she opened one of Angela's well-organized files. She was going to have a lot of work to do, but Meredith had never shirked from hard work and she didn't intend to now.

* * *

She'd been working late every night trying to catch up when she got a call a few weeks later from Gunther, who said he was coming through New York. But he didn't know when or if he could see her. He was as elusive as ever, and Meredith knew that Claudia was right about him. He was a heartbreaker waiting to happen to someone else. She didn't want or need to chase the impossible dream, and was smart enough not to take the bait. She wished him a good trip, told him she was busy too, and hoped he never called again. He wasn't even able to be a friend. And as a woman, she found him too dangerous.

The rest of the year slid by in a haze of disappointment. Nixon was elected, which she found depressing too, although her father was thrilled. And then her father got sick at Christmas, and was diagnosed with cancer, and much to her shock and her mother's, he died five weeks later, at sixty-four, a year after he had retired. Once he stopped working, he had just faded away, and her mother was a complete wreck when he died. She was unable to organize the funeral and incapable of making a decision. She cried all the time and was confused. She acted like she was ninety, not turning sixty, and Merrie was frustrated with her seeming helpless most of the time. Her father had done everything for her, and she couldn't manage her life, and called Merrie ten times a day with minor problems. The TV wasn't working, or the dishwasher. She had forgotten to pay her rent.

It was a welcome distraction when an elderly black man came to see her one afternoon. Someone had written her name down for him on a piece of paper, and he came to see her without calling first. He looked so dignified and respectful, sitting in her waiting area in a suit and tie, that she went out to talk to him and invited him into her office. They talked for a long time, and he told her that his son had been killed by a lynch mob in Mississippi ten years before for using a white restroom at a gas station.

But he'd come to see her about his job. He was seventy-six years old and had been a doorman at a building on Park Avenue for forty-seven years. He'd been an elevator man before they had put in automatic elevators years before. He said he was respectful to everyone, and knew all the tenants by name and their regular guests. He carried packages and luggage, and assured her he was still strong and claimed he had never had a sick day in twenty years. And he had been fired two weeks earlier and replaced by a man who was fifty-four years old, smaller than he, not as strong, and had a limp. He was undeniably younger, probably Russian or Romanian, and could barely speak English. She could easily figure out that his replacement was white.

His name was Jebediah Parker, and he said everyone called him Jeb, and Meredith gently asked him what he wanted. Did he want money from his employer, severance pay?

"No, I want my job back. I still got years in me. I'm not ready to retire yet." She smiled as he said it. He looked younger than his age, had a firm step when he walked into her office, and seemed energetic. "Can you make them hire me back?"

"I can try," she said honestly. "They may prefer to give you some kind of severance pay."

"I don't need that. I want my job. I can't get another job at my age. I want to work."

She wrote down all of his pertinent information, and his employer's, and he asked if he should pay her before he left, and she told him that they could settle it after she could see what she could do for him. She was hoping to threaten them with a discrimination case and unlawful termination for his race. She promised that she would write a strong letter to his employer and see how they responded to it. Jeb shook her hand firmly and thanked her politely before he put his fedora on his head and left her office. She wrote the letter and mailed it that night. She implied that they had grounds for a lawsuit, but assured his employer that what he really wanted was his job back. He had told her the building where he worked, and it was only a few blocks from her mother's apartment.

The response from his employer was swift. They made it clear that they didn't want a lawsuit, and were willing to give Jeb his old job back. They would put the new man on another shift. She called Jeb immediately and told him the good news.

"They said you can come back tomorrow," she told him, and he laughed.

"You must have scared them real good!" he said, sounding delighted.

"I think I did."

"I'll come by and pay you tomorrow before I go to work," he promised. "You did a powerful nice thing for me. I'm glad I came to see you."

"So am I, Jeb. And you don't need to come by. All I did was write a letter. This one's on me."

"I can't let you do that," he said, sounding worried. "You got me my job back."

"You can come to see me again if they give you any more trouble. I'll send you a bill next time." He thanked her half a dozen more times and then they hung up, and Merrie was still smiling when she walked home that night. She was delighted with the result. And she had other things on her mind when she went to work the next day, and saw Charlie grinning at her when she opened the door of her office.

"New romance?" he asked with a knowing look.

"Not that I know of."

"Secret admirer then?" And then she noticed the largest bouquet of red roses she'd ever seen sitting on the desk in her office. She couldn't imagine who might have sent them to her, and she opened the envelope with the card in it. In a careful handwriting, the card said "Thank you for my job. Sincerely, Jebediah S. Parker." She smiled from ear to ear as she read it.

"Well?" Charlie asked, still smirking at her.

"Satisfied customer."

He looked surprised by that. None of their clients had ever sent her roses before, and there were at least three dozen in the bouquet. "The man who came by to see me the other day, who'd lost his job as a doorman."

"Did he win a jackpot in Vegas?"

"No, he got his job back as a doorman, and he's a gentleman." She was still smiling when she sat down at her desk and got to work, and put the roses on the table in front of the window. She wrote Jeb a thank-you note, and couldn't have been happier with the result. Some days the good fight was easier than others. It made up for all the other times when it wasn't.

A few weeks later, on the way to lunch, she ran into Ted, whom she hadn't seen in several years, although he called her occasionally, and he looked thrilled to see her. She asked about Emily and the kids, and he seemed embarrassed for a minute.

"Actually, we're getting a divorce. She's having an affair with the tennis pro at our club. It's a humiliating soap opera, don't you think? But it wasn't working before that anyway." He tried to make light of it, but he was thirty-four, had four kids, and eleven years of marriage with a woman he'd been reluctant to marry. What was the point? It seemed like such a waste to Merrie. His parents had pushed him into it, and now his whole life was a cliché, and had been dictated by them. He had sold out to his father ever since college, with a divorce as the door prize a decade later.

It didn't seem worth it to her, despite the kids. Why bother? "I'd love to have dinner with you sometime," he said, with a gleam in his eye, still looking handsome and boyish. But she didn't want a child in her life, she wanted a man, and he'd never be one. She was happy to be friends with him, but the worst of it was she didn't respect him. "What are you up to?" He seemed genuinely interested, but their lives were so different.

"Work."

"No boyfriend?" he asked hopefully, which seemed pathetic to her.

"Not really." The occasional date he didn't need to know about. "My father died. He never got over my brother's death, and he retired too early. Now my mother is falling apart. No kids, but now I've got my mother to take care of and worry about." Since she didn't want to flirt with him, she decided to be real instead.

"Have you seen Claudia?"

"She's great." Meredith smiled as she said it and told him about Seth dying in Vietnam.

"I read about it," he said seriously. "Sad." They had all chosen their paths and paid their dues by then, some more than others. Ted and Seth had both given up their dreams to please their parents. She and Claudia had never sold out, or given up who they were. Claudia was still writing articles and working on books, and Meredith was still supporting the causes she believed in and establishing her law firm. She wondered what Ted was going to do now, and if he'd just find another girl to marry that his parents approved of and chose for him. It seemed like a dismal fate to her. They talked for a few more minutes, and she called Claudia and told her she'd seen him, when she got back to her office.

"How does he look?" Claudia asked, curious about him. "I ran into one of Seth's friends the other day, and he was bald and overweight. I didn't even recognize him."

"Ted looks the same. But there's something missing. I think he got lost along the way. I think you pay a price for taking the easy way out. He's still funny and cute, but there's nobody home. I'm not sure I could spend an evening with him. He never grew up, he's just Daddy's boy, his minion."

"It's too bad. Underneath all that, he's a sweet guy," Claudia said and then remembered something. "I need a favor from you, by the way. There's a book signing I want to go to tomorrow night in the city. Thaddeus says he has too much work and can't go. Will you go with me? My favorite author has a new book out and I'd love to meet her. I've read everything she's written, and she's really inspired me. Will you come?"

"I feel like Thaddeus. I have so much work. I really shouldn't. Ever since Angela left, I've been drowning, and I have two big cases I should be preparing."

"Oh, I hate to go alone." She sounded so disappointed that Merrie felt bad about it. She didn't want to let her down.

"All right, I'll go for an hour, but then I have to come back to work. Where is it?" The book signing was at Barnes & Noble downtown, not far from her office.

"We can't have dinner afterward?" she asked hopefully, and Meredith laughed.

"Don't push. I have to work."

"That's all you ever do," Claudia scolded her, as she had for a long time. "You need to get out and have some fun once in a while."

"Fun? Fun? What is that? My work is fun, so don't be a pain in the ass. Give the kids my love. I'll see you tomorrow." She promised to meet Claudia at six, and then go back to her office.

The next day, she groaned when she had to leave her office at five-thirty to get there. Her mother had been nagging her to spend time with her too. There just wasn't time to do everything, and her work was all-consuming. She could never figure out how women with jobs, a husband, and kids did it. There were never enough hours in her day, even single.

She hailed a cab when she left her office, it immediately got stuck in rush-hour traffic, and she arrived at Barnes & Noble ten minutes late. Claudia was already there.

"Sorry I'm late. I walked the last five blocks to get here, or I wouldn't have been here for another half hour."

Claudia was happy to see her and introduced her to the author, who was sitting at a table autographing a stack of books. She was an attractive Eurasian woman about their age, who had written two books about the war in Vietnam, and this was her third. Her bio said that she had been a foreign correspondent for *The New York Times*, based in Shanghai, Tokyo, Hong Kong, Peking, and Bangkok. She was half Vietnamese and half French, had left Saigon as a child, and grew up in London and Paris. And her father was a Pulitzer Prize–winning author. Meredith was fascinated by her, and Claudia bought her one of the author's books.

"She's certainly no slouch," Meredith said, reading about her. "How did you discover her?"

"I interviewed her once for the *Herald Tribune*. I've been following her ever since. Her views about the war are very interesting. She sees it more from the French point of view. They don't think we have a chance of winning, since they didn't, and I think she's right."

"So do I," Meredith said seriously and thanked Claudia for the book. "I'll try to read it when I have a break."

"God knows when that will be," Claudia said as they both saw the author, Louise Li, talking to an attractive, serious-looking man, who appeared to be about forty with graying blond hair. They were deep in conversation and seemed to know each other, and Meredith was surprised when he stopped to speak to them before he left. She and Claudia had stayed to have a glass of wine and chat. Claudia didn't come to the city much anymore. She was either writing or with Thaddeus and her kids in Connecticut.

The man who had been talking to the author introduced himself as Peter Watts, and the author came over to join them a few minutes later during a lull.

"I see you've met Dr. Watts," she said to both of them, and he looked embarrassed. He hadn't used his title of "doctor." "We met a long time ago, in my student days. I did a fellowship in Africa, and he was on a study there too. That was another lifetime, and now he's working with kids in Vietnam."

"What do you do with them?" Merrie asked with interest.

"I bring them to the States for medical and surgical treatment, and find foster parents for them if we can while they're here. Some of them are orphans, but many of them aren't and eventually will go back. And some we just don't know about, at least for a while." He had gentle eyes and there was something very humble and compassionate about him, as Claudia held up a hand.

"Please don't tell me about them," she said. "If I come home with a Vietnamese foster child, my husband will kill me. We have two children who run rings around us now," she said, smiling, and he laughed and turned to Merrie then.

"No, no, me neither. I'm a confirmed child hater and a workaholic. I don't even have time to take care of a plant."

He laughed again. "I was going to ask you what you do."

"I'm an attorney. I specialize in discrimination. If anyone discriminates against you, you can call me," she said, and he looked interested in what she said. "Actually, I've been arrested repeatedly for participating in antiwar protests, so I have a criminal record. Hard earned. I'd be a completely unsuitable parent." She smiled as she said it. Louise Li went back to her table to sign more books then, and Peter Watts chatted with them for a few more minutes. He went to hug Louise before he left, and promised to stay in touch with her.

"He's nice looking," Claudia commented after he left, and Meredith agreed that he was, and then said she had to go back to her office. If she stayed any longer she wouldn't want to go back to work, and she had mountains of files on her desk and a brief to write.

They shared a cab and Claudia dropped her off on her way to Grand Central Station to go home, and Meredith thanked her for an enjoyable interlude and the book. She had been very impressed by the author too.

"You should come into the city more often," she said to Claudia.

"And you should work a lot less," Claudia responded, and then they hugged and Merrie got out and waved as she drove away. It had been a nice break from her work, and half an hour later, she was buried at her desk. She stayed until midnight, but she got a lot done.

It was a hectic few weeks with several court appearances for old and new clients, and fully three weeks later Charlie told her there was a Peter Watts on the phone for her.

"I don't know one," she said, distracted by what she was doing. "Find out what he wants and take a message." And then suddenly she remembered his name from the book signing, and signaled to Charlie that she would take it, and picked up the phone.

"Dr. Watts?"

"Yes . . . Peter . . . I'm sorry to bother you. I'm sure you're busy."

"Are you being discriminated against?" she teased him and he laughed.

"Not lately."

"What can I do for you then?"

"I wondered if you'd like a tour of our center. We keep the kids there for a short time until they go to their foster homes. It's a happy place and they're amazing children." There was love in his voice when he said it.

"I'm not in the market for a foster child. I'm the last person you'd want to leave a child with. I'm single, I have no kids, I've never wanted any. And I work till midnight almost every night."

"That's not good for you, Miss McKenzie," he said, sounding like a doctor.

"Actually, I'm in love with my friend Claudia's children. You met her at the book signing. She was my college roommate. Other than that, children usually scream and hide when I walk into a room."

The truth was she never saw any except Sarah and Alex, and didn't want to. She had no urge to have children of her own.

"You might have some ideas for us if you come to see the center. Maybe someone you know would be interested in fostering one of our children while they get treatment here." She didn't want to tell him she didn't have any friends either. He'd think she was crazy or weird. She didn't want to see the center, but she didn't want to be rude either, and he was very persistent, which was something she understood and admired, for a cause he believed in. "Could you maybe spare an hour of your time?" he asked cautiously. He could sense how busy she was, but he had a feeling about her, that she was a woman who cared about some things deeply, and you never knew when someone like that would open the right doors. He hoped she would, if he could get her to the center and interest her in what they were doing.

She glanced at her schedule while she was talking to him, and saw that her six o'clock client had canceled. She had a thousand other things to do with the spare time, but she didn't have the heart to turn him down. He sounded so earnest and sincere.

"Would today at six o'clock work for you?" she asked him, and he thanked her profusely. In fact, he had an appointment somewhere else, but was going to cancel it for her.

"That's perfect." He gave her the address and she jotted it down. "See you then," he said, sounding cheerful and victorious, and Meredith hung up, wondering what she was doing, and scolding herself for being such a bleeding heart. She reminded herself that she had no room in her life for Vietnamese orphans, but at least she could take a look, thank him, and come back to work. There was no harm in that.

Chapter Seventeen

At five-thirty, Meredith took a cab to the small brownstone they had rented for their project. Peter Watts had said it was privately funded, except the medical care, which was paid for by the U.S. government.

The building in the East Eighties looked plain and a little shaky when she got there. Peter Watts was waiting for her downstairs, and she could hear the squeals of children on the floors above them. They didn't sound like children who were suffering, they were laughing and playing. And two of them almost knocked Peter and Meredith over as they raced down the stairs, chasing each other. Peter spoke to them in Vietnamese and redirected them gently up the stairs. One of them had a bandage over her eye, and the little boy only had one arm.

"Bottom line, they're just kids. They've been through a lot, and they have some hard times ahead of them, medically. But some of them are in pretty good shape and in surprisingly good spirits.

They're brave." As he said it, Merrie saw the warmth in his eyes. He was a gentle man who put his compassion into action, not just words.

They went upstairs then, and she saw a number of children sitting on cots, several nurses and volunteers playing with them, and a few children who looked withdrawn. A few were toddlers or even too young to walk. "All of these kids will be in their new homes by next week, or even in the next few days," he explained. "They just arrived. They're here to adjust until they seem ready to us. I'm going back to Vietnam next week, to bring back twelve more." She was impressed. It was a serious operation, and he explained that he had set it up himself with four other doctors, and raised the funding on his own.

"How did you get into this?" she asked him.

"I'm a pediatrician and I couldn't stand the photographs in the news of injured children in Vietnam with nowhere to go, or unable to get the medical care they needed. And many would be scarred for life or handicapped because of it. It's taken me a year to put it together, and it's working well," he said, smiling at her.

"It looks like you're doing a good job." She was touched by what she was seeing, more than she had expected, and he was so earnest, and kind with the children. It was obvious that they loved him.

"A lot of these kids will be adopted by their American hosts. Some won't. People are coming from all over the country to help us out. The kids with living families will have to go back."

They toured the rest of the facility, and Peter Watts walked her back downstairs. He was tall and appealing, and a few years older than Merrie. "Will you give some thought to anyone you know who might foster our kids?" he asked her, pleading with his eyes.

She nodded. "I will. But I honestly can't think of anyone offhand."

"I appreciate your coming anyway," he said sincerely, and she left then and thought about the Vietnamese children she'd met that night, even the little boy with one arm. She couldn't get them out of her mind, and was sorry she had no one to recommend.

Her mother was driving her crazy with calls all day long. Charlie and Peggy had an argument over cleaning the coffee machine. It was an annoying week. Nothing went the way she wanted. And three days after her visit to Peter Watts's center, she was still haunted by what she'd seen there, and she picked up the phone and called him. He sounded pleased to hear from her.

"Did you have an idea for a host for any of our kids?" He sounded hopeful.

"Yes," she said, sounding tense. "I had a totally crazy idea. You should hang up on me now." He waited. And she spat it out. "I'll take one." He could barely hear her, and was sure he'd heard wrong.

"Sorry?"

"I'll take one of your kids. I know nothing about children and my work life is crazy, but I'm not doing anything important, other than fighting with my mother and trying to teach her to run her own life without my father. I can spare a year to take care of someone else." All her life she had been determined to do the right thing, and this was part of it. It was different from what she normally did, but there was a need. And she had no social life to give up, and no love life. Why not make a difference to a child for a year? She'd been thinking about it since she'd seen them. And there was something so compelling about him and how much he cared.

"Are you sure?" He seemed amazed.

"No, but I'll give it a shot. If I can't do it, you'll have to find another home."

"We have a seven-year-old girl on the manifest for the next trip, with severe napalm burns. You might do better with a child that age than a really little one."

Meredith agreed and felt panicked. She was certain that she was truly out of her mind. She was about to foster a seven-year-old Vietnamese girl with severe burns. This was much crazier than getting arrested on a march. She wished she could talk about it with her father, or grandfather. Or someone. Her mother was too distraught to be of any help.

She called Claudia as soon as she hung up, and told her what she'd done. "We now know that I'm certifiably insane," Merrie said nervously.

"I think you're fantastic!" Claudia was bowled over, and full of admiration for her.

"I think I'm nuts." Meredith was overwhelmed by panic.

"When will she be here?"

"I don't know. I think in about three weeks."

"I'm sure that's how the Steinbergs felt when they adopted me. They had never laid eyes on me or even seen a picture when I arrived."

That put it in perspective for Meredith. And she had never thought to ask Peter Watts if the little girl was an orphan or not. It didn't really matter. She was going to foster, not adopt. "Did you ever hate being adopted?" she asked Claudia then, who laughed in response.

"Only when they wouldn't let me date at fifteen or wear lipstick at twelve. The rest of the time, I loved it. They never made me feel like an outsider or less important to them than my sisters. They did it well."

"I don't know what's happening to me. I never wanted a child in my life, and now I'm taking on someone else's, who needs skin grafts and surgeries. What if I'm terrible at this and she hates me?"

"You won't be," Claudia reassured her. "I think this is some kind of destiny. And you'll grow into it. No one knows what they're doing at first, even with one's own biological kids."

She spent the next three weeks worrying about it, while trying to do her work. She called Claudia every night while she agonized, and finally decided to tell her mother. And as soon as she did, she knew that was a mistake. Her mother told her she was crazy and had no time in her life for a child.

"That's true," Meredith said, her fears multiplying exponentially. "It's only for a year," she told her, trying to calm herself down.

"A year? How are you going to manage an injured child for a year?" Her mother looked as horrified as she felt herself and magnified Meredith's terror by voicing it.

"I don't know. I'll figure it out." Meredith called a domestic employment agency the next day to hire a nanny. She explained that the child would have medical needs, and she was hoping for a nursing student or someone with medical training of some kind.

The agency sent her half a dozen candidates, five of them inappropriate. All of them looked weird to Merrie, but the last one was a sweet girl who had taken a year off from nursing school after her mother died. Merrie hired her on the spot and had nightmares for the next week. And four weeks after she'd last seen Peter Watts, he called her. He was back in New York.

"I'm sorry we were delayed. We had to wait for two of the kids, who were too injured to travel. I've got your girl," he said as Meredith's heart sank. She was terrified of meeting her, and for a minute she was hoping he'd say she didn't come.

"Does she speak English?" she asked him in a choked voice.

"Not yet. But she'll learn quickly. They all do. When do you want to come and meet her? How about tonight?"

Meredith felt sick in the cab as she rode uptown after work. Only Claudia and her mother knew what she was doing. She'd bought a few clothes for the child, and put a narrow rollaway bed in her room for the little girl to sleep on. She had called the nanny after Peter's call, and she promised to come the next day at eight o'clock.

With new arrivals at the center, the noise level was even louder than the last time she'd been there, and Peter hurried down the stairs to greet her and smiled encouragingly. "She's a little tired from the trip," he said, as Meredith followed him up the stairs, and he walked her into a room full of children. Two of them were in wheelchairs and several were on crutches, and Merrie spotted her immediately. She was sitting on a little chair in the corner of the room, holding a doll they had given her when she arrived. She looked up with enormous eyes as Meredith approached her. And she had a pink bow in her hair. She looked perfectly normal and her injuries didn't show.

"Her name is An," Peter said gently, and Meredith held out her arms to her, and the child wouldn't come. She shrank further back in the chair clutching the doll, and Merrie sat down next to her on the floor. They just sat there together for a long time, and Merrie took her hand and held it. The little girl studied her face with interest and didn't say a word. An had dinner at the center with the other children, while Merrie sat with her. And after dinner, Peter talked to An and she nodded and he told Merrie that An had agreed to go home with her. "She thinks you're pretty," he said and smiled. He didn't say it, but he agreed.

An had one tiny suitcase with everything she owned in it, and she hugged Peter and the other woman when she left. She looked at Meredith with curiosity and interest in the cab, and they got out at Meredith's apartment and went upstairs. She showed An her bed and the clothes and a pair of pink sneakers she'd gotten for her, and a little teddy bear. An looked at everything and nodded, and then Merrie pointed to the nightgown, indicating it was time to go to bed. An nodded again. Meredith helped her take her clothes off, and was shocked when she saw the delicate young body and her severe burns. The only part of her that wasn't burned was her face and her hands, and Merrie had tears in her eyes as she helped her put the nightgown on. She took her to the bathroom, and then An climbed onto the bed and watched her. She said something that Merrie couldn't understand, and she realized she had to get some Vietnamese tapes to learn a few words so she could talk to her. She kissed the little girl on the forehead and turned off the light. An knew why she was there. The people who had brought her from Saigon had explained to her that she would be living with Meredith for a while, while American doctors fixed her burns.

After she put An to bed, Meredith called Claudia, who was dying to hear all about it. "How is she?"

"Scared to death, I think. Me too."

"So was I when I got here," Claudia reassured her. "How's her English?"

"Nonexistent."

"The Steinbergs didn't speak German either. And I didn't speak English."

Meredith promised to bring her out over the weekend, and then went and lay on her own bed in the dark, looking at the little girl, fast asleep on the narrow cot, and Meredith fell asleep holding An's hand.

The nanny, Pam, came promptly at eight o'clock the next morning, as Merrie was making breakfast for An. She seemed very pleased with the Coco Pops and Hershey Bar Merrie had given her for breakfast as the nanny laughed. She was a wholesome, pleasant girl from a big family in Salt Lake City.

"You might want to think about cornflakes and shredded wheat or she won't have teeth when she goes home!" They both laughed and An grinned at them and giggled and poured more chocolate cereal into her bowl.

Meredith spent another hour with her, dressing her and showing her a few toys she'd bought. And then she left for the office. Peter called her as soon as she got there.

"How's it going?" He was supportive and concerned for both child and foster parent.

"Pretty good. I gave her a chocolate bar and chocolate cereal for breakfast. She liked it." He laughed, and told Meredith when An's first medical appointments were, not for another month. They wanted to give her time to settle in, and she had to take English classes at the center, so she could eventually go to school. It all sounded overwhelming, and Meredith left work early, and was shocked to see her mother on the floor of the living room when she got home, playing with An. She had a little phrase book next to her so she could say things in Vietnamese, and Meredith was stunned. This woman who couldn't write a check, pay her rent or a phone bill, call a plumber, or make a dinner reservation was learning Vietnamese and talking to An.

"Mom, what are you doing?"

"I'm talking to An," she said as the little girl giggled furiously at something she said, which had obviously been wrong. "I've been listening to tapes ever since you told me. I'm never going to have a grandchild, I might as well enjoy her while she's here," she said, and Meredith went to get dinner ready for the three of them. The nanny said she'd be back the next day and everything had been fine. She said they had gone to the playground and walked a lot.

Her mother stayed for dinner and came back the next day too, and on the weekend, Meredith took An to meet Claudia, and they played with her babies and pushed them on the swings Thaddeus had set up for them. An said a few words in English that Meredith's mother must have taught her, or the nanny. She was a very polite, quiet child, and very sweet to the babies. Meredith wondered if she had siblings, but couldn't ask.

Over the next two weeks, it was all going surprisingly well. Meredith felt like she was getting the hang of having a child in the house, when her phone rang one night, and a male voice with a heavy southern accent said he was going to kill her. She had no idea who it was, and when she got to work the next day, someone had thrown a brick through the glass door to her office and Charlie had called the police.

When they arrived, she told them about the threat on the phone the night before. She had no specific enemies that she knew of, no dangerous cases at the moment or questionable clients. The vandalism to her office and death threat made no sense. She explained to the police that she had been involved in civil rights protests and marches for many years. But she had slowed down her activities considerably since Martin Luther King's death. She was busy with her practice, and had been more involved personally in antiwar protests in recent years. And she said she had worked for the ACLU, and was on their list of volunteers.

"Is it possible that someone from your civil rights days might have it in for you? Have you ever had threats from the Ku Klux Klan?" the policeman asked, and she said she hadn't. She hadn't been a known activist, just part of the support teams, unless someone knew about the activities in her youth, but her life had been very tame for the past several years.

It's probably just a random act of vandalism, they reassured her, and Charlie got the glass pane in the door replaced. They were both shocked when it happened again three days later, and they called the police again. And the southern male voice called and threatened her that night, and called her a "nigger lover," and then hung up. It was unnerving, but she didn't tell her mother. She was coming to visit An every day, and the little girl loved playing with her, as Janet tried new Vietnamese phrases on her. Merrie was trying to learn them too, while teaching An English at the same time. As stressful as her work life was, with half a dozen new cases that had landed on her, she relaxed when she got home to An at night, as soon as she came through the door and saw her. And she didn't touch her briefcase until An was sound asleep.

Peter called every few days to see how they were doing, and Meredith said they were doing fine. He said he'd like to come over and talk to An, and he brought Vietnamese food for all of them when he did. Janet stayed the night for dinner too. She had bought a Vietnamese cookbook and wanted to see how it was supposed to look. Meredith had never seen her so involved, and even though it irritated her at times to have her mother underfoot, it touched her that she wanted to form a bond with An. She was fully engaged.

"How's it going, really?" Peter asked her in a quiet voice as they put the food he'd brought on platters and into bowls in the kitchen.

"Better than I thought it would," she said honestly, and sat down for a minute so they could talk. "She's such a sweet little girl. And her burns are so awful. I dread what they'll have to do to her." For the first time in her adult life, she felt maternal and protective of a child, and one she barely knew.

"She'll come through it fine with you," he said gently, and she smiled. "Your mother seems very good with her."

"I haven't been able to get her interested in anything since my father died, and suddenly she's sprung back to life. I've never seen her like this before. And it's nice having An to come home to." She looked embarrassed when she said it, but did anyway. "I have a reason to come home now." He was easy to talk to and she was opening up to him more than she had intended. Peter had a sympathetic style that children and adults responded to, and she felt it herself.

"Whether you want it to or not, having a child, even in this context, will change your life," he said with a knowing look.

"I'm suddenly aware of that."

They put dinner on the table then, and An's face lit up when she saw the familiar food, and Merrie let her stay up a little later than usual, until Janet went home after dinner, and then she put her to bed. Peter had stayed, and she poured him a glass of wine and they talked for a while, sitting on the couch in her living room.

The vandalism at her office and anonymous calls at night were preying on her mind, but she didn't tell him about them. She didn't want him to worry about An. The calls were unnerving, but Meredith was sure they were safe. Peter lingered for a while, and they talked about his early work in Africa, and now in Vietnam. He said the work he did filled his life, to the exclusion of all else, and she smiled.

"That's how I feel about mine. It doesn't leave room for a social life, or romance, and now there's An."

"Some people seem to manage it. I never have," he said as he stood up and looked at Merrie. "Thank you for letting me hang around tonight," he said, seeming shy.

"You can come and see An anytime." An had told him she liked her American mother and grandma, and Pam the nanny was very nice.

"Actually," Peter said, feeling awkward. "I didn't just come to see her. I wanted to see you too." Meredith looked surprised to hear him say it, and was not sure how to respond. It had been so long since a man had shown any serious interest in her that she was sure he only wanted to be friends, which she barely had time for anyway, especially with a child to take care of now.

He left a few minutes later and promised to come again soon. She lay in bed thinking about him that night, and realized that his life was as full as hers, with the center to run and regular trips to Vietnam to bring back more children. He had as little time to date as she did, which she found reassuring. She had enough on her plate now, without adding to it. And she fell asleep feeling safe and at peace.

Much to her dismay, the vandalism at her office continued. They had an actual break-in a week later, and their computer was destroyed. Nothing was stolen but there was considerable damage. Charlie got everything repaired and replaced their computer. Peggy was terrified that the vandal would show up in broad daylight and attack them. And the anonymous calls at night were still happening every few days.

An had been with her for nearly a month when Merrie finally got seriously worried and admitted to Peter what was happening. It was one thing being at risk herself, but she didn't want anything to happen to An. Claudia suggested that Merrie leave An with her in Connecticut until the police caught the vandal and stopped the calls. And Peter seconded the idea. He was sorry it was happening to her at all.

She left work early that day and picked up An and Pam at the apartment. Janet had already left, and Merrie drove them to Connecticut, as An looked around with interest. They had packed some of their things in a suitcase since Merrie didn't know how long they'd be gone, and Pam was willing to go with her, and help Claudia with the kids.

Merrie could see that An was worried when she glanced at her in the rearview mirror, but she couldn't explain to her where they were going or why. When they got to Claudia's An didn't want to get out of the car, and Meredith carried her into the house, and she stood looking at Claudia sadly, until she went to play with Alex and Sarah again, as she had when they'd come to visit when she first arrived. They squealed with delight as soon as they saw Merrie, who picked each of them up and kissed them. An chattered to them in Vietnamese and they laughed and giggled with her. But she looked devastated when Meredith left after dinner. Merrie held her tight for a long moment and kissed her, and An watched from a window with tears rolling down her cheeks as her new mother drove away.

Meredith called to check on her when she got home, and Claudia said she was fine, and had settled down as soon as Meredith left. She was sleeping in one of their guest rooms with Pam.

That night, Meredith got another call, threatening to kill her. It was beginning to wear her down severely, and the police were no closer to finding out his identity. They hadn't been able to trace the call so far. He was calling from random phone booths around the city. Three days later, they put an unmarked car with a detective outside her office, and he saw a man break in to the outer door shortly after midnight. They arrived as he was breaking through her office door again with a sledgehammer, with the glass already shattered at his feet, and they arrested him and took him to jail.

A detective came to see her at the office the next day. The man they had in custody was a white supremacist from Mississippi who had somehow gotten the list of ACLU volunteers and had singled out a few names, including hers, to get even with them for their involvement in civil rights. He had already served time in prison for armed robbery and attempted murder, and was currently on parole. They would be sending him back to Mississippi in the next few days for parole violation, and he would be charged with breaking and entering, vandalizing her office, and stalking her. It was over, and Meredith was relieved when they left.

Charlie had already called to get the door repaired, and he walked into Meredith's office with a cup of coffee for her. She had a motion to file with the court, and then she was going to drive to Connecticut, pick up An, and bring her home.

"Well, that's over," she said, taking a sip of the steaming coffee Charlie had brought her before she set it down. "We're lucky we caught him last night," she continued, as Charlie perched on the arm of a chair in her office and looked as though he had something to say. "Are you okay?" she asked, and he nodded and didn't answer her for a minute.

"I am, but I've got something to tell you. I didn't want to bother you, with all of this going on." He looked sheepish and unhappy, and he hated to add more complications to her life. She had enough as it was, especially now that she had An, for the next year anyway. But there was never going to be a good time. Meredith's life didn't slow down. It hadn't yet.

"What's up?" Meredith asked, looking at him intently.

"I hate to do this to you," he hesitated, but he was poised at the edge of the diving board and had to dive in. It was too late to turn back. "I need a change. I've thought about it a lot. I'm moving to San Francisco." She felt her heart plummet to her feet. First Angela, and now him.

"When?" she asked in a grim voice.

"As soon as you can replace me. I've been out there a few times on vacation, and I think it's right for me." She nodded, with tears in her eyes. He made so many things easier for her, and Peggy was a sweet person, but a much weaker assistant and could never carry the load alone.

"I'll start looking right away. Are you sure?" She would have liked to beg him or bribe him, but he had a right to a life too, independent of her.

"As sure as one ever is, making a big change. I've been in New York for too long. It's stale for me. I want to try something new. I'm sorry, Merrie, I hate to do this to you."

"It's okay. I understand," it was a job, not a marriage, and she knew she was foolish to be so dependent on him. People quit jobs and moved away. But she had a heavy heart when he left her office and went back to his desk. And she felt somber as she drove out to Connecticut. She knew it was stupid, but she felt abandoned that he was leaving her, and she doubted that she would find anyone as good. Claudia could see that something was wrong as soon as she walked in. But An's face lit up the moment she saw her, and she flew into Meredith's arms.

"Charlie just gave notice. He's moving to San Francisco. I can barely handle my workload as it is. Without him, my life will be a mess."

"You found him, you'll find someone else," Claudia said philosophically, and smiled as she watched Meredith hold An in her arms.

"He's been with me since I opened the office."

"Life is long," Claudia said wisely. "You'll have a lot of paralegals before you retire. You'll find another good one."

"It's just a headache I don't need."

Claudia nodded, and Meredith thanked her for keeping An and Pam, and they left a little while later. She dropped Pam off at her apartment, and took An home. It was late afternoon by then, and she called Peter to tell him she'd brought An back, and he was pleased to hear that things were peaceful again.

"Can I bring dinner over tonight so we can celebrate?" he asked her cautiously, knowing how busy she was. She thought An would enjoy it, so she told him he could. She and An were playing a game when he arrived. She was good at Chinese checkers, and screamed with glee every time she beat Merrie. And from the moment Peter walked in, An talked a blue streak and didn't stop, until he held up a hand to slow her down and translated for Merrie.

"She thought you were giving her away to your friend," he explained to her. "She was sure you were never coming back." Meredith looked stricken when he said it and imagined how An must have felt.

"I would never do that to her. She's here until she goes home. You can say that to her." She wasn't available for adoption since they had found no trace of her family yet, and they didn't know if she was an orphan or had parents who had fled somewhere for safety and she got left behind during the attack on her village when she got burned. Merrie pulled An into her arms and held her, while Peter translated for her, and An looked up at her and smiled, and nodded, and delivered another long message for him to translate.

"She says she loves you," he said in the simplified version.

"Tell her I love her too," and it was true, she did. After barely five weeks together, Meredith was already deeply attached to her. They were starting her medical visits the following week, and Merrie was planning to go with her, with a translator the center was providing, so they could explain to An what was going to happen in the months ahead.

Meredith and Peter put their dinner on plates in the kitchen then, and she smiled at him as they did.

"If I hadn't gone to that book signing with Claudia, I'd never have met you, and An wouldn't be here."

"It looks like it was my lucky day then." He smiled at her.

"And mine. I never thought I'd have a child in my life," she said, looking pensive. "I was so busy doing other things, I just couldn't see it happening." And she hadn't expected her mother to fall in love with An either. An had changed their lives completely, in just over a month.

They had an easy, peaceful dinner together that night, with Peter translating back and forth, and a lot of giggling from An. After Meredith put her to bed, she and Peter sat and talked again for a long time. He was a nice addition to her life.

"What about you? When are you going to foster or adopt one of them?" she asked and put him on the spot, and he looked thoughtful.

"I'm responsible for all of them. That's about all I can handle. I know my limits."

"I thought I knew mine. I was wrong about it. Maybe you are too."

"I always figured I'd have kids of my own one day. But then I got caught up in a nomadic existence and fell in love with what I was doing, and it got away from me. I'm not sorry. I love what I'm doing."

"So do I. The causes I believe in were always more important to me. But it turns out that I have room in my life for An too. I thought I was crazy when I called you and said I'd do it."

"I have to admit, you surprised me," he said, smiling at her, and he gently touched her hand. "I'd like to have dinner with you one of these days, Merrie. Like a grown-up. In a restaurant, without An. Just you and me. How does that sound to you?"

She was smiling even before she answered. "Like a very good idea."

"You can tell me about your days as a Freedom Rider in Mississippi, and all the times you went to jail."

She looked pensive as he said it. "I'll probably wind up there again one of these days, for something I believe in. There's always another battle to fight. I even got arrested with my father once. I think he enjoyed it," she said, and Peter laughed.

And when he left her that night, he lingered at the door for a minute, and then he leaned toward her and kissed her, and what she felt for him was more powerful than she'd realized, as she closed the door softly behind him, half excited and half scared.

Chapter Eighteen

The first medical visit with An was more daunting than Meredith had expected. She had a number of arduous skin grafts ahead of her, but the doctors thought her prognosis was good. Janet had come with them, and the translator, and An didn't seem as upset as she would have expected her to, and the translator explained it to Meredith after the visit.

"She says that the more they want to do to her, the longer she can stay here with you." It was one way to look at it. The doctors were predicting that her surgeries would stretch over eighteen months to two years.

"We ought to do something fun with her in between, like go to Disney World or something," Janet suggested, and Meredith smiled at her. Meredith was thinking about getting a bigger apartment, so they would have more room to move around. And An needed her own room. It made sense, even if only for two years.

She dropped An and her mother off at the apartment, where Pam was waiting for them, and she went back to her office. Charlie had a stack of messages for her, and she was interviewing two paralegals that afternoon.

"How did it go?" he asked, looking concerned.

"It won't be easy, but she's a brave little girl. And my mother wants to take her to Disney World."

"The same woman who didn't know how to write a check or find her favorite show on TV two months ago?"

"The very same," Meredith said, smiling at him. She was still sad he was leaving, but was starting to adjust to the idea. Nothing lasted forever, and surely not employees in today's world. He wanted new adventures and was tired of New York.

They were both discouraged by the candidates for his job they saw that afternoon.

"I can't leave you with people like that, Merrie." One had been unpleasant, and the other one seemed just plain stupid. She wasn't looking forward to the mess in her office after he left. Even Peggy was worried about it. "Maybe California isn't such a good idea," he said. "Is it too late to change my mind?"

"Are you sure you want to? You sounded pretty excited about San Francisco." She wanted to be fair to him.

"I think I was just having a bad day. My romance had ended, and I thought geography was the only solution."

"Well, I'm certainly not pushing you to leave," she said, hopeful, but she didn't want to take advantage of him either, and keep him from a better life.

"San Francisco isn't going anywhere. Why don't we shelve the idea for a while, and see who I meet here?"

"Don't let your love life drive your life," she said wisely. "You can meet the right person anywhere, at the right time. I think it's all blind luck and good timing." And she thought both had just happened to her when she met Peter. They were planning their first dinner date when he got back from Vietnam. He was leaving again soon but only for two weeks.

He called her that night to see how the medical visit had gone, and after she told him, he said there was something else he wanted to tell her.

"An is available for adoption. We just got confirmation today. All her relatives are dead. If she goes back, she'll go to an orphanage in Saigon. There's no pressure on you. You can foster her for a year or two and then decide to adopt her, or send her back. I thought you'd want to know you have the option."

"And you don't call that pressure?" She laughed over the phone.

"It's information. That's always a good thing to have."

"Yes, it is," he could hear that she was happy at the news. "When are you coming home?" She was anxious for their dinner date.

"In two weeks. We're waiting for four more kids right now."

"That's a long time to wait for dinner," she teased him. She was looking forward to his return, and so was he. For years, there had been no time and no room in her life for anything but the causes she worked for, the battles she wanted to fight, and the people she wanted to champion. And now she had time for An, and for him, and maybe even for herself. And she still had room for the people who needed her help. Somehow a door had opened, and she could see new vistas ahead.

"Hang on for that dinner, Merrie. We'll do it as soon as I get back."

"I'll be here."

In six short weeks, An had brought joy into her life, and even created a bond with her mother that she had never had before. She had always felt that her mother disapproved of her, and even after all of her objections to Meredith taking on an injured child, she had finally done something her mother understood. And Janet was becoming someone she had never been able to be in her marriage, an independent woman with her own ideas. She had fallen in love with a little girl and was learning Vietnamese. An was an immeasurable gift.

"Take care of yourself, Merrie. I'll see you soon," Peter promised, and after they hung up, Meredith thought about him and what he was doing in Vietnam, bringing wounded children back with him for medical help and to find new homes for them when he could. In recent years, all her heroes had died, and now there was a new one, and he felt the same way about her. He was in awe of all that she had done and the life she had led. Instead of finding it shocking, he valued her all the more for it, and didn't expect her to give it up, which she never could. He had understood that too.

The next morning, Meredith found An sitting at the breakfast table in her nightgown, pouring chocolate sauce onto her cereal and looking pleased.

"Yes?" she said, looking up at her as Meredith considered the scene for a moment.

"Maybe not so yes," she said and then thought better of it: "Oh, why not?" She handed her a glass of chocolate milk to go with it. "Who says we can't make our own rules? I won't tell if you don't," she said, grinning at the little girl.

Danielle Steel

She had already made her decision after talking to Peter the night before. She didn't need to wait two years. Maybe one day she would take An to Vietnam when she grew up, so she could see where she came from, long after the war was over. But she was not sending her back to an orphanage in Saigon. She sat smiling at An and thinking about the future. They had lessons to teach each other, and she was going to teach her the same things her grandfather had taught her, and An would do with them what she wished. She would be her own person, with her own ideas and her own dreams.

Peter came back from Vietnam two weeks later, with twelve more children, and Meredith went to see him at the center the day he got home. She took An with her and she played with the others, laughing and squealing and running around, and Peter was happy to see them both. She told him about her decision to adopt An, and he was thrilled for both of them. After they left, he went home to get some sleep.

The next day they went to dinner, at a cozy neighborhood restaurant near her apartment. She told him what she'd been doing, and he told her about the trip. She explained a new case she'd taken on. It was a complicated racial discrimination suit, which would be a landmark case if she won it, and another victory in the battle that meant so much to her.

She was fighting the good fight, as she always had, and knew she always would. She had kept her promise to her grandfather. But there was room for Peter and for An now too. That was all new.

They walked back from the restaurant hand in hand, just enjoying the evening and being together, fully aware of how lucky they were to have met at the right time in their lives. And Meredith understood now more than ever, that despite the losses and the grief and fallen heroes, if you were brave enough, and stayed true to yourself, it all worked out in the end.

IN HIS FATHER'S FOOTSTEPS

A tormented past. A hopeful future.

April, 1945. As the Americans storm the Buchenwald concentration camp, among the survivors are Jakob and Emmanuelle, barely more than teenagers. Each of them has lost everything and everyone in the unspeakable horrors of the war. But when they meet, they find hope and comfort in each other.

Jakob and Emmanuelle marry, and resolve to make a new life in New York. The Steins build a happy, prosperous life for themselves and their little family, but their pasts cast a long shadow over the present.

Years later, as the Sixties are in full swing, their son Max is an ambitious, savvy businessman, determined to throw off the sadness that has hung over his family since his birth. But as Max's life unfolds, he must learn that there is meaning in his heritage that will help shape his future . . .

Available for pre-order

PURE HEART. PURE STEEL.